DEATH OF A PRODIGAL

As a young man, Mervyn Davies left South Wales for Australia under a cloud. When he returns to Pontyglas, forty years later, to collect a huge inheritance after the death of Edwin Edworth, his childhood friend and the town's richest bachelor, some people are surprised, others are disgusted at his good fortune – particularly Edworth's relatives who were left nothing in his will.

When Davies's severed head is discovered in a Tesco bag by the landlord's wife at the Coach and Horses, and other bits of him start appearing elsewhere, it's the relatives who have the obvious motive for his murder. But DCI Merlin Parry and DS Gomer Lloyd, sent from Cardiff to investigate, have to dig a lot deeper mentally to identify some less obvious motives, not to mention relatives, as well as physically to locate the remainder of the body before eventually cornering the killer.

This second Parry and Lloyd investigation is another delicious and authentic Welsh melange that easily matches the promise of *Last Seen Breathing*, lauded as 'tremendous' by Dan O'Neill in the *South Wales Echo*.

DEATH OF A
PRODIGAL

David Williams

HarperCollins*Publishers*

**This one for
Wallace and Ruth Grubman**

Collins Crime
An imprint of HarperCollins*Publishers*
77–85 Fulham Palace Road, London W6 8JB

First published in Great Britain
in 1995 by Collins Crime

1 3 5 7 9 10 8 6 4 2

© Copyright David Williams 1995

The Author asserts the moral right to be
identified as the author of this work

A catalogue record for this book is
available from the British Library

ISBN 0 00 232553 5

Set in Meridien and Bodoni

Photoset by Rowland Phototypesetting Ltd
Bury St Edmunds, Suffolk
Printed and bound in Great Britain by
HarperCollinsManufacturing Glasgow

1

The big man turned the corner of the solid Victorian house and found himself on a broad, stone-flagged south terrace overlooking the garden. The place was much as he remembered it from boyhood – or more as he had imagined it was from this side: he and Edwin would never have viewed things from the terrace.

It was a tidy-sized garden by anyone's standards – rolling lawns and grassy walks flanked by scalloped borders of carefully pruned rose bushes and shrubs, with well-sited, mature trees now bursting with bud. In the very early sunlight, under a still-hazy blue sky, the property looked as well tended and haughty now as it had done forty years ago. The empty aviary extending from the house on the viewer's right had not been there in his day, nor the glass and ironwork conservatory that balanced without exactly matching it on the other side. He noticed with approval that, like the house, both additions were in the Gothic style: he had always liked working on pointed arches himself. He saw the orchard was still where it had been, in the extreme south-west corner of the garden. He had good reason to remember the orchard. Some early apple blossom was showing in places there already – different from home, where the winter was just starting, not ending.

For the first time in several decades his thought process had stumbled over the word 'home'. When he was sixteen his home had not been, as it was now, in the booming city of Perth, Western Australia: it had been here in Pontyglas – pronounced Pon-tee-glas, with a short 'a', as in 'lass' – a middling-sized town in the county of Glamorgan, in South

Wales, a town that had got bigger in the interim but not prettier, or what he had seen of it had. Even so, as a boy, he had not lived in a grand house like this one, with its steep gables and three acres of garden. His gran's place had been across the town on a council estate.

He looked at the time, put down the worn, canvas holdall he was carrying, then moved a wrought-iron armchair so that it faced down the lawn before he sat in it. Like a lot of metal garden furniture of the type, the chair had been made for a smaller occupant. He wriggled his rump well back into the seat, then leaned his rain-jacketed trunk forward, running a callused hand over his forehead and the close-cropped, grey hair above it.

Peering thoughtfully across the grass, he sighed, and soon after this his eyes began to mist. He had never believed he would be here again, nor that he would ever want to be.

'Who the bloody hell are you, then?' The male voice had come from behind him.

The big man glanced about slowly. The challenge had surprised but not upset him. 'G'day to you,' he replied, in an accent that owed a lot to a long domicile in Australia and very little to his Welsh origins. He got up, but with some difficulty, as the padded jacket had caught on one side of the chair. 'Sorry I disturbed you so early. Didn't mean to. Let's see now, you'll be Mr Jarvis, I expect. I'm Mervyn Davies.'

The nonplussed newcomer was younger than the speaker. He was short, sharp featured, and weedy, with ears that were conspicuously large and protruding. He was wearing a stained, fawn-coloured raincoat over flannel pyjamas with the legs roughly stuffed into black gumboots. His stance and demeanour had, to this point, implied that the stout walking stick grasped tightly in both hands was intended for offensive action against intruders – except the holder seemed too slight and apprehensive to fill the role of vigilante in the face of an adversary as formidable as the one standing before him. He now seemed disconcerted as well as dishevelled – his hair uncombed, his cheeks rough with stubble, and the tired eyes, blinking furiously behind the round lenses of metal-framed spectacles, affirming that he had been roused from sleep as well as bed.

'You're Mr Davies, are you? But we weren't expecting you till Sunday. Sunday evening at the earliest, Mr Trimble told us.' Since it was now only a few minutes past six on Friday morning, Gareth Jarvis's surprise was explicable, and his heavy Welsh intonation seemed to have thickened in sympathy.

'Wasn't expecting to be here till then myself. The travel arrangements got moved up. I flew stand-by. That way, you take what you're offered, you understand?' Jarvis didn't look particularly understanding or even convinced as the man who had identified himself as Davies continued. 'Wish I could have been here for the funeral. On March the eighteenth, wasn't it?'

'That's right. At St Luke's. The wake was here, with outside caterers. A hundred people came. Lot of clearing up we had to do, after.' Jarvis's tight mouth set even tighter, and the small, nearly black eyes looked about as if searching still for abandoned sausage rolls and service sheets, three weeks after the event.

'You don't say? Ah, and this'll be Mrs Jarvis, I expect?' Davies moved forward with a hand outstretched. 'Very sorry to have woken you both like this, Mrs Jarvis.'

'It's Mr Davies, Mair. Mr Mervyn Davies. Come three days early, he has,' Jarvis inserted quickly as his wife and Davies shook hands.

'Yes, Gareth, I heard you say. How d'you do, Mr Davies. You're very welcome, I'm sure.' The slim figure now standing beside Jarvis was, like him, short, and some years younger than her husband, while, again in contrast to him, her appearance was almost bandbox. Her hair was bleached blonde and set in rigid, permanent waves. Her make-up had presumably just been applied, but it looked as if it could have endured already as long as her coiffure – although it threatened to crack in places if there was any deepening of the smile which was showing more in her cheeks than in her eyes. She was wearing a long, quilted dressing gown with large lilac-coloured rhododendrons printed on it, and a

7

lilac gauze scarf fluffed up about her neck. Her slippers were made of the same material as the dressing gown. 'Don't know why Gareth's kept you standing out here, I'm sure, Mr Davies,' she went on in a low, cheerful, bronchitic voice. 'Come inside, and I'll make you some breakfast, now just. You'll be hungry, I expect, after that long journey.' She was then suddenly consumed by a gravelly cough that made her eyes water.

'That's kind of you, Mrs Jarvis. I meant to sit here quietly till normal getting-up time,' Davies began to explain. 'And I haven't come far today. Only from Cardiff. On the first bus. I arrived there by train late last night. Well, at two-thirty this morning to be exact. There didn't seem much point taking a hotel room then, so I dossed down in the station till the bus was due.' He beamed at the others, and rubbed his chin. 'I could use a bathroom, all right, but I'll wait to have breakfast with you both when you're ready, if that's OK? I don't need much. Toast and coffee is fine.'

'I'll take that bag, Mr Davies,' said Jarvis after an urgent prompt from his wife.

'That's all right, Gareth. I can manage it. And I'd be glad if you'd call me Mervyn.'

'Oh, it'll take time for us to get used to that, Mr Davies,' responded Mrs Jarvis coyly. 'You do understand, I was Mr Edworth's cook and housekeeper, and Gareth was gardener and chauffeur? Well, we still are, of course, and proud to be of service, even though Mr Edworth's no longer with us, sad to say.' She paused briefly in reverence to the departed. 'Mr Edworth always had his meals alone in the dining room. We have ours in the kitchen,' she ended on a purposeful note of servility towards one whose importance to the Jarvises' future might prove incalculable, even if it was as yet problematical.

'I like eating in the kitchen,' Davies answered, beaming still.

'This is all the luggage, Mr Davies?' Jarvis questioned, looking at the bag that the other man was holding without effort.

'That's all I've brought with me, yes. I like to travel light. Means you can move faster.'

8

'And er . . . Mrs Davies didn't come with you, then?' asked Mrs Jarvis earnestly, trying to make the question sound less double-edged than it was.

'There hasn't been a Mrs Davies for years.'

'Oh, we wondered. I'm so sorry,' she responded, looking deep into his eyes, while primping one side of her hair.

'I'm not sorry. We're divorced. She's married someone else, God help him.' The speaker turned about and let his gaze sweep over the scene once more. 'Y'know, the last time I was here in the garden of Condleston Lodge would have been just about this time of day. But in September probably, not April. And with Edwin Edworth.' He turned to face the others again. 'Edwin didn't live here then, of course. And his parents' place in Raglan Avenue wasn't anywhere near as big as this one, either. You want to guess what the two of us would have been doing here?'

'Er . . . visiting friends, perhaps?' offered Jarvis tentatively, and pulling on the lobe of a massive ear while trying to seem interested.

'No. Thieving. That's what we'd have been doing. Not on the grand scale, mark you. Nicking apples. And pears. We were young devils in those days.'

'Well, boys will be boys, the world over,' said Mrs Jarvis with a tolerant smile, one hand rising to cup her delicate chin in a practised pose until the little tableau was spoiled by a further outbreak of coughing. 'Oh, dear. I always wheeze a bit, early morning,' she gasped, patting her chest delicately.

Davies nodded in sympathy, then turned to Mr Jarvis. 'Yes, we used to come in from the fields, over the stone wall at the end. Still there is it, the wall?'

'Oh, yes,' Mrs Jarvis affirmed, clearing her throat. 'The fields aren't though. Housing estate, that is now. Mr Edworth didn't like being overlooked, but he wouldn't move. Even though he had plenty of offers for the place. Big offers, he told us.'

'Is that right?'

'Not that the money would have mattered to him. It was the land they wanted, of course. For more building. But Mr Edworth was a real creature of habit. He used to say to me,

"Mair",' she paused pointedly. ' "Mair, I'm going to live out the rest of my life in this precious oasis, with my flowers, and my birds, and you and Gareth will always be welcome to live it out here with me." And that's what happened, wasn't it? Only he was gone sooner than any of us could have thought. So soon after his retirement too. Lovely man, he was.' This time Mrs Jarvis choked back a sob at the memory, and dabbed her eyes with a tissue – a colour-coordinated lilac tissue.

'I can tell you one thing, owning this place was a childhood ambition come true for him, Mrs Jarvis,' said Davies. 'Many's the time the two of us hid in the long grass, back of that orchard, guzzling apples, looking at the building, envying the people who lived in it. Edwin always said he'd own it one day. Can't say I ever believed him at the time. Belonged to a titled person then, as I remember.'

'Sir Oswald, that was,' put in Jarvis. 'In steel, he was. An uncle of mine worked for him.'

'You don't say? I'd forgotten that.' Davies looked genuinely interested by the fact. 'And Edwin became keen on birds, did he?' he went on, nodding in the direction of the aviary.

'Oh, more than just keen, Mr Davies. An authority he was,' Jarvis added quickly. 'The aviary was testament to that, all right. Many rare species we used to have here. Many. Valuable they were, too. No birds left now. Not since Mr Edworth gave away the whole collection. To that big aviary in Anglesey. That was three months ago. When he knew he hadn't got long. I used to be in charge of the birds when he was away. The feeding and that. Big responsibility that was, too. He used to travel all over photographing birds. That was his real hobby.'

'And Mr Trimble told me he never married?'

The Jarvises glanced at each other. 'He never did, no.' It was Mrs Jarvis who answered the question. 'Swore he had nothing against the ladies, mind you, but claimed he'd been too busy to think of marriage. That was while he was building the business, like, and then after, it was too late. Said he'd got too set in his ways. Well, it takes all sorts, doesn't it?'

She gently smoothed her rhododendron-decorated middle. 'Now, if you'd like to follow me, Mr Davies, I'll show you up to your room. It's got its own bathroom and everything,' she added, in an aside invested with a definite undertone of intimacy.

'What d'you think, then, Gareth?' asked Mrs Jarvis when her husband joined her in the kitchen some minutes later. She was still in her dressing gown, but he had shaved and dressed quickly, cutting his chin in the process.

'Don't know what to think. He's not what we expected, is he? I mean the way he looks, those clothes, the way he talks. He's not educated or anything. Wonder what he does for a living.'

'Well, it didn't follow because his friend made good, that he would too, did it? He didn't have the same advantages probably, for a start.' She was cutting the rind off some strips of fat bacon. A cigarette was clasped firmly between her lips in the left-hand corner of her mouth.

'Suppose not. Different backgrounds they had, I expect,' Jarvis continued. 'Mr Edworth's father was a builder. Ken Franklin at the Coach and Horses said Mr Davies didn't have a father, or a mother either, come to that.'

'Don't be daft, everybody has a mother and father.'

'Well, Ken says he was brought up by his grandmother.'

'And how would Ken Franklin know all that, anyway? He didn't live in Pontyglas in those days.'

'His wife Jacky did. He told me she knows more than she's saying about our Mr Davies. Even to Ken.'

'Oh, that's Jacky Franklin all over, that is. Always making out she knows more than she does.'

'Funny him coming all that way on the cheap, and no luggage to speak of.' Jarvis reverted to the earlier part of the conversation, shaking his head, then pressing at the piece of cotton wool attached to the cut on his chin. 'Doesn't look as if he's going to stay.'

'You can't tell from that.' Mrs Jarvis was cracking eggs as she spoke.

'Well, I'll bet you anything that one's not aiming to live in any Condleston Lodge.'

'You don't know, he might get used to the life. He could afford it.'

'That's not the point, is it? You don't own a place like this and eat in the kitchen with the . . . with the staff.' He had been looking for a more flattering word to describe the two of them, but there didn't seem to be one.

'I don't see why not.' After mixing the eggs ready for scrambling, she was busy now setting three breakfast places at the table. It was a modern kitchen table made of natural oak like the rest of the fittings in the room, which was light and airy. It had been completely and expensively done over five years before this.

'Suppose we won't be going to May and Arthur's party tomorrow now,' said Jarvis.

'Damn! I hadn't thought.' His wife frowned, and stopped what she was doing. 'Well, we'll just have to talk Mr Davies round to letting us go, that's all,' she concluded firmly, smoothing her narrow hips with both hands.

'So you're going to let him eat with us now?' asked Jarvis, standing with his back to the sink, his hands in his pockets, and watching his wife resume her brisk activity. It wasn't in his nature or upbringing to lend a hand in the house.

'I've laid for him in the dining room as well, so he can please himself. That's his privilege, isn't it? But he did say he wanted to eat with us.' She tapped ash from her cigarette into the sink.

'Only toast and coffee, he said, not eggs and bacon and the rest,' her husband cautioned.

'Well, he didn't mean that, you could tell,' she replied with assurance. 'Big man like him needs a proper breakfast to keep his strength up, and that's what he'll get so long as he's here.' She stepped back from the table to study it, the cigarette now back in her mouth. 'Ah, marmalade,' she uttered, breathing in fiercely, eyes half closed against the smoke. 'I knew there was something.' She went back to the larder. 'Look, Gareth,' she continued on her return, 'Mr Davies is an unattached gentleman, in late middle age, just like Mr Edworth. Only he's healthier.'

'Well, that's not difficult is it? Mr Edworth's dead.' Jarvis screwed up his nose in a kind of grin, then tightened the belt around his baggy, grey flannel trousers.

'That's not very funny, and anyway, you know what I mean.' She went back to the worktop by the cooker and began to slice bread for toasting. 'And as for whether he stays, just remember Mr Davies looks good for a few years yet – many years, most likely. So there's nothing to stop him leading the same life as his friend, if he wants.'

'The same?' He looked across at her sharply and rearranged the glasses on his nose.

'More or less,' she answered, still facing away from him, except he could see the side of her neck was going pink. 'And think what it'd mean if he did stay on. For the two of us.'

That was precisely what he had been thinking. 'But we'll have the pensions Mr Edworth arranged,' he said.

'Not for six years, you won't. Not till you're sixty. Ten years, in my case.'

'But there's the lump sum he left us, as well.'

'Which you said yourself wouldn't be enough to live on, not if we just used the interest on it. And Mr Trimble said we shouldn't even do that, not if we want it to put down on a cottage later on.'

'But we'll get another place if we're not wanted here.'

'You always say that, but it may not be so easy to find.'

'Well, we've got the dole on top of everything else, while we're looking.'

She had put out the cigarette under the tap, and was spooning coffee grounds into a large percolator. 'But what I keep telling you is, Mr Davies is our best chance of being wanted here. Here where we're settled and comfy. I don't understand why you won't see it.' She sniffed, rinsed the spoon she had been using, and wiped it and her hands on a paper towel. 'Right, now I'll go and dress properly. Then I'll give him a knock, see if he's ready. It'll be just like old times,' she completed lightly, but with an unmistakably speculative gleam in her eyes.

Jarvis's skinny jaw had tightened at his wife's last remark. He knew what she'd had in mind all right. He could tell from the looks she'd been giving Davies outside on the terrace. Well, he was damned if he was going to let her play around with the new owner the way he knew she had with the old one. He'd had enough of allowing another man to pleasure himself on Gareth Jarvis's preserve. He'd put up with it before for good reason, but the next dirty old man who lusted after his wife had better look out, because he'd have to pay for the pleasure differently.

2

'Not a bit. Glad you came straight away, Mr Davies. There's a lot to go through. Come this way, won't you?'

Dewi Ap-Evan Trimble, solicitor, was a quite short, muscular and hyperactive man whose speech was as rapid as his movements, and whose usual expression – thin eyebrows raised, cheeks hollowed, mouth half open – suggested a fairly permanent state of surprise bordering sometimes on apprehension. He had not been nearly so pleased as he was implying to find Mervyn Davies standing on the doorstep of his offices at twenty to nine with no appointment. Still, you could hardly turn away someone who'd come seven thousand miles at your own urgent instigation to collect a fortune. Plus there was the fact that with proper handling that fortune might still generate income for the legal partnership of Ablett & Trimble – something it had been doing for several decades past. Trimble hadn't needed to work that out in the last few seconds either. He'd done it some time ago, except that now he'd laid eyes on Davies again, it was easier to credit.

'We don't open for business till nine really, but I'm usually here by this time,' he went on, unlocking the solid front door of the two-storey premises on the corner of Crown Road and Pentre Street, not far from the town centre, and slotted between a building society on one side, and a hairdresser's on the other. He led his visitor through a sombre front office crammed with desks and computer stations. There was a bank of printers and photocopiers on one side, filing cabinets against most of the walls, a large old-fashioned safe in one corner, and an electronic switchboard alongside the desk by the front door. From the street, the smoked, plate-glass

15

frontage to this area had seemed to Davies more reminiscent of an undertaker's than a law firm – and it gave him almost the same impression from the inside.

'Early bird catches the worm, is it, Dewi?' asked the Australian as he had followed at speed between the desks, and been ushered through a door at the rear into Trimble's private office. This was nearly the same size as the other room, and the furnishings were to a degree less uncompromisingly functional – as if they were offering visitors more inducement to linger, if not for too long.

'The senior partner being early sets an example,' confided Trimble, but if the example was supposed to be encouraging early attendance by employees it had been singularly unsuccessful. 'Let me have your coat then,' he said. 'I'll put it with mine in the cupboard here. Take that chair, you'll find it more comfortable than the others. More comfortable, yes.' He held Davies's rain jacket between thumb and forefinger, at head height, and at some distance from his body, as though it were a species of dead creature infected by diseases and which he was about to consign to the nearest incinerator. The worn leather-winged chair he had indicated matched the one he was to take himself behind the heavy partners' desk. The other three chairs were stolidly upright with no arms.

Apart from the built-in coat cupboard, the remainder of the furnishings comprised two very large glass-fronted bookcases filled with expensively bound and suspiciously pristine legal tomes. There was also what might have been a drinks cabinet, and an immense, unyielding-looking leather sofa under the window at the back of the room, with a three-quarters closed Venetian blind behind it letting in some light, but no view of what lay outside.

'Yes, I'd have recognized you easily, Mr Davies. Even after all those years.' The welcoming smile that the pinstripe-suited Trimble beamed over the top of gold, half-moon spectacles, faltered slightly as it took in the tieless dark-blue sports shirt, the worn black blazer and the shabby corduroy trousers Davies had on.

'The name's Mervyn, Dewi. You know that.'

16

'Of course . . . Mervyn.' Trimble pulled a blue cardboard file from the briefcase he had been carrying and placed it on the blotter in front of him. 'And the Jarvises have made you quite welcome at the house, then?'

'Yes, thanks. I gather it's OK for me to stay there.'

'Of course. It's your house, or it will be once the will has been accepted for probate. And the Jarvises are being paid for another five months yet. That's in the will. In the will.'

'Very comfy quarters they've given me. I gather I'm in the main guest room.' Davies paused and stroked his chin. 'Like I said on the phone from Perth, I'm sorry I couldn't have been here for the funeral.'

'We did try to reach you.'

'I know. And that's the last time in my life I'll go on vacation without leaving word where I'll be. Trouble is, if you go fishing in the Duracks it's hard to be reached. Pretty wild country up there. Primitive. I like it fine, and normally it's unusual for anyone to want me.' He smiled ruefully. 'By the way, I bought the airline ticket with a credit card, like you said, but I didn't come first class. Got a stand-by ticket for a tenth of what that would have cost.'

'But Mr Edworth's estate would have paid, Mervyn.'

'I know that's what you said, but since I wasn't in time for the funeral, it didn't seem right somehow. Edwin was always pretty careful with money when I knew him.'

'Hm, he stayed that way, too,' rejoined Trimble with some feeling.

Davies had been studying the other man's features. 'You say we were in the choir at St Luke's at the same time, Dewi?' he questioned.

'Except I was quite junior to you. Children remember their seniors, not their juniors, of course. There's three years' difference in our ages er . . . Mervyn.' For the second time the lawyer busily straightened all the items within reach on his desk – blotter, diary, pen tray, memo pad, telephone, a silver-framed photograph of a formidable middle-aged woman with one arm around a slightly less formidable looking bull terrier that she vaguely resembled, and finally the blue file.

'That's why I don't remember you, I expect, Dewi. Of

17

course, I remember Edwin. We were great mates. He was a year and a half older than me, but he'd fallen back a form in school. That was after being off a year with glandular fever. He got over it all right, though. Very brainy lad.' Davies shifted in the chair. 'I . . . I didn't expect him to leave me anything. Not after all this time. We hadn't met since I left the old country. Or been in touch, except for the one phone call, six weeks ago.'

'When he never told you he was dying?'

'No, he didn't. We just talked about old times. He wanted to know what I'd done with my life.'

'And you told him about your two married sons?'

'That's right. He was interested in them all right. I figured it was because he'd never had children of his own. Never married even.'

Trimble nodded. 'Late in his life, he would dearly like to have had a son. But he had no time for his own relatives, I'm afraid. He always spoke of you with great warmth. Great warmth,' repeated Trimble, who was clearly in the habit of confirming his own points in this way. 'He said he owed you a great deal.'

'Then he had a long memory. Longer than mine.'

'He'd have been in touch with you sooner if he'd known where you were.'

'When did he find out I was in Perth?'

'A little under two months ago. Through an agency in Melbourne. It reunites people like yourself with relatives in Britain.'

'Bet they've never found any relatives of mine.'

'Probably not. But they were very efficient finding you. And they needed to be. You see, it was not till Edwin's cancer was diagnosed that I was at last able to persuade him to make a will. Even then, I fear, he obdurately refused to pay the quite trivial fee for the service. As a matter of principle. I'm afraid I indulged him over that. Our fees to him for other matters had been substantial for many years, and rarely challenged.' He gave a wan smile.

'And he left everything to me?'

'Yes. But he needed to know you were alive still, with

18

children of your own. He was quite firm on the last point. Quite firm.'

'But he never said he wanted to see me. In that one phone call, I mean. You'd have thought —'

'He was already too ill to travel,' the lawyer interrupted.

'I could have come to see him.'

'I suppose he thought the phone call was enough.'

'I wouldn't have.' Davies smirked. 'And he'd never made a will before?'

'Never. I'd been on at him for years to do it. Wealthy man like him.' Trimble shook his head vigorously. 'It's imprudent not to make a will. Even for a fit man. You never know, do you, when you might be killed in an accident? Never.' He lifted the blue file six inches, then let it drop, his open hands left poised in the air, eyebrows raised even more steeply than was usual.

'I suppose that's right, Dewi.' The other man seemed to be reflecting.

Trimble leaned forward. 'And you'd left Britain when you were nearly seventeen? That'd be after you and I had lost touch, I expect,' he offered, aware that the church choir was the only place where there had been any kind of contact between them. They had attended different schools — a private one in his own case.

'I was joined on to the young immigrant scheme, yes. Except I paid my own passage,' said Davies. 'I was an orphan. No close relations left after my grandmother died.'

'So you made a fresh exciting start in Australia,' the lawyer exclaimed, with romantic wonderment in his voice.

Davies's gaze dropped to study his scuffed leather shoes. 'Let's say I survived the first years there, in spite of the odds against.'

'You weren't looked after?'

'You could say that. But I was a big lad. Older than most of the others. I was sent to a sheep farm. I got my keep, and nothing much else. It was a hard life.'

'I'm sorry.'

Davies shrugged. 'That was a long time ago. Anyway, after two years in the outback, I did a bunk. Fetched up eventually

19

in Perth. Lived there ever since. At the start I was aiming to go to sea, but I never found a berth. I got work on a building site instead, and stayed with it. That's how I ended up a bricky.'

'A bricklayer?'

'That's right. Seems Edwin was a whole lot luckier. I remember his father was mad keen on him going into the ministry.'

'I'm afraid Edwin didn't realize his father's hopes over that.'

'Just as well. I don't think he'd have made much of a vicar. Too fond of the good life. How did his pa take it?'

'Badly, I believe.' Trimble wriggled in his seat.

'But Edwin didn't go into the family building firm either?'

'No, his older brother Gwilym did though, straight from school. He took it over eventually, as his father had always intended.'

'So the old man got his wish in one way? Is Gwilym still alive?'

'No, dead, I'm afraid.'

Davies accepted the news with a nod, but no special sign of regret. 'You know the father was a lay reader at St Luke's?' he asked. 'But of course you do. Narrow-minded bugger he was, excuse the language. Gwilym was the same. Should have been him his pa put into the ministry.'

'Gwilym wasn't academic enough for that. Edwin was though, and his father was very disappointed when he dropped out of university. It had cost a lot to send him there, after he'd done his national service. It was in the army he got his taste for cars. Crazy about them, he was.'

'And that's what he did. Sell cars.'

Trimble leaned back sharply, looking seriously surprised, almost affronted. 'That's putting it very mildly. Cars were his whole life for a very long time. He did get qualifications, of course. Did a regular apprenticeship in the Midlands. With the old Rootes Motor Company, I think it was. Then he worked as a garage mechanic before he set up his own small saleroom and service station, here in Pontyglas, behind the old bus station. It's still there, but it's a big place now, of course. There were a few hiccups at the start, but once he was over those, he never looked back. Never.'

'Ended up with two of the biggest car dealerships in South Wales, the Jarvises told me. Showrooms all over the place.'

'That's a slight exaggeration, but yes, he did well. Very well. He sold out and retired just under a year ago. Decided overnight he'd had enough. Wanted to devote the rest of his life to ornithology.'

'Birds? Don't blame him. Although he never got married, there's family here still, is there?'

'Gwilym's wife is still alive, yes, although er . . . she's not too well. Failing mentally, I hear. She lives in the town still. They had two children, a son and a daughter. The son, Charles, is married. He lives fairly close by as well. He's a production engineer at one of the larger factories on the industrial estate.'

'He didn't take on the building company from his father?'

'When it came to it, there wasn't anything to take on, I'm afraid. It had gone bankrupt. That was what sealed the rift between Edwin and his brother. Mark you, it'd been pretty firm for a long time before that.' Trimble began straightening the things on his desk again as he continued. 'You see, when Edwin had the setback with his first service station, Gwilym refused to help him with a loan. Later, much later, when the building company was in real financial straits, Edwin might have saved it, but didn't.'

'Getting his own back?'

'That's about it, yes.'

'Don't blame him. And what happened to Gwilym's other child? The daughter? Got a man, has she?'

Trimble's face reflected fleeting distaste at the question. 'Her name is Gail. She's a dental nurse here in Pontyglas. She's not married,' he completed somewhat stiffly.

'Seems none of them moved about at all. And how much did Edwin leave these people?'

'He left them nothing. He hadn't spoken to his brother since they quarrelled more than thirty years ago. The feelings went very deep. He didn't go to Gwilym's funeral, even.'

21

Absently, Trimble was moving the framed picture of the formidable woman further away from him.

'You don't say? But what about Gwilym's children? Charles and er . . . Gail?'

'I am not aware that Edwin ever met either of them.'

The big man opposite looked puzzled and slowly rubbed the knuckles of one hand with the palm of the other. 'And he's left me the thick end of two million pounds, you think?'

'That's an estimate, but after inheritance tax, your part of the estate should be worth close to two million, yes, not including Condleston Lodge.'

'Is there another part of the estate?'

'Yes. It's not significant, though. Just some small legacies, mostly to employees in his old company.' He opened the blue folder, withdrew a long document from it, and then a small envelope secured with red sealing wax. 'I'd taken Edwin's file home last night to study, remembering you'd be here shortly, though we weren't expecting you today, of course. I was to give you this envelope when we met.' He half rose from his chair, and passed the envelope across the desk in a purposely formal manner.

'Probably a letter from Edwin telling me not to spend all the money in one shop.' Davies turned the envelope in his hand without attempting to open it. 'Never had a letter sealed like this before.'

'And this is a copy of the will,' the lawyer went on. He smoothed out the creases of the document and turned over the first page. 'Yes. The largest legacy is to Mr and Mrs Jarvis. Twenty-five thousand pounds. That's on top of the private pensions they'll both get eventually. Edwin paid annual contributions on those, on top of their salaries, plus, of course, the statutory social security payments. They'd be wise to keep up the pension premiums themselves. In their next job. It's unlikely their next employer will do that for them. Edwin was very generous to them.'

'But if they go on with the payments themselves, that'll make their pensions bigger?' Davies questioned.

'Certainly it will.'

22

'And if I kept on the house and lived in it, d'you think they'd want to stay on?'

Trimble's eyes narrowed. 'Is that what you're intending, Mervyn?'

'Don't know. Too early to say.'

'If you did stay, I'd imagine the Jarvises would want to stay too, yes.'

'I don't know what I'd do with a chauffeur, all the same.'

'Jarvis hasn't done much chauffeuring for Edwin since he retired. Being gardener and odd job man keeps him fairly busy, I believe. There's usually plenty to do around an old house with a garden of that size.'

'And he looked after the birds in the aviary too,' said Davies, then leaned forward a long way in his seat, his huge forehead wrinkling: 'So tell me, Dewi, if I hadn't been alive, or if you hadn't found me, what would have happened to the money I'm getting?'

'I can't say for certain. It would most probably have been divided between a number of charities, all to do with the protection of birds. Edwin did discuss that possibility with me. In case you couldn't be found.'

'So there would still have been nothing left to the family?'

'That's right. In the end, I had the feeling he made a will as much to stop his relatives getting anything as . . . as . . .'

'As to make sure I got it all,' Davies completed for the embarrassed lawyer. 'I understand. So if I'd died before Edwin, but after he'd made his will, the money would have gone to the birds?'

Trimble shook his head sharply. 'No, no. Making you his main beneficiary was as far as Edwin would go. He wouldn't specify a successor beneficiary in the will.'

'Someone who'd inherit if I couldn't, you mean?'

'That's right.'

'Not even the bird charities?'

'Not even them, although they get some of the small legacies I mentioned. Edwin's sole concern at the time was not to die intestate.'

'That means without making a will, doesn't it? Because if that happens . . .'

23

'A person's estate has to be divided between his or her relatives according to formulas laid down by law,' the lawyer supplied.

'And Edwin wouldn't have wanted that to happen in any circumstances? He must really have hated his family.'

'I'm afraid so. He was a man with entrenched views and attitudes.' There was a knock on the door. 'Come in!' Trimble called, looking over Davies's shoulder. 'Ah, good morning, Annie. This is Mr Mervyn Davies. Mervyn, this is my indispensable secretary, Miss Annie Lewin.'

'Well I never. How do you do, Mr Davies. Come earlier than expected, have you?' Miss Lewin, in her late twenties, was bearing a handful of opened mail held out before her in her two touching palms like a votive offering. Pert faced and buxom, her dark hair, cut in a page-boy style, bounced in time with her breasts as she crossed the room. Her voice was low and musical, which Davies appreciated, also the waft of expensive scent, and the sight of her well-exposed cleavage as she rested the letters on the desk corner and leaned across to shake hands. 'No, don't get up. Can I get you anything?' She paused, holding his hand for a fraction longer than was necessary, and fluttering her eyelids becomingly before adding, 'Coffee or tea? There's both. Mr Trimble always has coffee, don't you, Mr Trimble?' She licked her top lip with the tip of her tongue, curled the front lock of hair under her chin with one finger, and stared playfully in the lawyer's direction as though there might be something revealing and deliciously sinful in his regular choice of beverage. He responded with a just audible snigger, as if to enjoin the same implication.

Davies settled for coffee too, and Miss Lewin moved around the desk to deposit the letters in front of Trimble. 'The extra tickets you wanted for the church supper are there on top,' she said. 'Perhaps Mr Davies would like one?' She gave the visitor a further wide-eyed smile that was both appraising and approving. 'St Luke's church is a hundred and fifty years old this weekend. There's an anniversary supper tomorrow night. In the new church hall. They built that in the old rectory garden,' she continued. 'Mr Trimble was telling me how he remembered you from the choir, when you were boys. There's lovely.'

'Not much of a churchgoer nowadays, I'm afraid,' said Davies sheepishly.

'Not to worry,' she said. 'Tomorrow's just the supper. Lots of people who've known St Luke's in the past are coming. From all over, they say. Probably plenty amongst them you'll know, Mr Davies. Isn't that right, Mr Trimble?'

'Oh, absolutely,' Trimble responded enthusiastically, his wife being the main organizer of the event that was so far embarrassingly under-sold. 'Come as my guest, Mervyn. Reception's at six-thirty. It's er . . . fairly informal,' he added, considering Davies's blazer again as he pushed a ticket across the desk.

'She's quite an eyeful,' said the Australian, a moment after Miss Lewin had left.

'Best legal secretary in the town,' the lawyer answered solemnly, as though the lady's looks were immaterial.

'Thinking about what you said, about the importance of a man making a will, d'you reckon I should make one, Dewi?'

'I think that would be sensible of you, yes.'

'When could we do it?'

'Just as soon as you've made up your mind who you'd want to make your heirs.'

'Oh, I can tell you that right now. I'll be leaving everything to my two sons. They're both married with kids. They'd manage nicely with a million each when I'm gone.'

The lawyer's cheeks hollowed markedly. 'You wouldn't leave anything to your divorced wife?'

'Would I have to? I mean, is she entitled to anything?'

'Not under British law. And not under Australian law either, so far as I know. Not if the children are grown up.' Trimble peered judiciously over the top of the half-moon spectacles. 'And you wouldn't want to leave anything to er . . . to Edwin's relatives? To Charles Edworth, and his sister Gail?'

'Definitely not. Not if Edwin didn't. I reckon he felt he had good reason for leaving them out.'

'Quite.' The lawyer cleared his throat, and looked as

25

though he intended adding something pertinent, then his features stiffened. 'Quite,' he repeated, looking down and pulling a white thread from his shirt cuff. 'If you like, when we've covered the business of Edwin's estate, I'll get Miss Lewin in and we can draft a will for you to approve, say, on Monday. That'll give you time to think of any extra legacies you might want to put in.'

'We can't do it all today?'

Trimble frowned. 'We could, no doubt, but I always consider it sensible not to rush over such a matter. There's plenty of time, after all.' He looked at his watch, as if to illustrate the fact, moved the pile of mail a little to one side, and opened the folder again.

3

'And so, to conclude the evening, let me say again how wonderful it was that so many were able to be here. I'm thinking especially of ex-members of the congregation who've come really long distances for the hundred and fiftieth anniversary of St Luke's. Two good people my wife Cloe said I forgot to mention earlier are Mrs Olwen Hughes, ninety-two years young, who's come all the way from Abergele in North Wales, and Mr Mervyn Davies, who arrived here from Perth, Western Australia, on Friday, would you believe? Well done, both of them.'

Of course, no one did believe that Mervyn Davies had come from Australia solely for the purpose just offered by the young Reverend Roy Gravler, a six feet two, slightly stooping, crosier-thin exemplar of Christian faith, enthusiasm and worthy endeavour. Not that anyone would have denied the well-meaning rector the right to use such a heart-warming interpretation of events for effect. Olwen Hughes had certainly been driven down from North Wales, but she came around this time every year to stay with her daughter. Too many, though, knew the real reason why Mervyn Davies had come back to Pontyglas, to the parish that, by all accounts, had shown no regrets when he'd been plucked from its midst, forty years before, as an orphan, and without concern being recorded by anyone, or interest in what became of him.

The likely size of Edwin Edworth's estate had been estimated in the *Pontyglas Gazette*, and there were rumours enough about who was to get most of his money. Davies was here, people knew, or thought they knew, to collect anything up to five million pounds – depending on which informant you believed.

'I'm sorry the bishop couldn't be with us because of pressure of engagements,' the Reverend Gravler continued with another half truth. Well, you could hardly announce that the bishop, who'd been invited a year in advance, was instead holding a confirmation service tonight at the other end of the diocese, because he'd forgotten to transfer the date to his new diary in January. 'But we're delighted to have had the archdeacon with us, and for his very witty and . . . inspiring remarks just now.' The rector beamed at the archdeacon, seated on his right, who had been close to dozing off, but who had come alertly awake, in a reflex way, when he had sensed praise in the offing.

The Reverend Gravler next allowed his approving beam to shine on everyone else present. Most were seated at the long table sprigs extending from the top table in the low-ceilinged, newish church hall. Slightly more people had come to the supper than advance ticket sales were indicating up to lunchtime. A last-minute surge in the numbers, possibly fuelled by the news that Mervyn Davies would be present, meant the event would cover costs, but it still hadn't been the success the rector had hoped. Of course, there would be a better turnout for the festival parish communion service tomorrow. The price of the tickets for tonight had been relatively high. His suggestion that the price had been too high had been ignored by Mrs Gwen Trimble, seated now on his left at the top table.

'Well, that ends the official programme, ladies and gentlemen,' the speaker added, crossing his arms tightly across his narrow chest as though he was preparing himself for voluntary embalming. 'But the cash bar in the room next door will stay open till ten for drinks and coffee. See you all again in church tomorrow, I hope. Good night, and God bless.'

'It's early yet, let me get you a drink, Mervyn,' said the garrulous, balding Geoff Godwin, catching up with Davies as everyone was moving away from the tables. 'We've hardly had time to talk yet. Sorry we weren't sitting closer. Nice meal. The rector goes on a bit, but he means well. Only been with us two years.' He waved at someone across the room. 'My wife Dilys has had to leave straight away. To drive our daughter and her husband home to Porthcawl, and then take their baby-sitter home after that. They don't have a car, see? I'll be walking home. We live just across the river. Above Newtown Fields. They're part of the park now. It's no distance really.' He took a short breath. 'Here, let me show you the old photo I've brought of the choir. Taken two years before you left, it was.' The well-nourished, deputy manager of the Pontyglas Council's refuse collection and street-cleansing department, and still a regular member of the choir, grasped Davies's elbow and steered him through the doorway towards the temporary bar.

'There we are, the two of us, side by side in the middle row, looking saintly in cassock and surplice,' said Godwin some moments later when the two were holding full beer glasses. The room, which was much smaller than the other, was filling up quickly. He pointed to the figures in the faded print he had produced from an envelope in his suit pocket.

Davies put on his glasses, then gazed thoughtfully at the picture. 'That's why I hardly recognized you tonight, Geoff. You were such a thin young fella. You've filled out and no mistake,' he said, grinning. 'And there's Edwin Edworth in the back row, with John somebody . . . John Sewell. Someone said he's here tonight.'

'He is. Let's find him. I'm sure he'd want to say hello, too,' offered Godwin, scanning the room, but with less real expectation on his face than his words suggested.

'John had a sister called Esme. Wasn't she in the choir too?'

'Yes. She joined the year this was taken. I remember she'd been chapel not church up to then.'

'What happened to Esme?'

'She left the town. You'd better ask John.'

Davies had gone back to studying the picture. 'And that must be Dewi Trimble sitting crosslegged in the front,' he said.

'That's right. Let's show Dewi.' Godwin stared about him again, but this time with more enthusiasm.

'No,' said Davies looking up, 'he and his wife weren't staying on. I was their guest tonight. They offered me a lift home, but I said I'd rather walk. Actually, I promised to have a drink with Annie Lewin who's just gone to the – '

'Dewi's wife Gwen, she's a marvellous organizer. Arranged all this tonight, you know?' Godwin interrupted. 'She gets things done, and no mistake. Great asset to a man's career, I should think, a wife like that,' he mused, either because he wasn't sure, or because his own wife lacked the qualities for the role. 'I suppose you'll be seeing a lot of Dewi, won't you? Over Edwin's will, like?' It was as close as anyone had got so far to quizzing the big man about his inheritance.

'So you are Mervyn Davies,' a spiritless female voice sounded behind Davies before he could answer Godwin's question. 'I thought it was, before we sat down. Before the rector said you were here.' The speaker was a thin, grey-haired woman of about sixty, with pale sunken cheeks, and penetrating grey eyes that suggested a burdened past and quite possibly an enduring resentment as a result of it. 'I'm Jacky Franklin. Jacky Morgan before I married. Alice Morgan's sister.' She paused, her lips tightening while she straightened the padded shoulder of her crocheted, beige jumper. 'It's been a long time, Mervyn.' There had so far been no warmth in the words. Mrs Franklin had offered plain statements of fact coloured with neither pleasure nor, as might have been expected with her last comment, any sense of regret that the lengthy separation had now ended.

'Glad to see you again, Jacky. You're er . . . you're married then?' Davies's words were warmer than the woman's, but not much warmer.

'With three children, yes. Grown up now. My husband Ken, he's landlord of the Coach and Horses.'

'And a very popular hostelry Ken and Jacky have made of it, as well,' put in Geoff Godwin with overplayed cheerfulness.

'Is your husband here, Jacky?' asked Davies.

'No. Saturday's our busy night. I wanted to be here though.

30

For old times' sake, I suppose.' But Mrs Franklin's voice was failing to suggest that the old times had been all that pleasurable, just as it was becoming increasingly clear that curiosity, not nostalgia, was what had brought her to speak to the Australian. 'Ken's not from Pontyglas. And before we took over the pub, I hadn't lived here for years myself.'

'How's . . . how's your sister? How's Alice?'

Davies's question seemed only to increase Mrs Franklin's coolness. It also evinced a nervous twitch at the corners of Godwin's mouth, as well as a sudden lowering in the noise level of chatter going on in other close-by groups.

'Alice? Alice died when she was very young. Seventeen, she was. I thought you'd have known that.' There was a twisted satisfaction in the tone.

The Australian shook his head. 'I never heard from anybody in Pontyglas after they shipped me out.'

'My family moved away soon after that. Very soon after,' Mrs Franklin said, her fingers stroking the silver cross hanging on a chain around her neck. 'We went to live in mid Wales. Near Llandovery. That's where Alice died.' She hesitated, breathed deeply, then added in a louder voice: 'Poor lamb.'

'Sorry to keep you waiting. There was a queue for the ladies. And here's someone else you haven't seen in a long time.' The effervescent tones of Annie Lewin, who had sat beside Davies during supper, at first brought relieved glances from both Davies and Godwin, and broke an awkward silence as the speaker squeezed through the crowd. The woman she was pulling behind her, by the hand, was a year or two older than Jacky Franklin. Short and stout, with a flustered expression on her red-veined face, she was wearing an unwaisted wool dress probably intended to make her appear less plump. 'You'll remember Winifred, I'm sure? She married Edwin Edworth's older brother Gwilym,' Annie continued, while resting a hand familiarly on Davies's arm.

'I remember Gwilym, all right, Mrs Edworth. Sorry to hear he'd passed away. Don't suppose you and I met that often, did we?' Davies responded carefully. 'Gwilym was very good to us younger lads. To Edwin and me.'

31

Mrs Edworth's tiny, sunken eyes darted to left and right. She was evidently confused, and before she could compose a reply, a male voice from behind her said: 'Well, that's more than my Uncle Edwin ever was to my sister and me in his lifetime. Or, it seems, after his death.' The young man who had spoken was thick set, with a shock of unruly black hair and a full beard, only lightly trimmed at the edges. 'My name's Charles Edworth, Mr Davies. I'm Gwilym's son,' he continued, looking from Davies to Annie, then pointedly at Annie's hand that was still resting on Davies's arm. 'Now if you'll excuse us, I have to get Mother home. She hasn't been too well lately. See you around. Good night.' He took Mrs Edworth's arm at the very moment when she appeared to be ready to say something – it seemed possibly to deny the suggestion that she hadn't been well. She still consented to being guided away towards the door, her parting expression indicating that she wasn't unduly disappointed that the encounter was over. Even so, it would have been clear, to a careful observer, that it had been Jacky Franklin's presence, not Davies's, which had caused Winifred Edworth's initial unease.

'They say Charles Edworth has a very promising career ahead of him,' put in Geoff Godwin quickly. 'Production engineer, he is. Pity his father fell out with Edwin.'

'Perhaps I shouldn't have brought Mrs Edworth over,' said Annie doubtfully, 'but she did ask if I'd seen Mr Davies since he arrived in Pontyglas. I just thought she'd like to speak to him again.'

Mrs Franklin made a loud tutting noise. 'Well, since you work for Dewi Trimble, Miss Lewin, you should have known she wouldn't really have anything to say to Mervyn. Not after the way his friend Edwin's treated her and her children. Or was it Charles Edworth you wanted over here for some reason? His wife wasn't with him tonight again, I noticed,' she completed, her penetrating, grey eyes staring unblinkingly into the young woman's larger, blue ones.

'I don't know what you mean by that, Mrs Franklin, I'm sure,' Annie answered sharply, but colouring.

*   *   *

'A very successful evening, if I say so myself,' said Gwen Trimble as her husband drew the Jaguar away from where it was parked outside the church. 'I'm leaving Cloe Gravler to see the caterers clear up. I hope she can cope. But really, I can't be expected to do everything. There's plenty of people to help her. She does little enough at the organization stage of anything. Keen but clueless, I'm afraid. The last rector's wife was much more on the ball. Older, of course.' She sniffed loudly before going on. 'I still don't see why Edwin Edworth left all his money to that man Davies. What could they have had in common, for God's sake? Edwin was strange in some ways, but he had a bit of style about him after all, and . . . and culture. Mervyn Davies is just a common Australian labourer.'

'Qualified bricklayer, actually, dear,' Trimble offered, but in a careful, uncontradictory voice.

'Exactly.' Mrs Trimble had been privately educated at a Gloucestershire ladies' college, in the fifties, and wasn't prepared to distinguish between labouring and a skilled trade.

'They had plenty in common in their younger days, of course. I remember Mervyn being quite . . . quite protective of Edwin. That was after he'd been ill,' Trimble reflected. 'Edwin was very sickly for a long time after. Bright mentally, but sickly with it.'

'But that was forty years ago. They hadn't seen each other in all that time. Or been in touch, you said. Turn the heating down, Dewi, will you?' She loosened the ranch mink jacket she was wearing over her green silk dress: it was late in the spring for furs, but not too late for Gwen Trimble. She had bought the dress at Harrods in January, during a special trip to London for the sales.

'A bond forged in childhood friendship can be very strong,' said Trimble in a romantic vein, while he lowered the climate control setting.

'Not that strong if there's no contact. Not usually. Not unless there's something else.' Mrs Trimble's eyes narrowed, and she gave an overtaking motorcyclist a hostile glare. 'He couldn't have had something on Edwin, could he?'

'What d'you mean by that?' Trimble sounded more

cautious than quizzical as he steered the car through the town square and on to the river bridge.

'I mean what I say. You know it's believed Mervyn Davies fathered a child, possibly several children, before he was deported?'

'Emigrated, dear. Before he emigrated.'

'All right, emigrated, but without the option, because he couldn't have stayed on account of the scandal. Or that's what they say. Mavis Turner was telling me one of the girls involved was the younger sister of that Franklin woman who was there tonight. The publican's wife. You must have known both of them. They were in the choir, apparently.'

'I think I may have known Alice, the younger sister, not Mrs Franklin. Not in those days. Anyway, I don't see what that's got to do with Mervyn Davies being Edwin's heir.'

'Unless Davies knew something like that about Edwin.'

'Like what? Putting girls in the family way? Edwin was only just eighteen at the time,' he offered, without embellishment.

'And I gather Davies was a year younger. Forward boy for those times, he must have been. It wasn't even the swinging sixties, was it? Could he have blackmailed Edwin?'

'You can't blackmail a man after he's dead.'

'You could if he'd done something terrible and wanted his reputation protected for ever.'

Trimble swung the car left after the traffic lights up Park Hill, the town's most prestigious area. They were nearly home now. They lived only a mile and a half from St Luke's, less than that, even, along the park footpaths. If he'd been by himself he would have walked there and back on such a fine spring night. 'If Edwin had done something terrible,' he said, 'I'd have known about it. He confided in me a lot, you know. Especially since his illness.'

'Well, even that's relative, isn't it? You've told me often how secretive he was by nature. No one would have known if he'd done something really illegal. You especially, I'd have thought. Only his best friend at the time, perhaps. Anyway, he didn't leave you any money.'

'If he had I couldn't have drawn up the will,' Trimble

34

answered pompously, and thinking again how hard he'd tried to steer Edwin Edworth into dividing his estate between his nephew and niece. 'In any case, he'd have thought we were too well off to need anything,' he completed.

'Well, that wasn't true for a start,' Mrs Trimble replied sharply, flicking imaginary dust from the front of her mink. 'Thank heaven Davies didn't want driving home. I was surprised you offered. He'd have expected us to go in for a drink and talk about . . . sheep shearing probably, or abolishing the monarchy. Will he stay on at Condleston Lodge after he gets the money?'

'I've no idea. He certainly won't need to go back to Australia or bricklaying, not if he'd rather do something else. Almost anything else.' Trimble was sounding increasingly preoccupied. They were halted in their own drive now, waiting as the automatic garage door opened.

The detached house was Edwardian, in much the same style as Condleston Lodge, though not nearly as large. It was matched by other, similarly prosperous-looking homes set well back from the road on both sides. Each house occupied an acre or so of ground, with those on this side of the road backing on to the open park.

'I need some exercise,' said the lawyer as he followed his wife into the house later. 'Think I'll take Hercules for a run.' Hercules was the name of the bull terrier now joyfully advancing on them, the remains of his docked tail wagging furiously.

'Good. I'm going straight up because I'm dead tired. Don't wake me when you come back.'

'I won't, dear.' It was what he had hoped she would say. He glanced at the time.

4

'You spoke to him, then? To Mervyn Davies?' In public, Ken
Franklin was as outwardly a cheerful person as his wife was
grave. In his case, though, what people took to be inborn
ebullience was for the most part a consciously manufactured
trait. He had determined years before to become the arche-
typal jolly pub landlord. His rosy cheeks, brawny arms and
weighty figure were natural enough adjuncts to the role:
the long bushy sideburns and flowing wide moustaches, the
hearty voice, the expansive gestures and the curled meer-
schaum pipe were all appendages aimed at enhancing the
'mine host' image in the minds of his customers. He had
played the part for so long now that he seldom dropped it,
except when he and his wife were by themselves. In reality
he was as much a melancholic as she was.

'I spoke to him, yes. Not for long though,' she said, in
answer to his question. It was just after closing time. She
had been back an hour before, serving as usual behind the
bar. They had just shepherded the laggards into the street
and cleared up the remaining empty glasses. Now they were
alone, and she was busy wiping over the bar tops.

The Coach and Horses in Pentre Street had recently been
refurbished by the brewery that owned it. The square, unpre-
possessing building had some right to its claim to have been
a coaching inn, though the fact had been effectively ignored
for over a century. While the place had been twice rebuilt
since the advent of the railway, the alley running northwards
at the side of the building had once led to stables, and a still
partly cobbled yard where the teams of coach horses had
been changed. Currently, part of this area was leased to a

motor mechanic who ran a repair and maintenance business in cramped, single-storey premises across the yard where the stables had once been. The yard itself was used mainly as a car park for pub customers.

As part of the refurbishment, the outside of the pub, previously redbrick, had been painted white. The name of the establishment was now displayed in large, free-standing Gothic-style lettering hung below a set of four carriage wheels with yellow spokes, their black hubs fixed level with the building eaves. At night the whole façade was illuminated from below.

The L-shaped main interior of the bar had been arranged with a series of dark oak snugs and alcoves around the walls, with chintzy cushions to the seats. There were extra tables and wheel-back chairs in the centre, including in front of the fireplace where the remains of a small log fire were still burning now. The mantel above this, like the surrounding wall space and lowered ceiling, was festooned with coachmen's whips, horse brasses, metal bits, and coaching horns, some of them genuine, but most of recent manufacture. Not to spoil the new Dickensian aura, the illuminated fruit machine and juke box had been placed out of the way, next to the washrooms, but where the clientele could scarcely miss them. Old customers, and there hadn't been many, had by now come to consider it all an improvement on the worn, nineteen-sixties interior that had been supplanted. Trade had increased since the redecorations, and while this was as much to do with the diligence of the Franklins as it was with the new decor, the improvement in profit to date had failed to come up to their own or the brewers' expectations.

'Changed a lot, had he?' Franklin was replacing some of the inverted spirit bottles in the row of optics behind the bar.

'Of course he had. But I'd have known him anywhere. He was always a big chap. Like you, he's put on too much weight.'

'What did you talk about?'

'Nothing much. He said he didn't know Alice had died.'

'Go on? Was that the truth, d'you think?' Franklin paused

37

for a moment to suck hard and pointlessly on his pipe which had been allowed to go out long since – it was a prop for his public image: he never smoked in private.

'May have been.' She grasped several used pint-glass tankards by their handles and plunged them into hot water in the sink under the bar top.

'Did you tell him Alice's baby had lived? That we brought him up?'

'Not then I didn't. It wasn't the place. Not in front of a lot of people. If I'd said Alice had died in childbirth, I don't think he'd have been interested. Well, not much, anyway.'

'The baby's survival had better interest Mervyn Davies. Now he's rich. Or going to be. Owen's his son, not ours. And the sooner he's reminded the better. All said and done, we know he's admitted being the natural father. Owen ought to get something for being who he is, and we should too for looking after him. Owen looks like him, does he?'

'No. Different colouring too. Mervyn's hair is dark, or was, till he went grey.' Their adopted son had carrot-coloured hair.

'Because he took after his mother, I expect.'

Mrs Franklin gave an exasperated sigh as she rinsed soapy glasses under a running tap. Even what he had just said was untrue: her sister Alice had been dark-haired. 'Ken, I've told you before, Mervyn is never going to accept Owen as his son. And anyway, I learned tonight he's got two legitimate sons in Australia.'

'He said that?'

'Yes. He's divorced now from the mother.'

'Well, I don't see why having two sons out there stops him accepting he's got an older one here. His rightful heir, you could say.'

'And I keep telling you there's no proof he was Owen's father.' She pushed hair from her eyes with the back of a wet hand as she went on. 'There's nothing on the birth certificate. Wasn't even a space for anything in those days. Not on the birth certificate of an illegitimate baby. It was only what Alice and Mervyn told my mam and dad at the time. Except Alice good as told me later the father wasn't Mervyn.'

'Well, nobody else knows that.'

'That may be, but Alice and my parents are all dead, aren't they? And they were the only ones Mervyn told.'

'Mervyn isn't dead.'

'He was a young boy when he said what he did. He'd have admitted anything to get to Australia. Putting himself in the wrong over Alice probably helped.'

'Not with the Australians, surely?'

'No, they wouldn't have known. I meant with the local authorities here. People were very puritanical then.'

'And did the local authorities know?'

'I'm not sure. I've wondered for years if my father put a word in somebody's ear. Or if Edwin's father, Dan Edworth, did. He had influence through the church. Oh, yes, plenty of that. And with the town council,' she added in a strangely bitter voice. 'Alice and Mervyn were too young to marry, and Dad wouldn't have had him in the family in any case. Poor Alice.' She was drying glasses now with unusual vigour.

'Well, she'd have done better to stay a virgin till she married, like you did,' Franklin pronounced flatly. His wife made no response. 'There's always blood tests to prove parentage,' he continued later, and reverting to the earlier point as he brought in a case of bottled beers from the storeroom beyond the bar.

'They don't prove if a man's the father of a child.'

'They prove if he could be, though.'

'Or that he couldn't be.'

'Suppose so.' He paused. 'But there's no one to say who the father was if it wasn't Mervyn. I suppose she knew herself, did she?'

'Oh, yes, she knew all right. Alice wasn't promiscuous,' his wife offered, still sounding bitter, and tightening her lips after she had spoken.

'Well, I still think Mervyn should be made to stand by what he admitted to your dad.' He joined her arranging glasses on the lower bar shelves as he went on. 'By the way, Owen was in tonight.'

'You never told me. Is he coming back? Staying the night?'

'Maybe. He came on his motorbike. On his way to see about a job in Swansea.'

'What sort of job?' She sounded suspicious.

'In er . . . in security. An evening job.'

'A nightclub bouncer again,' she deduced, without spirit.

'No, better than that, or so he said.'

'So what time was he here?'

'About six. Just after you left. We had a beer upstairs.' The Franklins lived above the premises. 'I er . . . I mentioned Mervyn Davies was in Pontyglas. He knew he was coming.'

'How?'

'I don't know. Somebody must have told him.'

She looked up at her husband quizzically. 'So what did he say about Mervyn?'

'Only that it was funny to be talking about his real father being just down the road, when he'd never seen him in his life.'

'Or wanted to before now. I wish he'd never been told.'

'Well, it was your mother who did the telling, not me. Didn't seem any harm at the time, of course. When he asked. How long ago was it? Twenty years or more now, must be. And he had the right, after all. Who'd have believed we'd hear about Mervyn ever again, let alone see him. Anyway, what's done's done. You can't go back.' He scratched his temple. 'Oh, and John Sewell was in too, early on. With his nephew. The one who's an army officer. Well, warrant officer. They were going to the church supper.'

'I know, I saw them there. Were they here the same time as Owen?'

'Yes, but he was upstairs changing. John Sewell said he'd noticed his motorbike in the yard.' He looked at the clock over the fireplace. 'By the way, Peter never brought those six chickens you asked for.'

'He didn't? But I need them for the lunches tomorrow. I'll brain that Peter for letting me down.'

'His van packed up. I said I'd go up and fetch the chickens myself. He's got left with a nice twelve-pound ham we can have as well. Cheap.'

'All right. But you'll have to go very first thing in the morning.'

'I'd rather go now and have the lie-in. Won't take half an hour to the farm, there and back, not this time of night.'

'All right. But don't stay yarning with Peter. Not too long anyway. And take this out first.' She was pulling an open plastic bin full of empty bottles from under the bar. 'I suppose you told Owen about Mervyn coming into Edwin Edworth's money?'

'Oh, he knew about that too.'

'I see.' But she sounded as if she doubted he was telling her the truth. 'Well, I hope he hasn't got ideas about asking Mervyn for money.'

'I don't see why not.'

'Because he might ask him for some for us as well, you mean? Except I've told you why Mervyn won't play that game, and it'll only shame us for asking. All of us. We've managed without anyone's help so far. Why look for it now? Especially from him.'

'Because this pub isn't paying its way, that's why,' he retorted hotly. 'Because Owen's unemployed again, and because Mervyn Davies is loaded. And he must know we all think he's Owen's father.'

She shook her head. 'Except Alice told me he wasn't,' she reiterated with a heavy, exasperated sigh.

'She could have been lying. She had to be lying to somebody. You, or your parents. Same applies to Mervyn. There are still people around from those days who know why your family left Pontyglas after he did. They can put two and two together as well. They'd believe he was Owen's father all right, especially if you said so.'

For a moment she seemed to be wavering, then her jaw tightened. 'No, you're wrong there. They might if it was just my word. But not while Mervyn's alive to deny it.'

'I remember Mervyn Davies when he was a boy. Remember him well,' said Winifred Edworth as she finished pouring the boiling water into the teapot. 'Big lad, he was. Bit rough with it. Your father never understood why Edwin made such a

41

friend of him. There was a reason though.' Her eyes clouded in thought as she stood stock still, with the electric kettle in one hand, and the top of the teapot in the other.

'Well, it'll come, Mother.' Her son Charles stroked his beard, and regarded her patiently for a few more seconds, before adding: 'Better put the top on the teapot, hadn't you?' He didn't intend to be here all night while she tried to conjure up reminiscences, but being with her for a cup of tea last thing seemed to settle her, especially if she'd been out. It was something his sister Gail didn't have the patience to understand – or didn't choose to.

'Oh, sorry, love. Miles away, I was.' She put the kettle down. 'And now I've even forgotten what I was trying to remember before. It's terrible getting old, isn't it?' she added, but lightly, as if this didn't truly apply to her. Then she moved across from the working-top next to the cooker to the matching yellow plastic table where she had set out the cups. 'Would you like a biscuit with your tea, Charles? They're fresh.'

He shook his head. The biscuits wouldn't be fresh, or at least they wouldn't be crisp because she kept putting them in the same tin as her cakes. It wasn't that she hadn't known better from girlhood not to leave brewing tea uncovered, or about not storing biscuits with cakes. These were just tonight's trivial manifestations of a serious and creeping malaise.

A week before this she had been found temporarily lost and disorientated two streets away from here, her home for over four decades, and in the town where she had lived since birth. She had made light of that too, afterwards, and he'd had to do the same for her sake. But it wasn't the first time it had happened.

Charles knew well enough that in her day, Winifred Edworth had been as acuitive a wife and mother as you'd find anywhere, but her mind was deteriorating rapidly. Her doctor had first treated her for depression, and now he was trying vitamin therapy, but neither strategy had availed much so far. It wasn't that she was particularly old, either. She was sixty-four, on the young side for Alzheimer's disease, the doctor had confided uneasily to her son – adding that perhaps it wasn't that: the vitamins might work wonders yet.

'Have you thought any more about giving up this house, Mother? Coming to live with Jane and me?' asked her son, as she sat down across the table from him.

Her whole body stiffened. 'No. And I'm not intending to either. I can look after myself, and Gail's in the flat upstairs. Well, she is some of the time.' Her husband had died five years before. The house had been divided more recently when her daughter had returned to Pontyglas to work for a dentist in the town. The idea had been to provide both women with independent quarters, and to give Winifred a feeling of security as she got older. 'I'm not ill, you know. Or infirm,' she claimed with spirit.

'Nobody says you are, Mother.'

'Dr Peebles does. He's only young, of course, with his tests and newfangled pills. Fat lot he can know about life when you're beginning to get on a bit.' Slowly, she put down the biscuit she had nibbled, then gave her raised open hand two delicate, short shakes over the plate to disperse any crumbs on her fingers. 'An extra hour's good sleep at night is all I need, but he won't give me the tablets he used to. The ones that worked for me.'

'I've asked him about that, Mother. They were pheno-barbital.'

'What were they?' she put in quickly, leaning forward to catch his words, eyes narrowing behind her glasses.

'Phenobarbital,' he repeated. 'Doctors don't like prescrib-ing those any more.'

'Why not? I remember that's what your father took for years.'

It was funny what she did remember, he thought. 'I don't know why not, Mother,' he said, leaning back, and running a hand through his mane of black hair – the same colour as his mother's had been, in her youth. In that way, both he and his sister had taken after her, not their father. He really didn't know, either, why the doctor was so obdurate, not in the circumstances. 'There are new sleeping pills now, of course, Mother,' he offered. 'Just as good. Like the ones he's given you.'

'Not for me, they aren't just as good.' She drank some tea, then folded her arms in her lap. 'Er . . . Jane wouldn't want me living in your house.'

'Now that's not true, Mother, and you know it. And the children would love you to be with us.' Except what she had said was partly true. Jane had only agreed as a last resort, because Winifred Edworth would pay them for her keep, and more. He supposed that his mother might have realized all that.

What to do with his mother was only one part of Charles Edworth's besetting problem. He had been planning to leave Jane and the two children for nearly a year, and it was certain his wife wouldn't take in his mother if that happened. He couldn't understand why his sister couldn't assume total responsibility for their mother – but then he was too selfish to be all that understanding. All he knew was that Gail had no other ties – well, none that she ever spoke about, and she seemed to see less of their mother than he did, even though Gail lived rent free in the flat above. She was out too often for a start: there had been no lights upstairs tonight, for instance. As he saw it, his sister being available to look after their mother had been the whole idea behind dividing the house.

'Worried about your job still, are you, love?' Mrs Edworth interrupted his thoughts after watching his tense face, and wanting to change the subject.

'No, no. Well, no more than usual.' And that wasn't true either. The firm had more production engineers now than it needed, and he was certain to be the next to go. In a way, being made redundant would force him into doing what he'd aimed to do for years – to set up his own consultancy in a bigger town: the severance money he'd get would probably be enough to finance him for a year, and he was sure he could make a go of it: in normal circumstances, that was. It was a question of priorities. Starting a consultancy might not leave him enough to cover a divorce settlement, plus ongoing family maintenance payments, plus possible contributions

towards whatever new living arrangements might be needed
for his mother. He knew that private nursing homes were
expensive, and beyond his mother's sole means, that's if she
lived for too long as an invalid, even assuming she sold the
house for a good price.

Altogether, Charles Edworth's financial future was in a
dangerous tangle, even if he kept his present job. 'Suppose
I'd better be going, Mother,' he said, swallowing the rest of
his tea.

Mrs Edworth looked quite pleased. 'Well, it was very good
of you to take me to the anniversary supper, dear. Meant a
lot to me, being there. Seeing old friends. So many of them.
I'm sorry er . . . er, oh dear, what's her name . . . ?' She
waved one hand despairingly in the air. 'Your wife . . .
er . . .'

'Jane, Mother,' he provided, tolerantly: she had known it
a moment ago.

'Yes, Jane, of course. I'll forget my own name next. I'm
sorry Jane couldn't be at the supper.' She had repeated the
name to make sure she didn't forget it again, at least until
after he left. Sometimes he made her so nervous.

'Well, it would have meant a sitter for the girls, and she
isn't all that involved in the church.'

'That's right. Pity about that. Still.' She reached up to kiss
him good night.

As he got into the car, he wondered if his mother counted
Mervyn Davies as one of her old friends, the man who was
inheriting Edwin Edworth's millions? By rights, that money
was his – well, his and Gail's, Edwin's only blood relatives.
He'd intended to see Davies that morning, to have it out with
him, the thing that had been festering in his mind since the
terms of the will had been revealed. His nerve had failed
earlier in the day, but he felt up to it tonight. He glanced at
his watch. There was probably just enough time to make the
other, more pleasurable call he had planned before con-
fronting Davies, who wasn't likely to be home yet. Besides,
he felt that the other call might help to strengthen his resolve.

5

'Alice Morgan was the prettiest girl in the town in them days,' said John Sewell, circling the remains of his beer around the bottom of the glass. 'And I can tell you, there was plenty of competition for the honour too, your mother included. Come to think, she was a close second to Alice for looks. Anyway, they was lovely girls, both of them. Good friends too. From school. Esme, your mother, she didn't join St Luke's choir till she was sixteen. That didn't please the family neither, her changing from chapel to church. Same as I'd done years before. That was to join the choir as well. The St Luke's choir was paid, see? Not for the ordinary services, but for weddings and funerals. Good money that was to us kids. Anyway, the family didn't do nothing to stop us.' His eyes became deeply thoughtful as he went on. 'Wouldn't have been the right thing to have a row about. Not then. Not with my dad working for Edworth's building company. All church and no chapel the Edworth family was. Most of their workers was the same.'

'And both my mother and her friend Alice died young,' said Sewell's sandy-haired nephew, Derek. He was a warrant officer in the regular army, dressed now in casual civilian clothes, and sitting on the other side of the fireplace where the coal fire was glowing red still. The two men were in the kitchen of the small terrace house that John Sewell shared with his semi-invalid wife, Iris, who had gone to bed before their return.

Both men were of medium height and wiry, the uncle pale and sinewy, in contrast to the bronzed soldier who was healthily spare and athletic looking.

John Sewell nodded at the last comment, and rubbed a cheek. His face and hands were ingrained with the black, telltale traces that seep into the veins, marking a man who has spent most of his lifetime working underground at the coal face. 'They died from different causes though,' he said, his left hand taking tobacco from his worn pouch, and spreading it deftly on to a cigarette paper. 'Your mother had pneumonia. They weren't quick enough treating her, and she was in a weak condition to start with. In London. By herself.' He tutted, keeping his gaze down, and not enlarging further. In any case, he knew no more than those bare facts. Not for certain. 'Alice was different. She did herself in. Not so many know that. Sinful waste in both cases.' There was steely regret in the eyes as well as the voice, and a brief, angry reddening of the cheeks. Mervyn Davies's presence earlier in the evening had brought back the whole sorry story as vividly as if it had all happened yesterday. The subject had come up after he had started to tell Derek how Jacky's sister, Alice Morgan, had been his girlfriend all those years ago.

'And they were both single parents?' Derek asked.

The other man paused after licking the edge of the cigarette paper and rolling it between his fingers. 'Unmarried mothers they were called in them days, Derek. Lot of shame went with it, too. Not like today. That's why your mam left home, leaving you behind. And why Alice's family left the town. Her baby was brought up by her sister like her own. Like you was brought up by your grandparents.'

'Who I never called anything but Mam and Dad. Still would, come to that, if they were alive. I don't think many people knew they weren't my real parents, either. I didn't know myself till I was fourteen, remember.'

'A lot of them as knew didn't let on to you, Derek. There was charity between friends in them days. Between real friends, any rate. They wouldn't have been the ones to cast the first clout, like the Bible says. And your gran was still young, too. She was only seventeen when she had me. Passed muster as your mam easy, she did.'

'I still want to know who my father was. Funny, I care

47

more about that as I get older.' The soldier emptied his own glass.

'Have another beer, Derek. There's plenty,' his uncle pressed.

'Only if we're sharing a can.'

'Right you are.'

'Then I'd better turn in. Ought to be on the road by half-five in the morning, if I'm going to make Heathrow by eight. And I won't disturb you, either. I'll have breakfast at the airport, after I've taken the car back to Hertz.'

'As you like, Derek.' John Sewell watched the man who had grown up in the guise of his younger brother stand up smartly and move to the table. Iris had left the cans of beer and glasses on a tray there.

John Sewell was proud that Derek had done so well in the Royal Engineers – got top promotion from the ranks, and learned a trade that would see him right when he left the service. He'd married a nice girl in Germany as well, and they had two lovely children. John just wished Derek had once been posted to South Wales, or at least near it, but he never had been: he would like to have known his nephew better. John had left home to work in the Rhondda Valley when Derek had still been very young, and they had never really lived in the same house after that.

The soldier was stationed in Germany now, near Düsseldorf. From what he had told John, he and the family lived in style there in comfortable quarters, with good schooling for the kids, and a Mercedes bought and paid for in the garage. John had only ever owned the small van that was at the back of the house now. Before Germany, Derek had been stationed in Carlisle, in the north of England, after two earlier spells of service abroad before he had married. He was only here today because he'd flown over to do a week's army course in Hereford, and had arranged to stop for a night on his way back.

John and Iris had appreciated the visit, short as it would be – also the gift Derek had pressed on them: they had no children, and no other family left besides Derek. It was Iris who had insisted that her husband should take Derek to the church supper that evening, saying she hadn't felt up to going herself. They had already bought two tickets which they could scarcely afford, but John sometimes got decorating jobs at the church, and at the home of Mrs Trimble, which they felt justified the outlay.

Iris had been right that nothing could have pleased John more than to parade his nephew before so many of the church's older members. Many of them had known Derek's background – some being even better informed about it than he was himself. John had only wished his guest had worn his warrant officer's uniform, but Derek had told him that soldiers didn't wear service dress off duty these days.

'I think I've told you before, your mam would never say who took advantage of her,' said the older Sewell, the twisted end of his cigarette now held tightly between nicotine-stained thumb and forefinger as Derek went back to his chair. Awkwardly, he moved his glass up and down along the chair arm, studying it closely as he searched for more words: the subject was one that they had never discussed at length. 'And . . . and that's what it was, see? Some bloody swine taking advantage. No doubt. She wasn't that kind of girl. Oh, not at all. Pure, she was, and innocent with it. And there's the trouble. Too innocent. Alice Morgan was the same. Exactly the same.' He couldn't leave Alice out. 'Wouldn't happen today, probably. Not in the same way. There's no innocence now. Or justice, that I can see.' He took a long draught of the beer, pondering his own words and the ultimate reaction his sister had suffered after that initial shock to her innocence.

'She didn't even tell her parents?'

John shook his head again, this time slowly as, over-deliberately, he stubbed out the remains of the cigarette in a black plastic ashtray advertising Manikin Cigars. 'Dad wanted to be fair, but he never really forgave her.'

'For getting pregnant?'

'Well, for that too. But I meant for not telling him who the man was. It was why she left home in the end. Couldn't stand him going on and on about it. Trying to force her to tell.' The eyes narrowed to slits. 'I think she believed he'd have killed him if he'd got the name. He might have, as well. He killed plenty of Jerry in the war, and that's a fact.' It had been the truth as he knew it – excepting only there was something more. He had always believed he knew who had seduced Esme – and Alice too.

'So why did my mother go to London?'

John Sewell didn't reply at first: his expression showed he was still preoccupied with his last statement. 'Sorry, Derek,' he said eventually. He blinked several times, then leaned forward, rubbing his roughened palms together. 'Why did she go to London? Same reason they say young people go there now who are not happy at home. Because it's big, and far away. And because the streets are paved with gold.' He gave a grim smile. 'She had a job to go to though. In service, it was. In an old people's home in Putney, I think. Yes, Putney. I remembered, at the time, because of the Boat Race starting there.'

'Doesn't sound as if it was much of a job.'

'It wasn't. But it gave her room and board at the start.'

'But she didn't stay long.'

John Sewell was hardly aware that his nephew was stating fact and not questioning any more. 'No, she didn't. And she er . . . she never accounted for her movements to Mam and Dad after that. She sent money though, to Mam. Every week. Regular as clockwork. Money for your keep. Not that Mam asked for it. She saved it for you. There was quite a bit in the end, because the postal orders kept getting bigger. I remember that.'

'So my real mother did care for me a little.' But the soldier's tone was grudging.

'Oh, she cared a lot, *bach*. The money was her way of proving it.'

'You know where she was living in the end?' Again it seemed the questioner knew the answer.

'Probably I did at the time.' The ex-miner rubbed his forehead. 'Let's see, was it –?'

'It was behind Paddington Station. That was her last known address. It was on her death certificate. Mam left that for me. As a matter of fact, I tried to see the place last year, but it's been knocked down. Block of flats there now. The duty sergeant in the local police station told me it was a change for the better. Used to be a cattery, he said. One of the best-known catteries in west London.'

John Sewell was bewildered. 'You mean a boarding place for cats? I've never been to London. Do they have –?'

'The sergeant meant it was a house that let off bedsitters to prostitutes. One of any number round there,' Derek interrupted. 'That's how my real mother ended up. Selling herself. And it wasn't just pneumonia she had either. It was pneumonia aggravated by syphilis. That's on the certificate as well. Didn't Mam tell you?' There was a despairing anger in his eyes now, but nothing to match the depths of outraged astonishment on his uncle's face.

'Mam never told me, no,' John Sewell uttered in a strained, shaking voice.

Mervyn Davies looked across St Donat's Place, the town square, and upwards at the new five-storey building, then quickly looked down again in an effort to steady himself. The drink seemed to be affecting him more than usual. His body hadn't got used to the change of hours yet, probably.

He hadn't been down this far into the town before. The last time he had stood in this same spot there had been a pork butcher's and a haberdasher's behind him, with a glimpse of the river in between. Then, the town hall, in classic style, with four columns and a pediment, had stood where the ugly new building was now. The shops he remembered had gone too, but at least the war memorial was still islanded in the centre of the square.

After they had left the church hall earlier, Davies and Geoff Godwin had walked back to Godwin's bungalow, using the river footbridge, and then the pathways through the park beyond, an area that had all been open fields in their youth. For his return route, Davies had chosen to go through the town centre, using the old main road bridge at the bottom of Park Hill. Godwin's place had been in a new cul-de-sac just off the hill.

On the outward journey, the two men had first stopped

at a pub near the church, and Davies had gone into Godwin's house for yet another whisky when they got there. He hadn't stayed long after that though. Godwin hadn't been drinking as much as Davies, and, aware that he was a bit fuddled, the Australian had wanted to avoid meeting Dilys Godwin, who was expected back from Porthcawl at any minute. He had also declined Godwin's offer to send for a taxi to take him home, insisting that he was perfectly capable of walking, and glad of the exercise. Now he wished he'd accepted the offer since he was suddenly very tired and a touch unbalanced. Still, it wasn't worth trying to find a taxi now: waste of money since he was nearly halfway home.

Bracing himself, he directed his deliberate steps past the St Donat's Arms, up shop-lined King Street, then right, opposite Trimble's office, along Pentre Street, and right again into the tree-lined Condleston Road. He wondered once again what had happened to Annie Lewin. She had told him that she lived somewhere near the station, on the north side of the town. He had offered to see her home but she had disappeared. Better luck next time, he thought ruefully. Still, he had enjoyed talking to Geoff and walking back with him. He stopped for a moment and looked about him. One thing hadn't changed: it was half past eleven, and even though it was a Saturday night, he had hardly seen a soul in the streets on his return walk. It would have been just that way forty years ago, too. Provincial towns had always rolled up the pavements before eleven, he ruminated, and probably always would. If people went out at night now, of course, they did so by car. There were more cars about than pedestrians, but few of either after he had passed the steepled St Luke's church, now deserted.

It was half a mile on, when he was in sight of Condleston Lodge, and with knees ready to give out under him, that he sensed he was on the verge of throwing up. He suppressed two bad waves of nausea before he reached the drive, increasing his pace, blearily brushing past a vehicle parked on the gravel, fumbling in his pocket for the back-door key but failing to find it. Knowing he couldn't now contain the nausea for more than a few seconds, he turned, gagging, from the door and, in a blind panic, thrust a way into the bushes at the side of the aviary.

A minute or so later, the big man staggered back on to the drive, bent headed, flushed, and wiping his mouth slowly with his handkerchief. It was as he raised his watering eyes that he heard a movement, but without sensing from which direction it had come.

'Somebody there?' he mumbled hoarsely, rocking on his feet, and looking back down the darkened drive. But the figure emerging from the shadow of the aviary had been behind him, and although Davies opened his mouth to call something more, the chance had gone for ever.

6

Jacky Franklin was up earlier than her husband on Sunday morning, as usual. In the days when he had been a British Rail engine driver, and she had been a cook in a factory canteen, she had always taken the children to church on Sunday mornings, and when they left home, she had gone by herself. Ken had never been much of a believer, and he'd enjoyed his Sunday lie-in when he hadn't been on duty, and he still did. More recently, Jacky had given up churchgoing, except at Easter and Christmas, but since they had been in pub management, with meals to cook and serve every day of the week, she needed to be in the kitchen before eight on Sundays, as she was on all other days.

The Franklins employed the minimum of help – just a cleaner three mornings a week, a part-time barmaid on weekday mornings, and a widow who did the cooking on Saturdays only, which was one of her two days off from doing the same thing at the local comprehensive school. There was no paid help on Sundays, the one day that bar food wasn't provided in the evening.

This morning Jacky had got up especially quietly because Ken had sacrificed some of his sleep the night before, fetching the chicken from Peter Baylis's farm. She had vaguely heard him coming back, but had been too sleepy to look at the time. In all probability he'd stayed for a beer with Peter. She didn't begrudge him that: he had little enough time to socialize with real friends. Both she and Ken liked Peter Baylis. He was young still, and a redundant coal miner. He and his wife had ploughed his severance money into a pig and chicken farm, supplying local pubs and restaurants. They were doing good business too, quite a bit better than a lot of their customers, including the Franklins.

Jacky had also heard Owen come in. He had long since stopped living at home, but he had a key to the back door of the pub. Although Ken Franklin had warned him to be extra quiet if he came back from Swansea to spend the night, his motorbike had woken Jacky. This time she had looked at the illuminated dial of her bedside clock: it had been twenty to two.

Get the chickens ready, that's the main thing, Jacky thought to herself after she had filled the kettle, donned her apron and switched on the radio at low volume. She'd take Ken a cup of tea at nine, and have a cup herself now, as soon as the kettle boiled. They neither of them bothered with a proper breakfast any more. She'd let Owen sleep in though, since he hadn't left her a note to call him.

She looked about the large kitchen, approving its shining stainless-steel equipment and working-tops. The brewers hadn't stinted on the new stuff they'd put in here – not that there had been much option about doing up this part of the premises properly, since the EU food regulations were very strict, too much so by the standards of most small caterers.

Ken had stowed the three chickens she would be roasting today in the fridge side of the big, two-door upright fridge-freezer. She checked that the other birds were in the freezer as she had instructed. She was looking for the ham he was bringing back too when she heard the door at the foot of the staircase to their flat open behind her.

'Morning, Mam. There's ravishing you're looking this lovely day.'

'Especially as you can't see my face,' she answered tartly, pleased all the same, and turning around to greet Owen. 'Thought you'd want to sleep on this morning.'

'No. Got to be in . . . in Cwmbran by ten at the latest. Promised to see a man there.'

'You want some breakfast, I suppose?' She pushed the hair away from her forehead with the back of her hand. Her eyes had brightened as they always did when Owen was around, even the times when he only came to borrow money.

'Yes, please, but nothing fancy. Just eggs, bacon, sausage,

tomatoes, and er . . . mushrooms if you've got any. Oh, and some kidneys would go down a treat as well. But don't go to any trouble.' He chuckled, moved across, took her in his arms, hugged her, then gave her a warm kiss on both cheeks. 'I'm only joking. Tea and toast is fine,' he completed.

'Well, we can do better than that for our special visitor who doesn't come often enough. But I haven't got any kidneys,' she said, in spite of her rational promptings not to indulge him, and in spite of all the things she had to do, without wasting time making hot breakfasts. He was her favourite still, despite his being her sister's child, and not her own. She loved her two daughters well enough. They were both married now, one living in Liverpool and the other in Canada. But she was even fonder of Owen, while hoping still that he would mend his ways, and be a credit to her and to Ken in the end.

Handsome, well-nourished Owen Franklin was over six feet tall, with a freckled, open face, and a full head of wavy, auburn hair. At forty he still had a supple physique, and apparent boundless energy supplementing a good brain and an engaging personality – none of which explained or excused his dissolute existence.

The less charitable of Owen's acquaintances could never credit why his lifestyle – including his fairly heavy drinking – hadn't taken its just toll by now. But he continued to thrive in his chosen role as an amusing drifter, living off his wives when possible – he had had three so far – and a succession of girlfriends when it wasn't. Between marriages, and girl-friends, he had tried various occupations – insurance sales-man, bus conductor, assistant in an abattoir, superintendent at a municipal swimming pool, security guard, and deputy manager in an amusement arcade. None of these positions had provided him with long-term prospects, which was no more than he had expected, even if he'd been invited to remain in any of them, which he hadn't been.

'Did you get the job?' Jacky asked, leaving the chickens, and fetching eggs and other things from the fridge for Owen's breakfast.

'Turned them down, didn't I?' he answered airily, helping himself to some grapes from a handy sprig. 'Mark you, they pleaded with me. On their knees, almost. I was touched, naturally. But, I asked myself, where's the future in wasting my undoubted talent and enviable experience as front-of-house manager at a bloody disco, all for a lousy three hundred quid a week.'

'They were paying that much?' she questioned in surprise.

'Well, not quite.' He grinned, sitting, back to front, on a kitchen chair. 'More like two hundred come to think, with a fiver a week extra if I had my own dinner jacket, which I have, except it's in hock at the moment.' He was usually frank with her, the more so when there was a special reason.

'So you didn't get the job,' she said flatly.

'Oh, you always find me out, don't you? Too old, they said, and not tough enough looking.'

'Too old,' she repeated, and sighed, while pouring cooking oil into a frying pan. 'From what your father said, I thought it was a bouncer's job.'

'No, no. But for a hundred and fifty a week –'

'You said two hundred just now.'

'Did I? Well, whatever.'

'I could lend you the money to get your dinner suit back.'

'And you're my very own darling still for offering. But I'd be better off staying on the dole than going to work there. Not that I couldn't have kept the dole too, not if I'd handled it right,' he ended ruminatively, tapping a rhythm on the chair top with his two first fingers and calculating how much he could say he needed for the dinner jacket.

'I wish you wouldn't say things like that, Owen. It's dishonest taking national security money, if you're working.'

'But everybody does it, Mam.'

'No, they don't. Your father –'

'Oh, let's leave him out of it, shall we? And no telling him I didn't get the job, either. Just say I turned it down.'

Her lips tightened. 'Why were you so late getting back? It's only half an hour on the bike to Swansea, specially the speed you go.'

'Ah, I had a few other things to do while I was there.'

'Norma, was it?' Norma had been his second wife. 'I thought she'd got married again?'

57

'She has. To a copper. I thought he was on night duty. He was too. Only not all night.'

'For shame. Why can't you leave that one alone? She was never any good to you. How many of these rashers d'you want?'

He half rose to look at them. 'Four, please.'

'And fried bread?'

'Yes, lovely. But you shouldn't be bothering like this.'

'Your father said you were asking about Mervyn Davies. Want to see him, do you?'

He shrugged. 'I might do, or I might not. Is he staying around?'

'You can't prove he's your real father, you know.' She was emptying the cooked eggs from the sizzling frying pan on to a plate she'd had warming.

'A lot of people wouldn't agree about that. Dad said he admitted it. Before he went to Australia.' He turned the chair round to face the table, and sat on it.

'Doesn't mean anything. And all the people he's supposed to have told are dead. You know he was married? In Perth, I think. Divorced since, but he's got children. Two sons. You want ketchup?' She put the laden plate down in front of him.

'No thanks, Mam. Bit of toast would be nice later.'

'Right, and I'll make the tea now.'

'Marvellous!' He sliced open the yoke of one of the fried eggs then dipped bacon into it. 'If I could prove he's my father, I reckon I'd be entitled to a lot of his money when he dies, don't you?'

'I don't know, I'm sure, love.' But she sounded a lot less negative on the subject than she'd been with her husband the previous night. 'You don't look like him. Not a bit.'

'That's because I've got the Morgan family good looks, like you. There's good sense for you.' His eyes sparkled as he went on chewing. 'Doesn't mean he's not my father. There's ways of proving he is. Well, one at least.'

'A blood test, you mean? That'll only prove he might be your father.'

'But if it did, he'd have to swear on oath he wasn't, and

I'm sure there's people who'll say he was. Enough for a court case, I'll bet.'

'Court case now, is it?' She gave a disparaging sniff as she brought the teapot to the table, and sat beside him. She was pleased that he was enjoying the breakfast she'd cooked. 'But nothing anyone said would be proof of anything. It's like many in the town still think your mother died in childbirth, Owen, in Llandovery. And that's something I'd rather they went on thinking. It's what I'll tell Mervyn Davies when I see him next. It's nearer the truth of what really happened than the bare truth itself,' she added bitterly. 'But if it came to proving, there's a death certificate that shows your mother took her own life three days after you were born. While the balance of her mind was disturbed. That's what it says. My own mother couldn't stand the shame of both things that happened. Alice being a mother and not married, then killing herself. It's what we've tried to keep to ourselves all these years. She was such a lovely girl, our Alice.' There were tears welling in her eyes as she went on. 'There's only one thing we can be thankful for. It wasn't my husband driving the train she jumped in front of at Llandovery station. It could have been though. Easy.' She shook her head at the thought.

Owen put down his knife and stretched out his hand to cover hers. 'I know, Mam.' He paused, squeezing her knuckles until he could feel she was over the distress. 'But the other's different really, isn't it? About whether Mervyn Davies is my father, I mean.' He went back to filling his fork. 'You're sure my mother never told you he was? I mean, you were sisters. You must have told each other things like that. Intimate things.'

'She never told me that,' she answered dully, and without hesitation, because it was the truth. She hadn't ever needed telling who Owen's father had been.

'Or hinted who it was?'

'No.' But this time there was stern resolution in her tone as she continued. 'And so far as I'm concerned, I wouldn't give Mervyn Davies the satisfaction of thinking he had any part in your making. Any part at all. Not for all the money in creation. I've cared for you since the day you were born.

You're my son, from my sister's womb, it's true, but that's the only difference. You're my son, and the son of the man sleeping upstairs who sacrificed more than you'll ever know bringing you up. You and our girls. We're your parents by right. You don't have to look any further than that.'

'No, Mam,' he replied, appearing for the moment to accept what she had said.

It was only ten minutes later when Jacky waved Owen goodbye outside. He hadn't got to the point of asking her for money, before she'd given him the twenty pounds she had ready in any case. She was too soft with him, of course, which was what she was telling herself after she'd got the chickens ready for the oven and was taking the tea up to her husband.

'Owen gone, has he?' Ken Franklin asked sleepily as he lifted himself on to his elbows in the double bed. 'His bike woke me when he came in. And just now. Pity he's gone. I wanted another word. Did he say anything else about seeing Mervyn Davies?' He smoothed his side whiskers slowly with the fingers of his left hand: that was always his reactive gesture when he awakened.

She put the tea down on the bedside table and went to draw the curtains. The bedroom was quite small and over-looked the yard at the back which the pub shared with the repair garage opposite. There was room to park a dozen cars there, and a notice reserving most of the places for pub customers. 'I think he wants to see Mervyn. But not today. He has to be in Cwmbran.' She looked down at their old Volvo Estate parked below, then up at the sky. 'Forecast says rain mid-morning. I hope it holds off till Owen gets there. It's so dangerous on a motorbike in the rain.'

'You've been saying that since he got his first one, and that was more than twenty years ago.'

'And he's had three accidents in that time, too.'

'None serious though. Stop fussing, woman. He can look after himself.'

She turned around. 'And where's that ham? It's not in the fridge. Didn't you get it from Peter?'

'Ham?' He slurped up some tea. 'Oh God! Must have left it in the car – which means I didn't lock the rear door. It was too much to bring it in with the chickens as well. I meant to go back for it, then it went out of my head. Damn! Hope it hasn't been pinched.'

'I'll get it.'

'It's in a Tesco bag. Lovely shoulder of ham on the bone.'

He was right, he hadn't locked the rear gate door of the Volvo, but when she lifted it a minute later, out in the yard, she could see the white bag with its blue strips and red lettering sitting quite far forward. That was a blessing, anyway. They couldn't afford to have expensive food stolen.

The bag was heavier than she had expected when she pulled it out of the car and held it, while pulling the rear door shut and locking it. Anyway, the ham would be perfect for lunchtime chicken and ham salads today, and through the week. It would do for sandwiches as well, except customers never seemed to appreciate home-cured ham in sandwiches, they'd rather have what she dismissed as the factory stuff. More fool them.

Back inside the kitchen she put the bag on the table and fetched a metal carving plate for the ham. Then she opened the bag for the first time.

Momentarily the blood inside the bag surprised her. It flashed through her mind that Ken might have picked up an uncooked piece of meat by mistake, or that Peter had handed Ken the wrong package. That was before she opened the bag wider. The whole of the inside of it was blood soaked, but at that point the mere presence of gore had ceased to be her concern. By then she was transfixed by the object she had disclosed. She staggered back from the table, head swimming, stomach heaving, fingers squeezing her cheeks, her jellified legs giving way under her.

'KEN!' she screamed, sinking on to a chair edge. 'KEN! HELP!' she repeated with all the volume she could manage, closing her eyes, unable to look again at the horror in front of her – at the blood-streaked object with the staring open eyes, the sagging, pig-like flesh drained to a ghostly, ghastly white. Except it was no part of a pig she had uncovered: it was the severed head of Mervyn Davies.

7

'You know it's nearly half past nine?' murmured the thirty-eight-year-old Detective Chief Inspector Merlin Parry, focusing his eyes on the bedside clock. He scratched the curly, straw-coloured hairs on his bare chest.

'My father always says it's sinful to be in bed after eight,' answered the lissom, naked Perdita Jones sleepily, snuggling herself closer against him.

'Depends if there's an incentive keeping you there, would you say?'

'I don't think that'd make any difference to my father.'

'Hm.' His broad brow knitted. 'And that's Sundays included?'

'Sundays especially. My parents always go to the eight o'clock service.'

'There's pious of them.'

'Not really. There's no sermon at the eight o'clock. My father hates sermons.' Perdita still had her eyes closed.

'Ah, I knew there had to be an incentive.' He had been studying her face. Now he ran a forefinger gently down her forehead and on to the tilted end of her nose, then he kissed her lightly on the lips. 'Happy?'

'Yes.' Her hazel eyes opened and stared gravely into his. 'I still feel guilty though. Because you're being so . . . so unselfish. It's shaming.'

'Well, you can start feeling innocent again. It's all part of my fiendish plot. I'm counting on you to keep me in my old age.' He considered for a moment. 'Or even in my middle age. The South Wales police are bound to be cutting back again soon.'

'I'll keep you if I qualify.' She moved away from him, raising her arms and running her hands through her longish, loose blonde hair which in the daytime she wore in a ponytail.

'I was wondering something in the night,' he said, dropping his head back on the pillow and staring at the ceiling. 'Does going back to medicine make you feel kind of easier about Rosemary?' He was raising a subject that had been in both their minds but never alluded to directly during a long and often tortuous discussion the evening before.

She leaned up on one elbow and stared into his face. 'I knew you'd think that eventually. Yes, it does. No, don't.' She put a hand gently over his mouth before he could reply. 'Don't be angry with me.'

'I couldn't be. Not with your hair over your eyes like that. It's very sexy. And the rest,' his gaze was on the curves of her pendant breasts.

She frowned. 'I'm being serious. About Rosemary. I know now it's what I need to do –'

'To square the account?'

'Something like that, yes. It's difficult to explain. It's not my main reason for doing it.'

'I didn't think it could be,' he put in.

'But . . . but it's the best one. I feel better about us now than I have since . . . since –'

'We started sleeping together,' he completed for her. 'I thought that would come into it.'

'Are you miffed?'

'No. Because, like you said, it couldn't be the only reason you want to be a doctor. But if it's the final balancer, so be it.'

'It is. And I love you. And I'll marry you when I've qualified. That's if you still want me.' She laid her head on his shoulder.

'I'll want you,' he answered with conviction. 'I've been thinking, I could probably get a job with the Met, or with one of the other forces close to London. That way we could live together.'

'Please, darling, don't think about that,' she came back

quickly, and he felt her whole body tense a little. 'For the next three years there won't be room in my life for anything except work. I don't know whether I'm going to make it, but it wouldn't be fair to either of us if –'

'If I got blamed for distracting you,' he interrupted.

'Especially if I failed. I'm just being practical. In any case, we both like working here in Wales. It wouldn't make sense for you to pull out now for a . . . a short-term reason.'

Inwardly he had to agree with her, except at the moment three years seemed longer to him than short term. 'So you reckon to sell the bungalow, and rent a London flat?'

'Yes. I thought of letting the bungalow, but it's a good time to sell.' She owned a bungalow in Tawrbach, a small market town some miles west of Cardiff. 'I think a friend may have found what I want already in London, near the hospital. Nothing grand. Two bedrooms though, so I can let one to another medical student.'

It pleased him that his place would be her Welsh base from now onwards. 'So how many weekends will you get off as a medical student?' he asked.

'Quite a few. I'll come down for some of them. Promise. That's until I start hospital work. It'll be tougher after that. The hours are diabolical. You can be on call for days and nights on end. The same as junior doctors.'

'I'm on call right now,' he replied, kissing her again, on the ear this time. 'It's really not too bad,' he added with a chuckle.

'Ah, that's not the same thing. In hospital you have to be on the premises the whole time. You can't swan off to some ritzy pad.' She looked around the room they were in. It was the larger of the two bedrooms of his flat – on the fourth floor of Lincoln House, Westgate Street, in the centre of Cardiff, the capital city of Wales. It was certainly an expensive property, but Parry leased it cheaply from a friend in a multinational company. The friend had been seconded to New York for an indefinite period, and he and his wife had just wanted someone they trusted to look after the place and its contents. Parry had sold his own house in Tawrbach, after the death of his wife, nearly two years before this.

64

'Well, it'll all be worth it in the end, Dr Jones,' he said, smiling, if a touch ruminatively.

'You realize, I'll be thirty-one when I qualify? Possibly thirty-two.'

'Well, so long as you keep your hair and teeth, we'll manage, I expect. Anyway, you'd be a lot older if you weren't half qualified already.'

'If I wasn't, I wouldn't have the courage to go back.'

In a way, of course, he still wished that had been the case.

Six years before, Perdita had dropped out of medical school in the fourth year, because she was getting married. She had later qualified instead as a physiotherapist. The marriage, which, like Parry's, had been childless, had ended in divorce after four years.

Rosemary, Parry's wife, had been Perdita's closest friend. Perdita and the widowed policeman had recently become lovers only after she had gone through months of soul searching. This was because the two had been attracted to each other before Rosemary's death, and Perdita had never overcome the fact that they had succumbed to that attraction for a brief interlude on the very evening before Rosemary's short and fatal illness had been diagnosed. Parry had been deeply affected by the episode too, but had come to terms with it a lot sooner, the more so because their fleeting affair had been technically unconsummated – if through force of circumstances, not intention. But it had remained a constraint in Perdita's mind, despite her pretence to Parry that she had finally dismissed it. Certainly it had been lingering with her still, until last evening when she had revealed her new career decision to him. Afterwards, she had been so uninhibitedly passionate in bed that he had easily divined the mental source of this physical release.

Parry's hope that they would marry soon had been dashed by Perdita's new plans, which she had announced with no prior warning. He had known that she had been vaguely contemplating going back to medicine ever since her husband had left her. He had always believed, though, that this had been as much self-justification by a bitter and rejected wife as it was a seeking after genuine fulfilment. He had hoped too that their new relationship would have ended any competing major yearnings. And things had gone against him now only because Perdita had unexpectedly been offered a place in the medical school of a London teaching hospital where one of her earlier tutors was on the faculty.

Although Perdita had promised that she would marry him after she qualified, she was firmly against a formal engagement before then. Marriage had destroyed her primary career plans before to no purpose, and she was determined to put her vocation first this time. Parry had been mature enough to agree about the wisdom of this.

'So you need to be in London in three weeks or four?' he asked.

'Three, really. To start cramming through the summer. I have to retake some exams in early June.'

'What happens if you fail?'

'I shan't.'

'Such confidence.'

'I passed them easily enough before. It's the next year that's daunting.' She was lying very close to him again. 'I'll give myself a two-week break at the end of June. We can still go to France, as planned. That's . . . that's if you want.'

It was the first concession she had offered since breaking the news. 'I want. So you're on then for a breezy drive to the Riviera. I'll start polishing the Porsche tomorrow.' He had bought the four-year-old, immaculate convertible from a bankrupt yuppie at the height of the recession. 'What about the rest of this month?'

'I have to work till the last minute at the hospital here. They've been marvellous about letting me go without reasonable notice. And I have to find someone to take on my private patients too.'

'So we'll still have the weekends?'

'The Sundays, anyway. I'll need to work Saturdays.' She sighed. 'There's so much to fit in.'

'I'll help.'

'Oh, darling, you are being marvellous.' She leaned over him, lacing her arms around his neck.

'I know. It's because of the wholesome way you have of

showing your appreciation.' He chuckled, running his firm hands down her back.

It was then that the telephone on the bedside table rang – with the extra stridency a telephone bell only affects when it's interrupting lovers.

'And does anyone know where the rest of this Mervyn Davies is, Gomer?' the irritated and frustrated Merlin Parry demanded sharply fifteen minutes later. He was gunning the Porsche up the ramp of the big basement garage under the flats without his usual concern for the sensitivities of a delicately tuned, cold engine.

'Not yet, boss. Local force is at the house where he was staying. In Condleston Road, Pontyglas, that is,' answered the chubby, fifty-three-year-old Detective Sergeant Gomer Lloyd, in a lower even than normal sepulchral tone. He was sitting in the passenger seat, the fingers of one hand agitating the bristles of his walrus moustache so determinedly as to suggest he might have lost something in it. The fingers had been thus engaged ever since he'd got into the car, their action a sign of his severe embarrassment. It was Lloyd who had phoned earlier from the Major Crime Support Unit in Rumney, on Cardiff's east side, where both officers were permanently based. 'Er, sorry again I had to get you out, like,' he completed.

'Up, as well as out, Gomer,' Parry enlarged as he turned the car left on to the wide and nearly empty Westgate Street.

'Worse still then.' Lloyd cleared his throat at a pitch that was a further half tone down the basso profundo scale. 'I thought you might . . . might have a visitor,' he said.

Lloyd and Parry had been friends since the time when both had been sergeants. It was a relationship that neither ever allowed to impinge on their official one. The reliable, efficient but unambitious Lloyd had been delighted when the young, high-flying Parry had got two promotions since then, and the sergeant and his wife had been an especial source of moral support and comfort when Parry's own wife had died. Lloyd was fairly well informed about the state of Parry's present love life.

'Perdita's staying,' Parry answered in a matter-of-fact voice. 'She won't be around here much longer, though. Going back to study medicine. In a London hospital.'

'Go on? That'll take years, won't it?'

'Three, in her case. Well, four at the most.' Parry was trying to be positive.

Now more relaxed, Lloyd folded his stout arms over his seat belt. 'That'll go quick enough, you'll see. Nice when it's over, though. Doctor of medicine. Well, well. Wish we had one of those in the family.'

'Your kids have done well enough.'

Lloyd had five grown-up children. 'I know, but a doctor's special. She'll be in the big earners after she qualifies, too. So could you, of course. You could be chief superintendent in four years, easy. Balance things nicely, that would.' The view confirmed what Parry had been trying to tell himself, but it was good to have it volunteered by someone else, even if the judgement was biased. Gomer Lloyd was respected for his objectivity, but as much, too, for being conscientious for the job's own sake, and not because he was after someone else's. 'Still, pity about you having to work today,' he added.

'Not your fault, Gomer. I'm on stand-by.' It seemed it was Parry's open season for gratuitous magnanimity.

'I know, but the super expected DCI Chambers to catch this one, except he's gone sick. Got that diverticulitis again. He needs to control his diet better.' Lloyd took a keen interest in other people's medical conditions. He and his ample wife credited their own robust health to factors as diverse as the consumption of organically grown vegetables, the use of homeopathic remedies when remedies were required, and to their still being regularly involved as active participants in a ballroom dancing society. He began searching for a roll of peppermints in several of the patch pockets of his short padded rain jacket.

'There are some mints in the glove compartment,' offered Parry: more magnanimity.

'Thanks.'

'You're welcome. They're probably yours anyway.' They had just turned left out of Castle Street into Kingsway with the high wall of the Gothic, fairy-tale Cardiff Castle on their left, and the white stone, baroque Law Courts, City Hall, and National Museum of Wales bathed in sunlight on their right, features of Cathay's Park, the most elegant of all Edwardian civic centres. Parry was heading north for the fast road above the city: that way they would be in Pontyglas in less than half an hour. 'So, the deceased left the town forty years ago?' he said.

'That's right, boss. Went to Australia as an orphan lad. Only been back two days. Came to claim an inheritance.'

'Bet he wished he stayed away, all the same. Big inheritance, was it?'

'Tidy enough, I should think. The story is, Edwin Edworth has left him all his money.'

'Edwin Edworth of Edworth Motors?'

'Yes. He died last month.'

'I remember reading. Related, were they?'

'Don't know, boss. Don't think so.'

'Anyone found a weapon?'

'Not yet. Only Mr Davies's head. In a Tesco bag. It should have been a shoulder of ham.'

'How d'you mean?'

'It's alleged there was a ham in the bag earlier on. The licensee of the Coach and Horses in Pontyglas, name of Ken Franklin, he bought it from a farmer in Llanharan last night. Went there after closing time. Says he left it in the back of his car by mistake when he got back. That was around midnight. The car wasn't locked. That was by mistake as well, he says. It was in the car park at the back of the pub. He'd taken something else inside, some chickens, it was, and forgot to go back for the other.' Lloyd had a notebook out now and was consulting it. 'That's what he's told the local CID so far.'

'And his wife found the head this morning?'

'Before he was up, yes. Gave her a nasty turn, too.'

'Well, that's not surprising. I wonder if she found it by mistake?'

'How d'you mean, boss?'

'Her husband seems prone to making mistakes, except this

69

could be a genuine one, if he left the head where it was on purpose. He could have been meaning to get rid of it later.'

Lloyd rubbed one cheek with an open palm. 'Ah, but he'd sent her to fetch the ham, as he thought, after she took his tea up this morning.'

Parry looked unconvinced. 'Did Franklin know the victim?'

'He says not. His wife did though. That's why she recognized the head. She'd been with him last evening. At a church supper. In the parish hall of St Luke's. That's in Condleston Road as well, next to the church.'

'I see. Did they leave together?'

'No. She says he was still there when she left. That was around quarter to ten. She was serving in the pub from ten to closing time.'

Parry absently pinched the end of his nose as they waited for a red light to change. 'And was Franklin on his own when he came back from the farm later?'

'I think so. He was when he got to the Coach and Horses, anyway.'

'And he'd left for Llanharan when the pub closed at eleven?'

'Bit after that. He and his wife cleared up in the bar first.'

'Why did he go so late? Couldn't it have waited till this morning?'

'Don't know, boss. We'll need to ask.'

The chief inspector nodded. 'All right, say he left at ten past eleven and he was back by midnight. Would it take fifty minutes there and back from Pontyglas?'

'Shouldn't think so. Not at that time of night. But he says he stopped for a drink with the farmer. Name of . . .' Lloyd hesitated while squinting hard at his own notes. 'Peter Baylis. We're checking on him now, and the time Mr Franklin left him.'

'Do we know when Davies was last seen alive?'

'There should be some gen on that by the time we get there, boss. Mrs Franklin said he was with a group of people when she left the supper.'

'Any background on Franklin?'

70

'Plenty. Aged fifty-nine. Ex-train driver. Sober citizen. No police record, well, he couldn't have, him being a pub licensee. Been at the Coach and Horses for fourteen months. Held two pub licences before that, for one year and three years.'

'Wife's age?'

'Sixty. She'd known the victim when they were both teenagers.'

Parry pouted before commenting: 'Could be a crime of passion, I suppose. Except they're all getting on a bit.'

'Like some more of us, boss,' Lloyd said with feeling.

'Do the Franklins live at the pub by themselves?'

'Yes. But they had a grown-up son staying last night. Arrived in the early hours this morning. But he'd been in earlier in the evening on his way to Swansea.' Lloyd scowled at his notes. 'Name of Owen Stanley Franklin. I thought I'd heard of him. I had too. When I was with Pontypool CID. He's on the central computer. No serious offences. Passing dud cheques, mostly.'

'Done time, has he?'

'Not yet. One suspended sentence, otherwise fines and cautions.

'Habitual crook, though?'

'Petty criminal, yes.' Lloyd was strong on official semantics.

'And he doesn't live with his parents?'

'No, no. He's not exactly a youngster either. Aged forty. Been married three times. Now divorced. His mother says he rents a cottage outside Brecon, but there was a Swansea address on the computer.'

'Con artists need to keep on the move. He and the father both available for us to see?'

'The father, not the son, boss. He'd left already on his motorbike. Before Mrs Franklin found the head, that was. Told her he had an appointment in Cwmbran.' The sergeant glanced at the time. 'He should be there by now, easy. Anyway, there's a call out for him.'

'We have the number of the bike?'

'Yes. And the make, engine size and colour.'

'Good. With no one else in the frame with a criminal record, we need him for questioning pronto.'

8

'And you'd never met Mr Davies, sir?' asked DS Lloyd. He
and Parry were sitting with Ken and Jacky Franklin in the
living room of the upstairs flat at the Coach and Horses.

'Never,' Franklin replied, while continuing to rock his
short body backwards and forwards on the edge of the sofa
he was sharing with his wife. The sofa was set opposite the
fireplace where the grate had been removed, and an electric
fan heater installed in its place. The heater was working now,
and making the room over warm.

'But he'd been a friend of yours since childhood, Mrs
Franklin?'

'Not a friend, exactly. I was two years older than him. I
only knew him in those days through the choir at St Luke's.'
As she spoke, Jacky Franklin's gaze had been fixed on the
handkerchief she was kneading in her lap.

'He was more of a friend of my wife's sister, Alice. Quite
a close friend, by all accounts,' Franklin volunteered. 'Alice
was more his age. Younger, in fact.'

'Sweethearts, were they, Mrs Franklin?'

The gaunt woman took a deep breath. 'I suppose you could
say that,' she answered quickly.

'You can say it for definite,' her husband blurted out. 'It
was he put her in the family way.' He moved further back
on to the sofa, and the fingertips of both his hands went to
smooth his flaring moustaches and sideburns.

Mrs Franklin gave her husband a look of stern reproach.
'That's never been proved,' she said to the sergeant. 'Nobody
knows for sure who the father was. She never admitted it
to me.'

72

'But she did to your father, didn't she?' said her husband with almost cruel insistence.

'She may have. Nobody was sure,' she responded flatly. 'It's wrong of anyone to say different.'

There was a brief, embarrassed silence. 'But your sister had a child that was . . . generally believed to be Mr Davies's?' asked Parry. He and Lloyd sat facing each other in wooden-armed, upholstered easy chairs set at opposite ends of the sofa at right angles to it. There was a television receiver at the sergeant's elbow. It was a small room, with very little natural light. The single sash window overlooked the narrow alleyway at the side of the pub, and a blank wall beyond.

Since his wife was sitting tight lipped and evidently wasn't going to answer the last question, Franklin did so for her. 'Alice had the baby out of wedlock,' he said. 'She committed suicide a few days after. Jacky and I adopted the child.' He picked up his pipe from the table beside him and blew into it.

Parry's eyebrows lifted. 'That'd be your son Owen who was here last night, sir?'

'That's right.' Franklin looked up inquiringly from the pipe. 'If he was Mervyn Davies's natural son, he'll be entitled to some of the money he's left, won't he?'

'I wouldn't know about that, sir, but is that what Mr Owen Franklin believes himself?'

'Of course he doesn't,' Mrs Franklin put in quickly, aware of the implications of her husband's question, and the damage it had done, even if he seemed oblivious of the fact.

'But presumably he knows he might be Mr Davies's son?'

'And that it's a very big might,' the woman rejoined, sharply this time.

'He must also know Mr Davies was here to collect a large inheritance,' said Lloyd, who had been looking at his notes.

'It came up in conversation, yes. Only casual, like,' Franklin offered in a more cautious tone than before.

'And when was that, sir?'

'Yesterday evening. Before opening time. When Owen dropped in on his way to Swansea.'

'And so far as you know, would your son have borne any grudge against Mr Davies?'

'Why should he have done that?' It was Jacky Franklin who had promptly challenged the question.

Parry gave a tolerant smile. 'Perhaps because he felt Mr Davies had deserted him as a baby,' he said. 'Or . . . or caused his real mother to take her life. Either reason would be natural enough in the circumstances.'

'For bearing a grudge, not for doing murder. Well, my son did neither, so let's have that straight here and now.' Mrs Franklin was sitting bolt upright, hands clenched tight against her stomach, her steely, hostile gaze directed at Parry. 'Oh, I know he's been in trouble sometimes in the past, but never anything serious. He's a good boy at heart, and he wouldn't harm a fly.'

'Thank you, ma'am,' the chief inspector responded without emotion. 'And is there any other member of the family who might have borne such a grudge against Mr Davies? I mean over his alleged fathering of your sister's child, and the er . . . the sad consequences?'

'Not anyone alive, there isn't. The rest of us have learned to forgive and forget. It was all a very long time ago. And I don't know why you think it's my son or other members of my family who'd be bearing grudges against Mervyn Davies. There's plenty in this town with better reason.' Her mouth closed more tightly still after this outburst.

'Such as, ma'am?' Lloyd asked, looking up from his notebook.'

'That's not for me to say, is it?'

'What my wife means is, with Edwin Edworth leaving all his money to Mervyn Davies, outside his own family, well, it could have started a lot of ill feeling.'

'In the Edworth family, you mean, sir?'

'I should think you could work that out for yourselves. Like Jacky says, it's not for us to point the finger. We just don't want it pointed at our Owen, for no reason.' Franklin glanced at his wife to ensure she had registered this attempted redemption of his previous lapse.

Parry cleared his throat. 'We shan't do that, Mr Franklin,

74

I promise you. But your son was the only person we know was in the car park after you'd left your car there last night. It's why we have to ask questions about him for our report.' He paused for a second. 'Did he mention to either of you last night, or this morning, that he'd seen Mr Davies since he got here from Australia?'

'He told me he hadn't seen him,' Mrs Franklin provided, while her husband nodded his agreement.

'And when you were speaking to Mr Davies himself after the supper last evening, ma'am, did the subject of your adopted son come up?'

'No. No reason why it should have, either. He asked me about Alice. I told him she was dead. He knew nothing about Owen.'

'You mean he didn't know he might have had a son in this country?'

She hesitated. 'He might have, I suppose. But it's only hearsay what my husband's told you. I keep telling him, it's never been proved Owen was Mervyn Davies's son.'

Lloyd leaned forward in his chair. 'Could I just go over what you said earlier about the time your son got in this morning, ma'am? You did say it was one-forty exactly?'

'That's right. I showed you just now, our bedroom looks over the car park. The noise of his motorbike woke me.'

'And you looked at the time on your bedside clock?'

'That's right.'

'But you hadn't done the same when your husband got back before that?'

'No. Because I was hardly asleep. I knew it wasn't late. I kept my eyes shut then, and when he came up. I didn't want to wake properly.'

'And neither of you heard any noises in the car park after that, except the sound of your son's motorbike?'

'I remember a car went down the alley just after,' said Mrs Franklin. 'It didn't stop though. Whoever put that head in our car must have been extra quiet about it. I'm a very light sleeper.'

Parry glanced across at Lloyd before saying: 'Well, I think we'll leave it there for the moment.' He slapped his thighs

75

with both palms, then stood up. 'And you'll let us know straight away if your son contacts you? If he does, please tell him to get in touch with me himself straight away on the number we've given you, or through any police station. It's in his own interests. Oh, and I have to ask you both not to leave the town for the time being without letting us know first.'

'Does that mean we're under suspicion?' asked Franklin, also rising.

The detective chief inspector gave a short, tight-lipped smile, which narrowed the shrewd eyes. 'It means we're not finished with our investigations, sir, that's all.'

Franklin nodded. 'And how long will you be keeping the car for, and those clothes I was wearing last night?'

'Only a day or two, I should think. For the forensic tests. We'll get both back to you as soon as we can. Right, then. We'll just have another look at what's going on outside. No need to see us out.'

A minute later, Parry and Lloyd had rejoined the group of detectives and civilian police employees at work in the taped-off car park. Most were enveloped in white, hooded coveralls with overshoes. They were working under the just-promoted Detective Sergeant Glen Wilcox, senior Scenes of Crime Officer. Parry nodded at the police photographer, who had finished his initial work and was waiting on further orders.

The recently resurfaced yard had a two-car width entrance from the alley, through an ungated opening in a high brick wall. The yard had been marked off with painted parking slots – except for an unloading area at the back of the pub, and a section in front of the car workshop opposite. Ken Franklin's Volvo Estate was parked immediately outside the back door Parry and Lloyd had come through. This was a private, not a public, entrance to the pub itself.

'Anything interesting-looking in the bedrooms and bathroom sweepings, SOCO?' Parry asked. A separate section of the team had been at work inside the pub and the flat when he and Lloyd had arrived to take over the investigation from local CID officers.

'Not to the naked eye, sir. The bags are ready to go to Chepstow with the car, and Mr Franklin's clothes. We're waiting for the low loader now,' replied Wilcox. He was a keen, young and ambitious officer, with a degree in sociology, a deeply serious manner, and a wife who was an equally dedicated Tupperware agent.

'And out here?'

'No signs of fresh blood, either in or outside the car, sir. We're doing a final sweep of the whole yard now.'

'So it's not likely the beheading was done in the car or in the yard?'

'Nor that the head was swopped for the shoulder of ham while both were in the car, sir. That's assuming the Tesco bag it was in was the same one allegedly used for the ham.' Wilcox never assumed anything he couldn't prove. 'We've taken fingerprints from Mr and Mrs Franklin, and we've got an incomplete set of what we believe may be the son's. They were taken from the bedroom and the things he used at breakfast. I gather his dabs are on record for comparison, sir?'

'Should be, yes. And there's no sign of the ham?' Parry's eyes widened amiably as he put the question.

'No, sir.'

'Pity. Mrs Franklin is hoping it'll show up. So am I. And er . . . has the victim's head been taken away?' He and Lloyd had examined that gruesome exhibit earlier.

'Collected five minutes ago, sir, by the hospital.'

'Good. And you've got another group at Condleston Lodge?'

'On the way, sir. The property was taped off earlier. I couldn't send anyone from this team, of course, in case of contaminating DNA evidence,' Wilcox added unnecessarily: Parry was well aware of the rules and the hazards.

'Right,' Parry responded. 'Detective Sergeant Lloyd and I will go there after we've talked to Mr Godwin, the last person seen with the victim.'

'Uniform and local CID went to Condleston Lodge just after nine, boss, as soon as Mrs Franklin identified the head,' said Lloyd, as he and Parry moved off to where they had left

77

the Porsche at the front of the pub. The sergeant had just been talking on his radio. 'The live-in gardener and house-keeper just got back,' he continued. 'They were away for the night. And Mr Peter Baylis, that's the farmer outside Llanharan, he's been interviewed. Says Mr Franklin arrived there at eleven-thirty last night in his Volvo, and left ten minutes later. Mrs Baylis confirms it. And they both said he was wearing a maroon jacket, like the one he showed us.'

'Which has gone to forensic in Chepstow. So, if everyone's telling us the truth, Franklin hardly had time to cut Mervyn Davies's head off and dispose of the rest of the body. Not before he got back here again at midnight. If he did, there ought to be blood on his clothes, and in his car.'

'And if Mrs Franklin was right about the time he got back, boss. She didn't look at the clock, of course.' Lloyd sounded doubtful on the point.

'But it was before the son got in,' observed Parry. 'Unless they're in a conspiracy together, which isn't likely. They weren't coordinated enough in their statements for that. And I don't believe Franklin did in Davies because he'd been making love to his wife since he's been back, or even forty years ago.' He sniffed. 'Mrs Franklin certainly saw the need to shield the son before her husband did.' He looked up at the decorated front of the Coach and Horses before he unlocked the car door. 'Did stage coaches really have yellow wheels, d'you suppose, Gomer?' he mused, without ex-pecting an answer. 'Must have taken a lot of effort to keep clean.' He beamed at the gleaming bonnet of the Porsche, then he glanced along Pentre Street. It was a relatively nar-row thoroughfare that had remained so, because it was less important to Pontyglas than it had been before some parallel, new road building had, in effect, bypassed it. It was lined with small, nondescript, two-storey shops, all built around the turn of the century, and which hadn't been candidates for modernization. Local shopping had become more concen-trated, moving to the bigger outlets closer to the centre of the town, or else to the shopping centre a mile back, beyond its outskirts, on the Tawrbach Road. The Coach and Horses was the only building in sight to which any recent care had been given. Even so, one of the SOCO team members, a local man, had just remarked that it would take more than a murder on the premises to make the pub more popular than it was.

'You don't rate Ken Franklin as a suspect, boss?' the sergeant asked when they were in the car.

'Not yet, no. Do you?'

Lloyd frowned and took a peppermint from the packet in his hand. 'He'd have been daft to leave the head in his car like that, and then send his wife out to find it.'

'Daft or ice cool. Anyway, better to leave them both be for now. I'm a lot more interested in the son, Owen. We need him, Gomer, and fast.'

'The general call for him's been out for over an hour, boss. He shouldn't be that far away.'

'That's what bothers me. Cwmbran may have been a blind.' Parry sniffed. 'Put another call out, covering a hundred-mile radius from here. And this time say he should be approached with extreme caution.'

9

The youthful, heavyweight Police Constable Alwyn Evans was sitting back in the saddle of his stationary BMW 1000cc motorcycle, listening to the police frequency on his radio, finishing a Mars Bar, and planning what he'd be doing this time tomorrow on his day off. He was also keeping a dutiful eye on the traffic joining and leaving the M4 motorway at Junction 41, in the rolling countryside six miles east of Swansea, as well as on the vehicles passing along the motor-way itself.

Despite his own wide field of vision, too few of the drivers briefly within PC Evans's purview were aware of his presence. This was because he was parked below a small knoll and between the stanchions of a lofted road direction sign. His superiors had long decided that the sight of a station-ary police patrol at a busy roadside did more in the aggregate to reduce speeding than a moving patrol, which, perforce, was likely to be moving in the opposite direction to a lot of the law-breaking motorists. This logical decision also had the merit of reducing police petrol costs.

Thus, although there was nothing in his orders forbidding Alwyn Evans to be stationary, he was supposed to be visible as well. This was why lurking below the direction sign had only been a very temporary ruse. It allowed for the consump-tion of the Mars Bar, without detracting from the public image of a larger than life lawman in shining black leather and a space invader helmet sitting astride a multi-antennaed machine that looked capable of anything, including vertical take-off if circumstances demanded.

The policeman had just finished his snack when he spotted

a motorcyclist, on a red machine, moving eastwards along the motorway at what in his tutored estimation was a speed well in excess of a hundred miles an hour.

Since it was still only ten-thirty on a Sunday morning, there was relatively little traffic about. While this encouraged the slightly over-the-limit speeding overlooked by authority, it definitely didn't license the M4 as an alfresco race track – which was what Evans was thinking as he started to give chase.

Touching a hundred and twenty himself, he quickly brought his quarry back into view. Dropping his speed slightly, he held the red motorbike in sight for a measured mile, noting the common speed, but not closing the gap. Then, with an extra surge of power from the BMW, he overtook the other rider, and signalled him to draw on to the hard shoulder.

'Can I see your driving licence, MOT and insurance certificates, please, sir?' Evans demanded some moments later, after walking back from where he had parked the BMW, three yards ahead of the offender.

'Over the limit, was I, mate?' the lanky Owen Franklin questioned cheerfully, while dismounting from his machine. He lifted his helmet visor and zipped open the parka jacket he was wearing. 'A lovely day and an empty road – makes you forget the regulations for a few magic seconds, doesn't it?' he offered lyrically, and with no nervousness in his voice.

The demonstrably unmatey constable was giving no visible sign that he enjoined any of the last romantic and hopeful sentiments. He took the documents from Franklin after waiting patiently for them to be produced. 'What speed would you say you were doing when I passed you, sir?' he asked, woodenly.

'Oh dear. Over eighty, I expect, was it, Officer?' Franklin replied, trying a more respectful form of address. 'Really got carried away by –'

'A hundred and twelve miles an hour, sir. That's forty-two miles an hour higher than the limit on the motorway.'

'Go on? I wouldn't have thought my old bike was up to that.'

'To be honest, neither would I, sir,' Evans responded drily, glancing across at the mud-spattered Yamaha 500cc, with its six-year-old licence number, then back again at the papers in his gloved hand. 'Did you know this insurance certificate is out of date, sir?'

'Never!' Franklin made as if to move forward to examine the offending document but changed his mind when the look in the policeman's eye firmly suggested he should stay where he was.

'Expired at the end of January, Mr . . . Franklin. You are Mr Owen Stanley Franklin, sir?' the policeman asked, reading the name from the insurance document.

'Yes, that's me all right. Probably the new certificate's in the post, or sitting in somebody's in-tray. Terrible people, insurance brokers. Never get anything out on time. I'm positive I paid the premium months ago.'

'I see, sir.' But Evans didn't really appear to have been much interested in the last comment. 'If you'll just stay right where you are for a minute, Mr Franklin, I have to check something on my radio. Won't keep you long.'

'That's all right, old chap. I've got all the time in the world.' He raised his open right hand, arm bent at the elbow, like an American Indian offering peace.

Evans was involved in an intense, low-voiced exchange on his radio for rather more than a minute, while watching Franklin throughout. 'Did you come from Pontyglas early this morning, sir?' he asked on his return, his gaze sterner than before.

'That's right. Anything wrong with that?'

'Aren't you supposed to be on your way to Cwmbran, sir?'

'I might be, yes. Who told you that, then?'

'But that's on the other side of Pontyglas from here,' the policeman continued, ignoring the question. He was glad to be making amends for almost overlooking the earlier broadcast details of a wanted motorcyclist who hadn't been expected to come in this direction. Happily, the colour of the machine had stayed in his mind.

'I know. I had to go to Swansea first.'

'I see, sir. D'you mind telling me what you've been doing in Swansea?'

At first, Franklin's expression – or what could be seen of it under the open visor – suggested he minded a good deal. He wet his lips. 'I er . . . I left something there last night,' he replied warily. 'Last evening,' he then corrected.

'What was that, sir?'

'My er . . . my wallet. Look, I don't know what this is about, but –'

'You don't mind if I look in those pannier bags, sir?' Evans interrupted, nodding at the red Yamaha.

Franklin hesitated, then shrugged. 'Help yourself. There's nothing much in them. I'd still like to know –'

'And you stayed at the Coach and Horses in Pontyglas last night, sir?'

'That's right. My father's the licensee,' he completed, this time with a touch of pride which seemed also to bring a return of confidence. He straightened his back, an action which made him taller than the policeman.

'And what time did you get there, sir?' Evans was bending over the back of the Yamaha now, but standing on its far side so that he could continue to watch Franklin.

'Can't remember. It wasn't that late. After midnight, I should think.' A long, high-sided articulated lorry with French markings thundered past close to the two as Franklin was speaking, drowning his words.

'Sorry, sir. I missed that. What time did you say?'

'About er . . . half-one. Maybe a bit later,' Franklin corrected.

Evans was arranging the items taken from the first pannier on the saddle of the Yamaha. There was a black blazer, a pair of grey trousers, a roughly folded white shirt and a striped tie, both in the same clear plastic bag, a pair of scuffed brown suede shoes, two unopened cans of lager, and a copy of the *South Wales Echo*.

'I had to dress up last night. For an interview. In Swansea,' Franklin volunteered. 'Got offered the job, too,' he lied, because the claim put him in a better light.

'Congratulations, sir,' responded Evans, but in a detached

sort of voice, as he replaced the items in the pannier. Next, he leaned over the machine to the bag on the other side, releasing the securing clips. This time the trove amounted only to a dirty pair of fawn overalls before the searcher delved deeper to the very bottom of the pannier.

'That'll be it on that side. I don't use it much,' said Franklin. 'Wasn't expecting to be away for the night, either.'

'Something happened to change your mind, sir?'

'Not specially. I just thought I'd look in on the old folks, that's all. They like me to stay a night occasionally.'

'And your home's in Brecon, is it, sir?' That's what it had said on the driving licence, except he'd been told police records had him listed as domiciled in Swansea.

'That's right. Got a pad up there, I have.' He was looking at the white bag now in the policeman's hand. 'What's in that?'

'You don't know, sir?'

'No. First time I've seen it.'

'Is that so, sir?' Evans had rested the bag on the red petrol tank of the motorcycle before he opened it. After taking one long look inside the bag he swallowed, then glanced up at Franklin. 'Right, sir. I have to ask you to wait with me here till we have transport to take you and your vehicle to Swansea Police Station. You're required there for questioning.' As he spoke, he removed the ignition key of the Yamaha and pocketed it.

'Why's that? What am I supposed to have done, for God's sake? This is a fit-up, isn't it? If you think because –'

'Lie face downwards on the ground over there, Mr Franklin, please, arms and legs extended, and look smart about it now,' the policeman ordered.

'Do what?'

'Lie face down, sir, please. Now.'

Franklin shook his head in bewilderment. 'But this is crazy, I –'

'Are you refusing to obey a police order, Mr Franklin?'

Scowling, the other man moved a pace further away from the inside lane of the motorway and, with his back to the traffic, did as he was told.

The policeman made a careful weapons search of the spreadeagled body. 'Right. Now put your hands together behind your back, sir, please.'

Franklin sighed, but this time did as directed, expecting a further search, until he felt the handcuffs on his wrists. 'Hey, what the hell?'

'You can get up now, sir. Sit side-saddle on your vehicle if you want.'

Franklin struggled to his feet. 'Look, if this is a joke it's gone –'

'Owen Stanley Franklin,' Evans cut in, trying to keep his breathing easy but with his pulse pounding. 'I'm arresting you for being in possession of suspicious items. You're not obliged to say anything, but anything you do say may be taken down and used in evidence.'

'What bloody suspicious items?' demanded the outraged Franklin, still standing.

The young policeman had never made a lone arrest of a suspected murderer before, let alone one he'd just been informed should be approached with extreme caution. It was also the first time he had officially used the handcuffs, which were his own property – a Christmas present paid for by a doting mother. The whole successful exercise had made a change from dealing with speeding or drunken drivers. He relaxed even more, relieved that his prisoner had given no trouble. 'Well, for a start, you've got a machete in this bag with what looks like blood on it,' he answered, 'and there's a severed human hand in with it. Fair enough?'

'And to think I said good night to him at this very gate last night,' said the normally cheerful, but now deeply grieved Geoff Godwin. 'This is a terrible shock. Terrible.' He drew in a long breath through his open mouth. 'You'd better come in, Chief Inspector er . . . sorry, I've forgotten your –'

'Parry, sir. And this is Detective Sergeant Lloyd.'

They followed Godwin, his head bowed, up the concrete drive beyond the double wrought-iron gates which he had been opening as the Porsche had pulled up outside. The brick-built, semi-detached bungalow in Park Rise was mock

Georgian, with a pedimented front door and white wood-work. Beyond the low street wall, the small front garden consisted of a circular rose bed arranged around a sundial. There were glimpses of a trim lawn and a freshly dug flower bed at the back of the house, seen through a lattice gate under the brick arch that joined the main building to the garage on the right. A glistening blue Rover Metro had been backed out through the still-open garage door. The concrete around the car was wet.

'If you were just going out, Mr Godwin, there's no need for us to come in. We shan't keep you long,' Parry offered, partly because Godwin had hesitated as they came up to the car, but also because the policeman was anxious to move on to Condleston Lodge. He wasn't expecting this witness to shift the case along much.

The grey-suited Godwin turned about. He was still evidently dazed by the news he had just been given. 'As a matter of fact, the wife and I were off to church. It's the big anniversary Eucharist at eleven. When I tell her about Mervyn, she'll be upset something terrible. She'll still want to go to church, though. I'm certain of that. We both will. He'd promised to be there, d'you see?' He let out a heavy sigh. 'And he was coming back here with us after, for Sunday lunch. I've just cleaned the car in his honour, too. The better the day, the better the deed, like. Oh, dear me.' He paused again and looked blankly across at a neighbour, two doors down, who was washing a nearly identical car in front of a nearly identical house. Tears had welled in Godwin's eyes, behind his glasses, as he returned his gaze to Parry. 'We'd known each other over half a century, Mervyn and me,' he said, directing a watery as well as supplicant expression at the chief inspector. 'But who would do such a thing? To cut a man's head off?' The speaker's chubby hands did up the centre button of the tight-fitting jacket, then undid it again, before his arms dropped listlessly to his sides.

'That's what we're here to find out, sir. Knowing Mr Davies's movements last night is a first step. We understand you left the parish supper together at five past ten.'

Godwin swallowed. 'That's about right, yes. Then . . . then

we walked back here. Dilys, that's the wife, she had the car. She was taking our daughter and her hubbie home.'

'Did you stop anywhere on the way, sir?'

'Yes. We had another beer before we started back. At the King's Head.'

'That's a pub close to the church, is it, sir?' asked Lloyd.

'That's right. When we got here, Mervyn came in for a last drink. Whisky, it was.'

'Can you remember what time he left, sir?' Parry put in.

Godwin ran a finger along the roof ridge of the car. 'Yes. Just before half past eleven. I remember because Dilys came back soon after, when our hall clock was chiming the half hour.'

'And Mr Davies walked home, sir?'

'Yes, Mr Parry. I offered to drive him if he'd wait for Dilys to get back with the car, but he wouldn't hear of it. Said I'd be above the alcohol limit. He might have been right too, except I'd been watching my intake all evening. Got a weight problem, see?' He patted his stomach in an almost reflex way. 'Anyway, I don't believe Mervyn wanted Dilys to think we'd been drinking all evening. I did offer to ring for a taxi, but no, Mervyn wanted to walk. Through the town this time, to see how it looked. We'd come by the shortest route, through the park and over the river footbridge.'

'So you'd both had a few drinks, sir?' Lloyd commented.

'Yes. Beer mostly. But I was on halves. I had two pints in all, including the half at the church hall before we left.' Godwin frowned, then took off his glasses and began polishing them with his handkerchief as he went on. 'I think Mervyn had four pints altogether. He was fond of his beer. Australians are, aren't they?'

'And you both had wine at the church supper, sir?'

'Only one glass, and only because it was included in the price.' He grinned sheepishly. 'Wine's not my tipple really.'

'And you drank whisky when you got here, sir?'

'Mervyn did. I just had soda water to keep him company.'

Parry nodded. 'So he'd have been fairly . . . merry when he left you, sir?' he said.

'Mellow, he was, yes. Not tipsy though. Nothing like. He'd

enjoyed the evening, I know. And praise God for that, being it was his last.'

'Were there many people he knew at the supper, sir, from his boyhood, perhaps?'

'Quite a few, yes. Some of them are in this picture.' He had put on his glasses again and produced the old choir photograph from his pocket. 'There's Mervyn and me,' he said, pointing. 'And Dewi Trimble in the front row. Solicitor now, he is. Mervyn was his guest at the supper, but Dewi didn't stop after. And there's Jacky Morgan, Mrs Franklin as she is now.' He looked up. 'There's shocking for her to find Mervyn's head like that. He talked to her for a long time in the bar.' He tutted several times.

'Can you remember what time Mrs Franklin left the church hall, sir?' asked Lloyd.

Godwin looked up and frowned before replying. 'Not exactly, no. But it was long before us.' His gaze dropped, and his finger was tracing over the picture again. 'And there's John Sewell. He was there, but I'm not sure whether he spoke to Mervyn. John had his er . . . his nephew with him, the one people always thought was his brother. Anyway, he's an officer in the army. I think Mervyn knew John's sister Esme in the old days. She died. In London. And that's Gwilym Edworth in the back row,' Godwin continued earnestly. 'He's dead now, but his wife Winifred was there. She talked to Mervyn, and her son Charles did as well, but not for long, either of them.' He paused, wetting his lips. 'Charles made it clear enough the Edworth family wasn't happy about Edwin leaving his money to Mervyn. Well, that's understandable in a way, but it's a free country, all said and done. You can leave your money to who you like.' He rubbed the end of his nose. 'Fat lot of good Edwin's money has done for Mervyn, in the end. I suppose it'll all go to his sons in Australia now. He did tell me he was making a will himself, and he wasn't leaving anything to the Edworths. Because Edwin Edworth hadn't either. That's what he said. It was all in confidence, of course.'

'Mr Davies wasn't threatened by Mr Charles Edworth, was he, sir?' Lloyd questioned.

'Good Lord, no. Nothing like that.'

'And do you know if there was anyone else present last night who bore Mr Davies a grudge, sir?'

Godwin shook his head. 'No one I know of.'

'Did you know some people think Mr Davies is the father of Owen Franklin, sir?' Parry put in.

'Oh yes. But that's an old story. The mother was Alice Morgan, of course. Jacky's younger sister.'

'Did Mr Davies ever admit to you that he was the father, sir?'

'No. Not before he left the country, and not when I saw him yesterday. We didn't discuss Owen last night. Too many more interesting things on the agenda.'

Parry's eyebrows lifted a fraction. 'You don't like Owen Franklin, sir?'

Godwin shrugged his shoulders. 'I hardly know him. I've got no opinion of him one way or the other. It's generally thought though, he hasn't been a credit to the couple who adopted him.'

'Thank you, sir. So, we must let you and your wife get off to church. I see you've done your spring digging at the back there.' Parry nodded and smiled as he moved closer to the lattice gate and peered through it.

Godwin's face brightened for the first time. 'Ah, I'm changing over the bed you can see from annuals to herbaceous. Less work in the end. Have a look before you go.' He moved forwards and opened the gate to lead the others through.

The rear garden was a quite modest rectangle and well established with planted borders around the lawn, all undisturbed, except for the flower bed nearest the gate. There were daffodils and tulips in plenty elsewhere, mostly around flowering bushes, some of which were also in bloom.

'Very nice, sir,' said Parry with a smile.

'Lovely garden you've got,' Lloyd volunteered. 'I'm a bit behind with mine this year.'

'Ah, you've got to keep on top of it, of course,' Godwin replied seriously. 'I dug this bed over last week. Put plenty of horse manure in too. Good gardening's all in the preparation, isn't it? Surprising how quick things dry out though, if there's no rain.' As he followed the others back through the gate and down the short drive, he added, 'I've got more time for the garden here now I've given up my allotment.'

'You kept an allotment as well, sir?'

'Oh yes, for years. One of the council allotments at the end of Greenlow Street, beyond the railway, and the police station, of course. I had it for the vegetables. We miss them, too, but it was getting too much at my age. Bigger than the garden here, it was.' He straightened his back which made his large stomach more evident. 'Well now, if I can be any more help to you over the tragedy, let me know. You can always reach me here, or in working hours at the Council offices.'

Parry was unlocking the car door when he looked up again and walked back towards Godwin, who was standing at the gate. 'Just one last thing, sir. Since Mrs Godwin got back last night so soon after Mr Davies left, you didn't by any chance go after him, in the car? To give him a lift home after all, forgetting to mention it to us just now?' He watched Godwin's face redden as he continued. 'Going after him would have been the natural, friendly thing to do, of course.'

Godwin hesitated, blinking several times. 'Well . . . as a matter of fact, Mr Parry, I did,' he said, in a lowered voice. 'How did you know?'

'Because I think you'd have worried about him if you hadn't, sir. Anyway, I assume you didn't find him?'

'That's right. He wasn't on the bridge or in St Donat's Place. After that I gave up and came home. I thought he'd probably gone across the park after all.'

Parry smiled. 'And, let's say, it all slipped your mind just now, especially since you'd had a few drinks last night, and thought we might figure you'd been drinking and driving?'

Godwin looked sheepish. 'That's it, Mr Parry, in a nutshell. I'm sorry. It was the shock, d'you see? I wasn't thinking straight.'

'Well, we're not in the drink drive business today, Mr Godwin, so you needn't have worried.' Parry was looking over Godwin's shoulder at the recently cleaned car. 'So you

90

left just after eleven-thirty, was it, and got back at . . . ?'

'Oh, I couldn't have been much more than ten minutes. Fifteen at the outside.'

'And your wife will be able to confirm that if necessary, sir?'

Godwin turned his head to glance back at the house. 'Oh yes. Dilys could tell you right enough.' He had been in time to notice, like Parry, a slight movement in the lace curtain at one of the front windows.

10

'I could see something had happened there. Soon as we come in the drive,' said Gareth Jarvis. He had just led Parry and Lloyd through the side door of Condleston Lodge and into the kitchen where Mair Jarvis was making tea. The two policemen had been at the house for nearly twenty minutes already.

'Well, that was clear enough if you knew the way the place was supposed to look, I expect, sir,' said Lloyd in a conversational way. 'Our local colleagues didn't notice anything wrong. Not when they first got here.'

'Ah, because they're not gardeners. A gardener could have seen straight off someone had been in those rhodies. Fallen in, probably. And the rest.' Jarvis paused, wrinkling his nose. 'With someone being sick in them as well. Disgusting,' he added.

'But the police were more concerned to get into the house, of course,' Lloyd offered, while looking about the room which he and Parry had been through once already.

'Why?' demanded Jarvis dismissively. 'No one's broke in. You could see that. The place was as tight locked as when we left yesterday. Anyway, the alarm hadn't gone off.'

'It was very observant of you, Mr Jarvis, noticing the damage to the bushes,' Parry cut in with what sounded like a compliment, although Jarvis was beginning to bore him. 'The investigating team out there will get a lot of information from that patch of ground.' At first he had hoped they might even have produced a body from it, but that hadn't happened.

'I heard one of your blokes in white say there's blood there,' Jarvis added in a questioning tone.

'Tea's made,' announced Mrs Jarvis, turning to greet the three men with a gushing smile which, as always, threatened to crack open her make-up, though it never did. She had a pinafore tied around her shocking-pink sweater and matching skirt. Pink and lilac seemed to be her favourite colours, since she never wore any others. 'Why don't you sit at the table.' She gave a heavy sigh as she put the top on the teapot. 'This is our first sit down since getting back. I still can't believe Mr Davies is dead.' She carried the pot to the table making tutting noises all the way.

The Jarvises had returned to Condleston Lodge from their night away only half an hour before Parry and Lloyd had got there, but some time after DS Wilcox had arrived with his SOCO group. The team Wilcox had working at the Coach and Horses was now matched by this second wave of men and women dispatched earlier from Cardiff by police minibus.

It was Jarvis who had first noticed that there had been a disturbance in the bushes above the horseshoe-shaped drive on the short, western side of the house. It seemed that quite a large quantity of blood might have soaked into the earth under the rhododendrons, with some of it clinging still to the evergreen foliage. The area involved was fairly close to the side door, and to a stone-flagged path that led from the drive to the south terrace: the aviary was to the right of this.

A search of the grounds and the house had failed to reveal the remains of Mervyn Davies's body, assuming the spilled blood was his. Nor was there yet any clue as to how he might have left Condleston Lodge, whether he had been dead or alive at the time, and, if dead, whether he had already been decapitated. It seemed unlikely that he or anyone else had entered the house the night before, although the police were not as convinced of this as Jarvis had been. The burglar alarm could have been disarmed and later reset.

'If we could just cover your own movements, Mr Jarvis, and yours, Mrs Jarvis,' Lloyd asked, producing a notebook. 'You left here together at what time last evening?'

'At six.' It was Mrs Jarvis who answered, patting the side of her wiry coiffure with the pink-tipped fingers of one hand. 'Right after Mr Davies left for the church supper. It was ever so good of him to let us go for the night. It was my sister May's silver wedding, see? My older sister,' she added pointedly. 'We'd arranged to be there months ago. Long before Mr Edwin Edworth passed away, it was. Then, after the funeral, Mr Trimble, the solicitor, said Mr Davies wasn't due to get here till late today, so we hadn't cancelled going to the party. We thought it'd still be all right.' She began pouring tea as she continued. 'My sister and her hubbie would have been so disappointed if we hadn't been there. Bitterly disappointed, wouldn't they, Gareth?'

'Bitterly,' her husband echoed, pulling at the lobe of one of his formidable ears. 'They live in Porthcawl. Behind the seafront. The party was in the banqueting suite of the Esplanade Hotel. Went on till one this morning.'

'Fancy,' said Lloyd. 'Porthcawl's not very far away though, Mr Jarvis. You hadn't thought of driving back here after the party ended?'

'No, we hadn't. Not in the first place. But we did on Friday, that's after Mr Davies arrived unexpected.'

'Except he wouldn't hear of it,' Mrs Jarvis put in quickly. 'Nor of our not going to the party either. "You go and enjoy yourselves," he said, "and stay the night. You don't want to drive back after you've had a drink or two." Well, that was very thoughtful of him, wasn't it? There's milk and sugar in front of you, Mr Parry. Of course, it'd all been fixed in the first place that we'd stay at my sister's. And that's how it ended up. But only because Mr Davies insisted, like.' She paused for breath, but only briefly. 'It was a godsend to us, I can tell you. I don't drive a car, and Gareth hates driving at night, except you did run my Auntie Olwyn home, didn't you, Gareth?' she added, passing Lloyd his cup. 'But that was earlier on. She doesn't like sleeping away from home, and she doesn't like going in taxis either.'

'A lot of older people are like that,' said Lloyd in a sympathetic tone, while helping himself to two spoonfuls of sugar. 'And they don't like staying up late either. So whereabouts does she live then, your Auntie Olwyn?' he inquired, and sounding as if he was genuinely interested in auntie's wellbeing. 'In Porthcawl, is it?'

'No, no. In Kenfig Hill. She's in sheltered accommodation there. Private, not council, of course.' Mrs Jarvis's lips closed and tightened while she allowed her audience to digest what she clearly considered to be a socially significant point. 'Lovely, it is, too. Isn't it, Gareth? Self-contained, and not too far from me or my sister.'

'That's a comfort to your aunt, I'm sure, Mrs Jarvis,' said Lloyd. He looked across to her husband who was on the opposite side of the table to himself, and who hadn't yet been given the opportunity to give his invited opinion on the loveliness of Auntie Olwyn's accommodation. 'And what time did you take the lady home, sir?'

'I'm not sure. Must have been around eleven.'

'And you got back to the party at what time, sir?'

'Can't remember that, either. Must have been before midnight, though. We had the main toast at midnight. Today being the real date they got married.' Jarvis's expression darkened suddenly. 'Why d'you want to know?' he questioned, in a bellicose way.

'Just routine, sir,' Parry intervened, in a let's-get-on-with-it tone. 'And did Mr Davies mention he might be meeting anyone here after the church supper last night?'

'Not to us, he didn't,' said Mrs Jarvis, lighting a cigarette.

'He wouldn't have, would he?' her husband added, stretching to the end of the table for his cup of tea which his wife had poured but omitted to pass to him. 'Not if it was someone we wasn't supposed to know about, like.' His eyelids lowered, and he looked from Parry to Lloyd, then back again.

'Like a lady friend, you mean, sir?' asked Lloyd.

'Well, with us away for the night, he knew he had the place to himself –'

'For shame, Gareth,' his wife interrupted, blowing smoke at him, like a small but angry dragon. 'We don't know he was like that. Anyway, he didn't have any lady friends in Pontyglas. For one thing, he hadn't been back here long enough.'

'What about the ones he had before he left?' countered her husband defensively, before draining his teacup.

'Had he mentioned any, sir?' asked Lloyd.

Jarvis frowned. 'No,' he admitted, with reluctance. 'But I reckon he had an eye for the women all right.' His own eyes were directed at his wife as he spoke, and his expression had made her whole frame stiffen.

'You think the same, Mrs Jarvis?' asked Parry.

'I think he was a normal single gentleman. More normal than some I know. And more of a gentleman as well. He didn't forget to compliment a lady on her appearance, for a start.' The Jarvises were now exchanging looks of mounting hostility as Mrs Jarvis continued. 'Mr Edwin Edworth was the same as Mr Davies, of course. They were both gentlemen, and now they're both gone.' She appeared gamely to be holding back her tears – though conceivably because she knew that shedding them would damage her eye shadow.

'Would you and Mrs Jarvis have been staying on here with Mr Davies, sir?' asked Lloyd.

It was Mrs Jarvis who answered again, before her husband had opened his lips. 'We might have been,' she offered, then drew deeply on her cigarette. 'Though nothing definite had been said. Mr Davies might or might not have been keeping on the house. He hadn't made up his mind. We were to be paid six months' wages in any case. That's whether we were needed or not. That was in black and white. In Mr Edworth's will. Of course, on top of that we were –' She stopped speaking when Parry's mobile phone began buzzing in his pocket.

A minute later the two policemen were eschewing further prognostications about the Jarvises' future, and were back in the Porsche heading in a hurry for Pontyglas Police Station.

The Traveller's Break, a modest, fast-food wayside restaurant, was six miles north of Pontyglas on the road to Aberdare. Charles Edworth and Annie Lewin, who had been lovers for more than two years, had been using it since the previous summer. They met there at times of day when Edworth might have been noticed going into her flat in Woodford Road, behind Pontyglas railway station. They had never seen anyone they knew at the restaurant which had no appeal for locals. The trees that screened the car park at one end were not yet in leaf again, but the couple still found the putative cover there reassuring. It was where they had drawn up their cars under the branches now, isolated from the few others in the park. Annie had left her Mini and was sitting with Edworth on the back seat of his big Toyota.

They had just finished a long first embrace and she was holding him still, not speaking, but stroking her fingers through his beard.

'Couldn't wait to see me again till this evening, is that it?' he asked softly.

'Bighead,' she answered, now running a hand inside his shirt and down his chest, which was almost as hairy as his chin. 'We are on for tonight, aren't we?'

'Yes. That's definite.' He was supposed to be driving to Wolverhampton and spending the night there, prior to an early business meeting in the morning. Instead, he planned to stay with Annie and to leave her place before first light.

'Good. Because last night hardly counted. Not for me, anyway. Bit of a fast job, wasn't it?' she added petulantly.

'Couldn't help it, love. I didn't leave my mother's till late, and —'

'And you had to be home with Jane and the children before you turned into a pumpkin, I know,' she interrupted. But now there was less irritation in her words than a recognition of a depressing fact. She was acknowledging that for the time being she had no better than second-class rights over him.

'I'm sorry. Actually, it isn't as simple as that,' he said. They kissed again, more tenderly than before.

'I said I'd leave the church supper early as well,' she offered when their lips parted. 'I had some quite attractive offers before I left, too. One, anyway.'

'From an Aussie millionaire, was it?'

'Yes. I thought I told you that last night. Or were you in too much of a hurry to hear? But there won't be any more offers from that direction.' She had moved a little away from him and was sitting upright, her eyes on his and her tone suddenly more serious.

'How d'you mean?'

'It's why I rang you. Mervyn Davies is dead.'

'Who told you that?' He sounded more interested than surprised.

'A neighbour of mine passed the Coach and Horses at ten this morning. The place was alive with policemen, she said. She knew one of them. He'd been one of the first there. Told her they were investigating Mr Davies's death. He probably shouldn't have, of course.' Her training as a legal secretary had prompted the last remark.

'What's the Coach and Horses got to do with Davies? Is that where he died?'

'They don't know. But they found his head there.'

'Just his head? What about the rest of him?'

'No sign of it yet. Or that's what this policeman said.'

Edworth took her hands in his. 'So was Davies in an accident, or something?'

'Sounds more like murder, doesn't it?'

There would have been silence for several moments had it not been for a fight going on between several jackdaws in a tree immediately above the car.

'I went to see him last night,' said Edworth eventually, his gaze on their still-clasped hands.

'I thought you might have done. Straight after you left me, was it? Why didn't you tell me?'

'I didn't want you to know till after. In case he turned me down. I was going to ask him if he'd give my mother some of Edwin's money.'

'Not you? Your mother?'

'It would have been the same in the end. I mean, what was left after she died would have come to me and Gail. I just thought he might shell out for my mother, even if he wouldn't for Gail and me.' He frowned. 'I mean, as the widow of Edwin's brother she was entitled to something.'

'I suppose that's right.' She sounded doubtful, even so. On Friday she had told him that Mervyn Davies had told her boss that he wasn't going to share the inheritance with Charles or his sister. She was aware at the time that she shouldn't have divulged confidential client information of that kind, but it had seemed only fair to her lover. He had been building his hopes for weeks on getting some of Edwin's money. She had even disclosed to him that in the draft will she had already typed, ready for Davies to approve on Monday, he had left everything to his two sons in Australia. 'You weren't going to ask him to put up money for your consultancy?' she went on tentatively. They had earlier agreed there had to be a chance of such a request succeeding since it would have been a business investment, not just a gift. Annie herself expected to benefit as well. Charles had definitely promised to leave his wife for her as soon as he had the funds to get the new company started.

'I was going to come to that after we'd talked about my mother,' he replied quickly.

'But you never did?'

'I didn't see him. I drove over to Condleston Lodge from your flat. There was nobody there. No lights or anything. I hung about for a bit. But it was getting late. I'd promised Jane I'd be coming straight home when I left Mother. She might have rung to find out what had happened to me.'

'Did anyone see you at Condleston Lodge?'

'I don't think so. I parked in the drive. It's well sheltered from the road.' He lay back on the seat. 'So that's that. The end of any chance we ever had of getting help from Mervyn Davies. I should have gone to see him Friday. I wonder who killed him?'

'It's not definite he was murdered,' she commented uneasily. 'Shall we go inside for a coffee? I could use one.'

He looked at the time. 'OK. But I have to be home by –'

She put a hand over his lips so that he couldn't complete his words. He would never know how much it hurt her every time he made the same excuses about having to leave her. 'Ten minutes,' she said, opening the car door. 'Come on. Live dangerously.'

She watched him glance about, apparently to no purpose, as they walked towards the restaurant doorway. She knew, though, that he was surreptitiously checking the cars in the car park, their makes and number plates, just in case one of them belonged to someone he knew, someone from the factory, perhaps, which wasn't far away. He always did this, even though they were both aware that no one living in the area ever came here: there were far too many better and cheaper places to eat in or near Pontyglas. Now she sensed he was watching the road entrance for the same reason. He would hesitate when they walked into the restaurant too, ready to bolt if he spotted anyone who might give them away to his wife.

She hated these signs that he was afraid to be seen with her. They demeaned her, even though she understood the logic behind them. For her, they equated with his being ashamed to be seen with her. Sometimes she was on the point of purposely giving their secret away herself, and to hell with everyone else involved. But she had never acted on the impulse. She wasn't nearly enough certain that he'd ever forgive her if she did. He had this fixation about his children not finding out about them until everything was arranged – whatever that meant. She was still positive that he wanted to come to her, though, to leave Jane – otherwise she wouldn't have persevered. He had made enough fervent pledges. Sometimes she even felt he loved her enough to do something desperate.

'You know his dying now may be better for you? For us?' she said, dropping his hand, and putting her arm through his in a possessive way.

His face clouded. 'How d'you mean?'

'You really don't know?' She was looking up, straight into his eyes, as she asked the question.

'What's there to know? My Uncle Edwin left his fortune to a childhood friend, and nothing to anyone in the family. Now the childhood friend has died and the money goes to his sons. End of story.'

She smiled, wanting to believe him more than anything else in the world. 'I'm not sure it is the end of the story. Not legally. Ever heard of the rules of intestacy?'

'Vaguely.'

'Only vaguely?' The honesty she detected in his answer was hugely important to her – except she couldn't help remembering that he'd been deceiving his wife with his lies for years.

11

'But, Mr Franklin, if you were innocent, why did you need to escape arrest in the first place?' demanded DS Lloyd, rubbing the fold of his double chin with an index finger. He was seated beside Merlin Parry on one side of the table. Owen Franklin was on the other side with a middle-aged, prim-looking woman solicitor called Avril Norris. They were in an interview room on the ground floor of the newish, redbrick Pontyglas Police Station in Greenlow Street. It was exactly noon.

'I didn't escape. I came here, didn't I? Straight off. To complain of police harassment.'

'You came on PC Evans's motorbike. Which you stole.'

'Borrowed. Only because he had the key to mine, and I couldn't get it off him.'

'After you'd disabled him by headbutting him in the stomach with your helmet on, and kicking him in the crutch. Viciously.'

The staid Mrs Norris winced as though it was she who had been kicked so indelicately. Without actually moving her chair, she leaned a bit further away from her client, and pulled her skirts further over her knees. Normally, Mrs Norris only did property conveyancing: her senior partner coped with the criminal work that came their way, but he was in Venice on holiday for the weekend. He had been duty solicitor for this Sunday – on the roster of lawyers in the town covering legal aid work at nights and weekends. Instead of changing places with someone else – which he had done too often recently – he had got Mrs Norris to stand in for him in the very unlikely event of anyone being needed. After the police had called her earlier at home, when she was preparing lunch, she had desperately rung round two lawyers in other practices who might have been ready to take on the present assignment, but neither had answered the telephone.

'It wasn't a vicious kick. I just winded him, that's all,' Franklin objected, looking at his solicitor. Because there was no sign of sympathy from that quarter, he switched his angry, protesting gaze to the uniformed constable covering the door whose stony expression remained unaltered. 'I had to get away, see?' he went on. 'I knew the whole thing was a fit-up by the Swansea police. They've got it in for me. Or Percy Trout has, and they're backing him because he's one of them.'

'So you broke out of the handcuffs —'

'Didn't need to. Your PC Evans hadn't closed them right. Not the one on my left hand. He needs practice most probably. In self-defence as well,' he added gratuitously, with a smirk, while swivelling on his chair to reach the cigarettes in his back pocket.

'OK. So you released one hand from the cuffs, left PC Evans winded on the roadside, and rode his bike straight here?'

'That's right.' Franklin lit a cigarette. 'Smoke, anyone?' He offered the pack to the other three at the table, but got no takers. Only Mrs Norris leaned even further away from him.

Parry cleared his throat. 'Why do you believe PC Trout and the Swansea police have it in for you, Mr Franklin?' he asked, in a quietly level voice that suggested they might have been engaged in settling some abstruse, academic question.

'Because of Norma, my second wife. She's married to him now. She's Mrs Trout. Only I er . . . I see her sometimes. Like last night.'

'You were with PC Trout's wife last night?' Parry inquired, again in an interested, unchallenging tone.

'Not all night. Worse luck. Percy came home unexpected, see?' The speaker turned a knowing grin on Mrs Norris who, taken unawares, grinned back. She then reddened, and applied herself to writing the date on the blank top page of the massive notepad she had brought with her.

'So PC Trout surprised you with his wife?'

'No. Because I saw him first.' Franklin beamed in a self-congratulatory way, tilting his chair back on two legs and inhaling heavily on the cigarette. 'He was coming up the path to their house. I nipped out the back. Half dressed, I was. Well, you know how it is.' For some reason, the speaker shot a conspiratorial sort of glance at Lloyd, before continuing. 'I dropped my wallet in the rush, too. Anyway, he must have heard me. Starting my bike, probably. He came after me then, shouting blue murder. He didn't catch me, but I reckon he had all his mates out looking for me this morning.'

Lloyd leaned further forward over the table, despite the smoke the prisoner was blowing across it. 'The whole South Wales Constabulary was looking for you this morning, boyo, for quite a different reason,' he growled. 'PC Trout hadn't reported you for being at his house. There wouldn't have been any point in his doing that. It wasn't police business.'

Franklin shook his head. 'Maybe not official police business. But I reckoned some of his mates at Swansea nick were out to get me unofficially, and PC Evans was one of them.'

'So what exactly did you suppose was going to happen to you, after you were taken to Swansea nick?'

'I reckon they'd have beaten me up, then cooked up something to charge me with.'

'There was nothing cooked up about the bloodstained machete and the severed hand, Mr Franklin,' Lloyd responded firmly.

'There was if they were in my pannier, because I never put them there. Anyway, PC Evans never showed them to me. Only said they were in that white Tesco bag. He could have put them there himself, couldn't he? Before or later — like after he'd got me to Swansea, even.'

Merlin Parry leaned back and folded his arms. 'What you've just said is a very serious accusation, Mr Franklin,' he put in with due solemnity. 'You were warned this interview was being taped,' he went on, indicating the recording machine on a small table close to Lloyd. 'I imagine your solicitor will advise you to retract the accusation, in your

103

own interests.' He gave Mrs Norris a prompting smile.

The woman lawyer swallowed. 'I'm sure my client wasn't meaning to accuse PC Evans, Chief Inspector,' she responded quickly, though she was evidently confused. 'If he inferred that the constable put the items in the pannier bag he now withdraws . . . unreservedly withdraws the inference, don't you, Mr Franklin?' There was more hope than certainty in her voice.

'Sure,' said Franklin, shrugging his shoulders and bringing the front legs of his chair down on the tiled floor with a bang. 'But if they were there, someone must have put them there, and it wasn't me.' He had planted both bent elbows on the table, and was staring defiantly at the two officers, closed fists butting each other, his eyes screwed up by the wreaths of smoke rising from the cigarette between his lips.

'But you didn't see PC Evans put the bag in your pannier, Mr Franklin?' Lloyd pressed.

The arrested man hesitated. 'No. But I wasn't watching him all the time, was I? Like when he had me lying face down in the bloody dirt.'

'While searching you and handcuffing you. PC Evans's report, his verbal report, says the bag was produced before he ordered you to lie down.'

'He still didn't show me what was in it, did he?' Franklin replied sullenly.

'For your information, Mr Franklin,' said Parry, 'that was because PC Evans recognized the items were probably valuable evidence in a murder inquiry. He knew they'd need to go for forensic examination without their being tampered with any more than was absolutely necessary. If you're as innocent as you say, that could well be in your own interests.'

Franklin scowled but made no reply.

'So at what time did you leave PC Trout's home last night, Mr Franklin?' Lloyd asked, changing the line of questioning.

'Ten past one. If you don't believe me, ask Percy Trout. He was supposed to be out all night on a surveillance job, or so he'd told Norma.'

'We've asked PC Trout, Mr Franklin, and he confirms the time.'

'Good. And has he told you he sent his mates out to get me this morning?'

'PC Trout sent nobody out to get you,' Parry put in with as much impatience as irritation. 'I sent a message to all divisions about you at ten o'clock this morning. I was trying to locate you to ask you to come to this police station to help us with our inquiries. PC Evans was only doing his duty.'

'By arresting me? Or trying to?'

'Yes, since he found you in possession of suspicious items. Incidentally, you didn't take the white bag with you after you'd assaulted the constable. Why not?'

'I was going to, but he was lying on it.'

'Did you touch the bag? And think before you answer,' Parry advised.

'No. I didn't exactly have time to spare.'

'So what time this morning did you reach the Coach and Horses in Pontyglas?'

'One-forty, or close on. My mother'll tell you, probably. She's a light sleeper, and I expect I woke her up. She'll have looked at the time if she woke.'

'She did, Mr Franklin. You were also seen turning your motorbike into the alley beside the pub near the time you say.'

'Well, that's all right, then, isn't it? Swansea to Pontyglas in half an hour, that's better than average. With no speeding, of course.' He favoured his solicitor with one of his normally infectious grins. 'So what am I supposed to have done on top in the time. Murdered somebody, is it? And cut up the body into handy pieces?'

'Did you know a Mr Mervyn Davies?' asked Lloyd flatly.

'Never met him, no. I know who he is though. Some say he was my father. He's all right, is he? It's not his –'

'Did you call at Condleston Lodge after you got back to Pontyglas last night, either before or after you arrived at the Coach and Horses?' Lloyd interrupted.

'Where's Condleston Lodge?' Franklin asked in an innocent voice, looking from Mrs Norris to Lloyd, then back again.

*   *   *

'I can't stay long,' said Dewi Trimble, with an air of importance, as if his being present at all was a concession. 'I'm giving Hercules his run now. Got up too late to take him before church.' He was holding the barrel-chested Hercules by a short, heavy chain. 'Gwen's making our lunch,' the dapper lawyer went on in the manner of a field marshal sharing top intelligences with his ADC. 'It'll be ready at one.' He straightened his shoulders.

'Oh, lovely. Am I invited, sweetie?' asked Gail Edworth in a playful voice. She closed her front door behind Trimble, and kissed him first on the forehead, then more feelingly on the lips. As she drew away from him again, the lower part of the long frilly dressing gown she was wearing fell open to reveal the maximum length of one very shapely leg. 'Shall I be all right like this?' she giggled, leaning back a little, hands on hips, and crossing one bare leg over the other in a provocative pose.

'Of course you're not invited.' Trimble wasn't in the mood for tomfoolery. 'Your mother isn't in downstairs?' He moved at a clipped pace from the hall into the prettily furnished living room, then towards the window so that he could see out, but not so close to it that he could be observed from Raglan Avenue. The entrance to the upper-floor flat was via an outside staircase screened by mature cupressus. This was at the side of the detached end house which was set in a neglected garden.

'I told you, it's Charles's turn to have Mother this Sunday,' said the young woman. 'He called for her earlier. Why don't you relax? Sit down. Have a drink. Want a drinkee too, do you, old Curly boy?' The dog wriggled its rump as she smoothed its back.

Trimble's face registered fleeting displeasure. He wished Gail wouldn't abbreviate the name Hercules – especially to Curly. In an almost reflex reaction, he ran his hand sensitively over his balding head.

'I was just going to get dressed,' Gail offered next. 'Unless you have other ideas, my lovely?' She put her arms around him from behind, whispered 'Ooo' in his left ear, then, keeping her mouth where it was, blew gently into the same orifice, before drawing in breath sharply and noisily as she dropped her hands down his stomach.

Gail Edworth was an essentially physical woman – an attractive brunette, with tousled hair, laughing eyes, and a well-developed body which she kept taut with exercise. Her voluptuous mouth matched her flared nose. To a purist in such matters, the mouth might have been considered a touch vulgar and the nose also a bit on the large side: Trimble thought both noticeable features quite splendid.

His mistress tended to mother Trimble, who was thirty years her senior. He was also shorter by two inches. Although he had suited and amused from the start, for her there was to be nothing enduring in their attachment: she wasn't ready yet for a new emotional entanglement. Trimble had come into her life shortly after she had broken with her lover of five years, a Cardiff dentist who had also been her employer. At the start, that affair had been romantic and exciting, but when she sensed the ardour was beginning to wane, hers more than his, it had been hard to pretend that things were not as they had been – particularly when the two were thrown together in their daily work, in a closeness that threatened to become irksome and embarrassing where once it had added hugely to the pleasure. To keep the memory sweet, Gail had abruptly ended the loving and resigned her job. That had been a year or so back, when she had returned to live and to work in Pontyglas.

Dewi Trimble was a patient of Gail's present employer, and they had first met, as it were, professionally. He had been unexpectedly bold, as well as eager, in his approaches to her, and to a degree, even matter-of-fact. After sending her red roses, out of season, he had asked her to meet him for dinner at an extremely expensive country hotel near Cardiff. Over the brandy, he had announced that he had reserved a double room for the night which he hoped she would share with him since it would be a pity to waste it. Impressed – even entertained – by such unpredictable audacity, she had succumbed to his invitation, and not regretted it.

From the start, Trimble had proved to be a more than satisfying lover, and it went without saying – because neither of them ever raised the subject – that each met the other's current amatory needs, and without complications. At Gail's own suggestion, there had been no more visits to expensive hotels since she had a perfectly good flat of her own. It was enough that Trimble took to making her regular presents – latterly always of money. This was precisely the form of gift she made it plain pleased her most, since dental nursing was not the best paid ancillary job in medical practice.

For the lawyer's part, the relationship was nearly perfect. It fed the often most pressing of his appetites, with no obligation to indulge it more often than was needed, or to have to linger after every repast, so to speak. Nor did the affair jeopardize his marriage, or threaten his respectable status in the community. Gail was undemanding not only of his time, but also in the way she made it plain she had no ambition to become the second Mrs Dewi Trimble.

Few clandestine affairs being free of complications, Trimble still had problems, of course. A minor one was having Mrs Winifred Edworth in the flat below while he made love to her daughter. This was something he, a married man with old-fashioned conservative values, found unsettling – also sometimes unnerving enough to put him off his stroke. More importantly, at the very start of his relationship with Gail, he had purposely given her the impression that he was far better off than he really was. He had subsequently done nothing to destroy the illusion. Sadly for him, one of the reasons for his relative impoverishment had been his habit over the years of, as it were, over-compensating a string of previous lady friends. By now he should have learned better, but he hadn't. Being bluntly realistic, he believed that the longevity of the affair with Gail was probably dependent on the frequency and size of his gifts. In that sense, he felt it certainly wouldn't do to give her the impression that he couldn't afford her. At one point he had even unnecessarily suggested that he might set her up with a cottage of her own nearer the coast, an extravagant and unaffordable idea prompted on the spur of a moment, and primarily through his determination to distance their lovemaking from her mother.

He turned around now to face Gail, which involved Hercules, still on the lead, awkwardly having to swivel about where he had seated himself so that he could just see out of the window. 'You won't have heard that Mervyn Davies is dead,' Trimble announced, in the solemn manner of a Neville Chamberlain declaring that a war had been declared.

'Well, good riddance to bad rubbish. Mean bugger,' she responded with spirit.

Trimble, mildly shocked at this reply, cleared his throat. 'Yes, well, the rector made the announcement at the end of the service this morning. A lot of people knew already. There was a good deal of talk about it in the parish hall after. They think he might have been murdered.'

'Go on?' She dropped on to her soft, billowy sofa. 'And which worthy citizen performed this public service?'

Trimble suppressed a disapproving sigh: most of the time he encouraged the free and irreverent way she expressed herself because it served to loosen his own linguistic inhibitions. 'It's very serious,' he only half admonished. 'He . . . er . . . he was a client, after all.' His face clouded at the seeming inadequacy of the remark, though on consideration he had to admit to himself he couldn't find grounds for saying anything more warming.

'I know he was a bloody client,' said Gail. 'You told me on Friday he wouldn't be leaving anything in his will to Charles and me.'

'You haven't mentioned that to anyone else?'

'Of course not, silly.'

'Not even to Charles?' The second inquiry was more pressing than the first.

'Certainly not.'

'Good. It wasn't a new will. It was the first he'd ever made,' he continued pedantically. 'He never signed it, and now, of course, he never will.'

'His sons will get the money anyway, won't they?' She took his thoughtful silence to indicate agreement. 'Mervyn Davies being dead doesn't alter the fact he was a mean bastard.' She tucked her feet up and patted the cushions beside her. 'Come and sit by me. Worried are you? Will it make a difference to your business?'

Trimble bent down and undid the dog's lead, then moved across to the sofa. Hercules, a disciplined creature of habit, still got up and followed him.

'There'll be complications over the estate,' said Trimble, sitting alongside her and absently starting to caress one of her legs. 'It could affect you and your brother.'

'You mean we could get some of the lolly after all?'

'Possibly quite a lot of it. That's if I arrange things the way I intend.' It was strategically important that she should credit him as the putative source of her future riches. Even so, he well knew that she could scarcely avoid coming into a quite large inheritance if the law took its normal course − even his secretary could attest to that, and, unknown to him, had virtually done so to Charles Edworth earlier that morning at the Traveller's Break. The financial outcome, following on the death of Mervyn Davies, might not be clear to the police yet, and one had to allow for complications − the most unsettling of these resting with how the man had died.

There were two, possibly three, people Trimble knew might be suspected of murdering Davies. These were the people who would benefit directly and substantially. In addition, there were several others who would do so indirectly. He was fondling the lower limbs of one of the direct beneficiaries at the moment. It was almost unthinkable, of course, that Gail should be suspected of murder. But the same stricture would not apply to her brother, which in turn could introduce the possibility in some policeman's mind that Charles could have recruited Gail as an accessory.

'Do you know where Charles was last night?' he asked.

'Yes. He took Mother to a dreary church supper,' she answered. 'He asked me to go too, but I'd arranged to see a play in Cardiff, with Adele. She's that nurse I used to work with.'

'I know about the supper. It wasn't dreary. Gwen organized it.' He was nothing if not loyal in normal circumstances. 'We were there too. So was Mervyn Davies. I meant, what was Charles doing later in the evening?'

'He brought Mother home, and they had tea together. She told me, when I went down to see her mid-morning.'

'What time did he leave?'

She ran a hand across her forehead. 'It was late, Mother said. Which could mean anything, of course.'

'You didn't hear him leave?'

'No. I wasn't here. Didn't get home till midnight myself. Adele and I had a pizza after the theatre, then I drove her back to Tawrbach. We er . . . we had a natter at her house for a bit.'

'I knew you were out. I walked over with Hercules after we got home. There weren't any lights on.'

'Shame. You should have said you were coming.' She reached for the hand that wasn't caressing her thigh and squeezed it. Then suddenly she sat bolt upright. 'Hey, you aren't thinking Charles could have done in Mervyn Davies?'

'No, but it's conceivable the police may.'

'Because we'll be getting some of the money? But how? You haven't told me that yet.'

'Better to wait till I've done some fact finding. I'll need to be in touch with Australia tomorrow. Then there's the question of the cause of death. With only Davies's head available so far, the coroner will almost certainly delay the inquest.'

'Until they find the rest of him?'

'Yes. Well, the delay will be for a reasonable time. The legal situation over all won't be straightforward.' Trimble was doing his best to build up the complexities, despite the fact he knew well enough what the end of the matter would be. 'Meantime, don't get all excited, but rely on it, I'll be doing my best for you.' He checked the time. 'Now I must go.'

'Oh, but you've made me all excited already,' she insisted mischievously, wetting her open lips with the tip of her tongue.

'I'm afraid I'll be too busy to get here tomorrow evening after all,' he went on dispassionately, except he was undoing the bow of her gown as he spoke. 'But all in a good cause. Make up for it at other times,' he completed.

'Or in advance, like now, sweetie? Let's build up your

appetite for Gwen's lunch, shall we?' She lay back on the sofa and pulled him towards her.

As one of those who would indirectly benefit, but significantly, from Mervyn Davies's death, through his relationship with an appreciative and wealthy Gail Edworth, Dewi Trimble had decided it was better they had no contact with each other after this morning, and for the immediate future. Even so, making love to her now was nothing less than he had coolly intended when he had walked Hercules here in the first place.

The pink-eyed bull terrier marked their passionate and protracted parting by advancing stiff-legged to the sofa and licking one of the lady's wriggling feet.

12

'If it was Owen Franklin, and if he was getting rid of the hand and the machete, why did he leave the head?' questioned the shirt-sleeved Merlin Parry, pacing the floor, and pausing occasionally to take short sips of scalding coffee from a plastic cup. 'There'd be no logic in it, Gomer.' He came to a halt, changed the hand holding the hot coffee, and stared through the half-glazed partition walls that separated the small corner office he and Lloyd were in from the larger room from which it had been carved, and which it looked on to on two sides. The whole low-ceilinged area accounted for a quarter of the top floor at Pontyglas Police Station. Normally used for data processing and storage, it had been made over, since late on Sunday, as an incident centre for Parry and his investigation team.

'There's no logic in it, boss, not if he was going to destroy the body bit by bit. Otherwise, why leave the most identifiable part on his parents' doorstep?' Lloyd, standing behind a desk, was sorting paper, and drinking tea. He had a half-empty plastic cup in his hand, and another, full one, steaming on the desk, with a Danish pastry beside it. 'Can you smell paint?' he added, wrinkling his nose and looking around at the walls, none of which had been decorated recently.

'No,' replied the preoccupied Parry. 'But if Franklin didn't do the murder, the head and the hand may have a significance we haven't understood. So we'll have been wasting time. Expensive time. Too much of it,' he ended, the phrasing characteristically clipped.

'Meaning the person who did it could have left the bits and the weapon just to implicate Owen Franklin?'

'Or for a more subtle reason.'

Lloyd never credited criminals with being subtle, and he had seldom had occasion to regret the fact. 'What reason's that then, boss?' he questioned.

'No idea.' Parry gave a disarmingly self-deprecating smile – the smile that his late wife had said made him look even more like the actor Anthony Hopkins, her second most favourite Welshman. 'We'd better have an idea soon though,' he went on. 'The head and hand were left in separate places. Found by different people. If more bits of body turn up, perhaps that'll show us a pattern. Too soon to say, I expect.' But his eyes indicated he was working on it. 'And where's the rest of Mervyn Davies? Buried? Burned? Refrigerated? Bodies don't disappear into thin air. And he was a big chap.'

It was now eight o'clock on Monday morning, and there was plenty of activity in the big outer room. A dozen men and women, police and civilians, all permanent members of the Cardiff Major Crime Support Unit, were still setting up equipment – telephones, fax machines, computers, printers, tape recorders, a slide projector, photocopiers, and shredders – most of which had arrived from Cardiff in the last two hours. Extra desks, tables, chairs, and filing boxes had been borrowed from within the building.

Local maps and diagrams were being fixed to pinboards around the walls, with blown-up photographs of the garden at Condleston Lodge, and some enlarged fact sheets giving the victim's background, his movements on Friday night, the clothes he'd been wearing, and the names and addresses of the people he had been with since his arrival in Pontyglas. Dominating all this, in the centre of the wall display nearest the door, was a large colour photograph of the victim, not a grisly exhibit of his head after it had been separated from its body, but a shot of a smiling Mervyn Davies spooning up fruit salad and ice-cream at the parish supper on Saturday night. The rector's wife, the amateur photographer responsible for this indispensable, clear study, had nervously offered the undeveloped film to DC Lucy Howells, the team's Exhibits Officer, on the previous afternoon. It had provided the only likeness of the victim yet available, apart from the one in the group photograph of the St Luke's choir taken when he had been fourteen years old.

As well as the team members here at the police station, a larger number were already at work in different parts of the town. Some were at Condleston Lodge, others, armed with smaller copies of the church supper photo, were interviewing householders along all the routes the victim could have used after leaving Geoff Godwin's house on Saturday night.

If the cost of government resources – British and Australian – expended on Mervyn Davies through the whole of his fifty-eight-year lifetime had been added together, the total could scarcely have equalled what had already been spent on him by the South Wales police in the thirty or so hours since his death, or so Parry was thinking as he watched what was going on through the open connecting door of the offices. He was pleased with the evident energy being applied, while overly aware of what it was costing a police force already strapped for cash.

'SOCO had covered the Condleston Lodge garden by nightfall yesterday, boss,' said Lloyd. 'It's a big area, as we saw. It didn't seem there'd been any fresh digging from the night before. If there had been, it should have been possible to tell, just by looking. Well, a gardener could have.' The weighty sergeant and his equally ample wife were keen gardeners. They continued to grow enough organic vegetables in their own kitchen plot to satisfy the needs of themselves and their five children. But since four of the children had married and left home permanently, and the fifth was away most of the time at college, it was neighbours and friends who now chiefly benefited from the results.

'You can't be sure of that, Gomer. Not if it was a gardener who was arranging things to fox us,' replied Parry, no gardener himself.

'Ah, but that GPR machine should be here this morning,' Lloyd continued confidently.

'The what?' Parry demanded.

'Ground Penetrating Radar machine, boss. Coming from Gloucester. We'll go over all recent diggings with that. It'll tell if the ground's been disturbed anywhere in real depth. Marvellous invention. Save hours of labour. It's the veg and flower beds we're interested in still. And the weeded areas in all that shrubbery. Mr Jarvis did say he was halfway through with his spring digging.' He picked up the Danish pastry. 'Funny, I can still smell paint.'

'Really? Well, it's probably me.' Without enlarging on the point, Parry turned about, dropped his crumpled cup in the wastebin, and moved briskly over to the chair behind one of the two metal desks butted together in the centre of the room. A set of transparent coloured folders were laid along the join of the desk tops. They held copies of all police and witness reports, transcripts of interviews, faxes and messages available so far.

Parry had left Pontyglas at ten on the previous evening. He had spent the night at Perdita Jones's place in Tawrbach, partly because it had been closer than his flat in Cardiff, but mostly to compensate for their not having spent the rest of Sunday together. Perdita had been painting her bedroom when he arrived – improving the sales appeal of the bungalow, she said. He had helped her finish before they had fallen into bed in another room, tired and reeking of Dulux. He had left her still sleeping, and returned to the town by seven o'clock. Lloyd had arrived later, after first going to Condleston Lodge. He had then joined Parry who had been interviewing Owen Franklin again. A bright-eyed Mrs Norris had been in attendance: her senior partner had not yet returned from holiday. After her awkward performance the day before, she had been keen to prove at least that she was good at early starts, a trait demonstrably not matched in her client.

The two police officers had afterwards held a briefing meeting with the whole team in the big office. After that they had sent to the canteen for the coffee and tea – and Lloyd's Danish pastry – that Parry had called breakfast. Lloyd had already consumed a plate of eggs, bacon and lava bread before leaving home.

The detective chief inspector leaned across and picked up the transcript of the previous interview with Franklin, flicked through the pages, then dropped it back on to the desk. 'He hadn't altered his story one iota this morning,' he said.

'Going to let him go, are we, boss?'

Parry sniffed. 'We'll have to tonight anyway, unless we can charge him with the murder.'

'We've still got him for assaulting a policeman.'

'Always supposing the Crown Prosecutor's office is prepared to proceed on that one, and I don't think it will be. He'd get bail in any case. Even with a lawyer as switched off as Mrs Norris. She must have figured by now that fit-up story of his could be made to hold up in court. Just.'

'You don't believe it's true though, boss?'

'Not that he was being fitted up by the Swansea bill, no. But, in the circumstances, he could have believed he was. He's bound to claim provocation. Pity PC Evans hadn't shown him what was in that bag.'

'Evans should also buy his private equipment from the police approved list.' Lloyd gave a low chuckle. 'Those handcuffs Franklin came in were straight out of toytown.'

'The fact remains, Franklin didn't leave Swansea till ten past one Sunday morning, and he was here in Pontyglas at twenty to two. Both times verified by policemen. The Swansea time by the off-duty PC Trout whose wife he was shafting.'

'And she admits he was with her the four hours before that,' Lloyd put in.

'That's right. Then Franklin was seen half an hour later turning into the Coach and Horses by two constables on mobile patrol, one of whom even knew him by sight. He couldn't be better alibied to that point if he'd been arranging the police rotas himself. On top of that, his prints aren't on the machete, the severed hand, the shopping bag, or the Volvo.'

'Wouldn't have been if he'd worn gloves, boss. And there's nothing to prove he stayed at the pub after he got there. He could have taken the Volvo and nipped round to Condleston Lodge. The car was open, and he might have had a key for it anyway, or known where his folks kept a spare.'

'Except his mother would have heard him go out again,

start the car, and bring it back.' Parry pulled out the chair and sat in it as he spoke.

'Partial, she'd be, though. And he could have warned her not to say anything to us.'

'But Dr Ironmonger, the pathologist, he isn't partial.' Parry picked up his own notebook. 'He couldn't give an exact time of death when I phoned him last night. Not with just the head and hand to go on. But, as I said at the briefing, his guess is that Davies died between eleven-thirty and two in the morning. He'd have put it between six in the evening and two, he said, if he hadn't known the victim had been alive at eleven-thirty.'

'That's according to Geoff Godwin, of course,' said Lloyd slowly. 'At least the doc confirmed the hand belonged to the same body as the head. Awkward if it had come from another one. And he's absolutely certain the machete was used both times?'

'Yes. And that Davies was alive when his head was severed.'

'So that was the cause of death, boss?'

Parry shook his head. 'Ironmonger won't commit on that till he's examined the rest of the body. There could have been an earlier fatal wound to another part of him.'

'Fair enough,' Lloyd replied, but sounding as if he thought the point too pedantic. 'The hand was cut off after he died, though?' he said, eyeing the remains of the Danish pastry as if it was all that might lie between him and threatened starvation, before slowly lifting it towards his mouth.

'Yes. Very soon after, he thought. Let's hope we get more today on the machete. It looked pretty ancient. Made by Brade's, it says in the report.'

'They mostly were, boss. The older ones. I've got one of theirs at home. Belonged to my dad. Mr Jarvis says it definitely didn't come from Condleston Lodge. His tool shed was well locked up, and the machete he keeps there was in place on the tool rack. Chances are he wouldn't have had two.' Lloyd drained his second cup of tea, then rubbed an open hand across his moustache. 'So if Owen Franklin's the murderer, he only had about twenty minutes to reach Condleston

118

Lodge, get Mr Davies up, and do the job. Then he had to chop off the hand, do a disappearing trick with the rest of the body, reset the house alarm, assuming he knew the code, clean out the back of the car, assuming he was using it, and get back to the Coach and Horses without anybody seeing him. Oh, and without waking his mother again, that's if she's telling the truth. Tall order that, boss. And according to that first forensic report, there was no blood in the Volvo. Only what was inside the bag with the head.'

'Yes, it's a tall order. That's if the estimated time of death is reliable, of course,' Parry commented. 'And he couldn't have known the alarm code for the house unless he forced it out of Davies. Though that's always possible.'

'Dr Ironmonger didn't know what happened to the ham?' Lloyd asked, with a grin.

'No, but he mentioned there were traces of cooked ham in the bag.'

'So the same bag was used for the ham and the head.'

'No. He wouldn't commit on that either. Said there could have been ham in it when it was first used at the store.'

'Careful blokes, pathologists.' Lloyd sat down heavily in the chair behind the second desk, and opposite Parry.

'So what did you mean about Geoff Godwin, just now?'

The sergeant's face clouded. 'Well, I've been thinking since the briefing, so far we only have his word for it that Mr Davies left his place alive. I mean, he could have done him in when they got back to his house, and buried the body in the garden, then or later. In that flower bed even, the one he'd dug over last week.'

'So why would he have admitted going off in the car to find Davies?'

'He didn't, boss. Not till you challenged him, and he didn't want to risk a direct lie. But that's when he could have left the head and the hand at the Coach and Horses.'

Parry shook his head. 'Not the hand, he didn't. He said his wife would confirm he was back in fifteen minutes. Owen Franklin's bike wasn't there till one-forty. And if Ken Franklin was telling the truth, the Volvo wasn't there till midnight, either.'

'So Mr Godwin's wife could be covering for him. And remember, he'd cleaned his car inside as well as out before we got there,' Lloyd continued, aware that his Godwin theory had just lost some of its credibility.

'What about the blood found on and under the bushes in Condleston Lodge?' Parry asked thoughtfully.

'He could have planted that there later, to keep himself out of the frame. Or to put someone else in it.'

'Or maybe he didn't murder Davies at the house. Maybe he found him when he went after him with the car, drove him back to Condleston Lodge, and chopped him after they got there.' Parry paused. 'But what was his motive for murder?'

'Anything from a childhood hatred that'd festered over the years, boss, to . . . to a violent quarrel over something last night . . . when they were alone and er . . . and in their cups,' the sergeant finished with an affirming nod, and a trifle breathlessly. He searched for the roll of peppermints he had put down somewhere on the desk when he'd arrived.

'All possible, yes, but it doesn't match Owen Franklin's motive,' said Parry. 'Anyway, haven't other people confirmed Davies and Godwin were bosom pals in their youth?' He half reached for the report that said as much, then decided not to.

'I thought Mr Davies was supposed to be closest to Edwin Edworth, who left him all his money,' Lloyd offered. 'Or perhaps they were a trio? He didn't leave Mr Godwin anything, though. Not that we know of. So Mr Godwin could have been jealous, couldn't he? There's a motive, if you like.'

Parry pouted. 'OK. What are we going to do about him?'

'For a start, I'll have that GPR machine taken over to his place, when they're through with it at the Lodge. We'll tell him his garden has to be eliminated as it's the last place Mr Davies was seen. We'll check for blood traces as well. And if there's no machete in his tool shed, we'll find out if he used to own one.'

'He's not likely to tell us if he did, is he? Not if it's gone missing.'

'Ah, one of his neighbours might, boss. Very observant,

gardeners are. Given to borrowing each other's tools as well.'

Parry leaned back, clasping his hands behind his head. 'What about checking the municipal rubbish tip? I should think Godwin's in charge of it. Isn't he manager of the Borough Cleansing Department?'

'Deputy manager. And we had four men there yesterday checking. They didn't find anything. We had a look at his old allotment after that as well. The report's being typed. Mr Godwin arranged to have one of his blokes help with the search of the rubbish tip. To drive the bulldozer they use there. He offered that when we asked him to have the place opened up for us. It's why I don't think he'd have dropped the body there. Not if he's the murderer.' He took a peppermint from the roll discovered under his copy of Monday's *Daily Express*. 'You still think Owen Franklin had a better motive, boss?'

'A more obvious one, yes. If he can prove he's Davies's natural son there must be at least a chance he's entitled to some of the Edworth money.'

'His adopted father thinks he is Davies's son.'

'Yes, but his adopted mother denied it.'

'If Mr Davies died later than Dr Ironmonger says, Ken and Owen Franklin could have gone over together and done the murder during the night,' Lloyd suggested. 'Got him out of the house on some pretext, and chopped him by those bushes. It would have given them the time they needed, and two of them could have handled the job a lot easier than one.'

'What if they'd woken Mrs Franklin again?'

'The two of them could have squared her, easy, boss.'

'I'm not so sure. In practice, a wife usually makes a lousy defence witness in a murder case, especially one who's out of sympathy with what her husband's done. I don't believe Jacky Franklin would have sanctioned Davies's killing, whoever did it.'

'Not even if it was her husband *and* her adopted son, boss?'

Parry considered for a moment. 'Possible, but I'm still not sure she could carry it off.'

'The same might apply to Mrs Godwin, of course,' the

121

sergeant observed. 'And we don't know yet whether she's as strong a character as Mrs Franklin, even.'

'That's right. The case against Ken and Owen Franklin still has holes in it, of course. Even if the doc is wrong with his times. Davies's bed hadn't been slept in. And the burglar alarm was set. He'd have turned it off if he'd gone into the house earlier. They couldn't have known the code.'

'Except two of them could have got it out of him, boss.'

'I wonder.' Parry paused. 'What about the Jarvis couple? There's nothing to suggest they'd want to get rid of Davies, is there?'

'Not really. They get their legacy from Edwin Edworth, and their wages are paid for six months, that's even if they're not kept on at the house. You thinking Mr Jarvis took too long getting Auntie Olwyn home to Kenfig Hill?' Lloyd was flicking back the pages of his notebook. 'Yes, there was probably enough time for him to get back here as well, do in Mr Davies, and drop the remains of the body in the sea at Porthcawl before going back to the party.'

'But he was too early to leave the head in the Volvo and the hand in Owen Franklin's motorbike.'

Lloyd shrugged. 'He could have done that later in the night.'

'Right. So what if Davies was sending them packing? A living-in couple like that do as well from their free bed and board as they do from their wages. But, no' – he shook his head – 'you don't kill someone for the sake of six months' board and lodging.'

'According to Jacky Franklin, Mrs Jarvis supplied Edwin Edworth with extra room services, like. She says it was rumoured Mrs Jarvis slept with him.'

'How would Mrs Franklin know that, I wonder?'

'She wouldn't say exactly, boss, but that's what she told me when she was showing us over their flat. According to her, Mrs Jarvis is a bit of a boaster when it comes to advertising her charms. Publicans' wives do pick up a lot of gossip, of course.'

'But surely it would have been a reason for Jarvis to do in Edwin Edworth, not Mervyn Davies.'

'Not if he thought his wife had started offering the same services to Mr Davies, boss. And the way he was talking yesterday, she might have been thinking just that. She's got a roving eye, all right.'

'Aimed it at you, did she, Gomer?'

'I got the feeling she wasn't far off it. I suppose she's quite sexy in her way.'

'Well, she couldn't lure me out of a burning building.'

'Nor me, and I'm more her age,' Lloyd responded defensively. 'Might have appealed to Mr Davies though, like she did to Mr Edworth.'

'*If* she did,' Parry cautioned.

'Yes. She's a lot younger than both of them were, of course.'

'Hm, well, we've still only got Jacky Franklin's word that she was sleeping with Edworth,' Parry said doubtfully, then his tone sharpened. 'Someone's getting corroboration from this Auntie Olwyn?'

'Yes, boss. This morning.'

Parry checked the time, then looked through the glass partition. Activity in the bigger room was now less manic, and the number of operatives there had thinned. More people had left for outside assignments. 'Right, Gomer, breakfast break's over,' he said, pulling his chair up to the desk. 'We've only got staffing priority from Superintendent Gore for two days. After that we'll lose half the team, back to the jobs they were on before this one. So, let's you and I tie up those loose ends first on Owen Franklin. His motive's one of them. I want to know what his real chances are of inheriting anything. He's still our best prospect.' His hand went out to the list of people Davies was known to have seen since his arrival in Britain. 'Have all the people in that old choir photo been seen? The ones who were at the church supper, I mean?'

'I'll check, boss.'

Parry continued to study the list. 'This Dewi Trimble, the lawyer, he can give us the legal gen on illegitimate heirs. We need to see him next in any case.'

'He and his wife were at the church supper. His secretary,

a Miss Annie Lewin, she's supposed to be the girlfriend of Charles Edworth.'

'That's the late Edwin's nephew?'

'Yes. They were both at the supper too. Not together, though. He's married, but his wife wasn't with him.'

'Who said Trimble's secretary is Edworth's girlfriend? Mrs Franklin, I suppose?'

'That's right, boss.'

'Bit of a troublemaker, quietly, our Mrs Franklin,' Parry commented half questioningly.

13

'I'll get it, Heidi,' called Warrant Officer Derek Sewell. He had been halfway down the stairs, doing up his belt over his khaki jersey, as the telephone rang.

'Could you, Derek? The children are late already. Why are you being so slow this morning, Peter?' His buxom, flaxen-haired, German wife was bundling their two offspring out through the front door. 'If it's Susie, say I'll ring back in a minute, will you?' she called back in her high, penetrating voice, the 'will' as always emerging as 'vill'.

Briefly, he glimpsed her following the children in the direction of the bus stop at the end of the road, as he closed the front door behind them. He took deep pleasure in the sight of her lusty, athletic figure, especially the strong, well-shaped legs.

There was no real reason why Heidi had to shepherd the two of them any more, Sewell thought, after he stopped thinking about her legs. Well, not quite as much as she did. Shirley was nine now, and Peter nearly seven. They could perfectly well see themselves on to the school bus. It wasn't as though they lived in a town, well, not a town in the accepted sense, though where they did live had most of the amenities of one, and few of the hazards.

'Warrant Officer Sewell,' he said into the phone briskly, glancing around the lounge – inspecting it. They'd had two of his army colleagues and their wives to supper the previous evening. It had been a welcome home party Heidi had arranged for him. The guests had stayed until very late, but Heidi had the place pristine clean and tidy already, used coffee cups and glasses gone, carpets swept, cushions fluffed up. The kitchen had been matchingly spick and span. She had done it all while he'd been out jogging – that as well as getting everybody's breakfast. She was a model wife, a treasure, inexhaustible in all departments, including bed.

'Morning, sir. Post Office, here. I've got Captain Clark for you.' There was a click, but no further response for a moment, until the female operator came back with: 'Sorry, sir. I'm to transfer you to Major Denison instead. Could you hang on a sec? Or I can ring you back?'

'I'll hang on.' He knew Captain Clark, in the Adjutant's Office, but not Major Denison, and he never risked keeping strange senior officers waiting. He was in no particular hurry, and wasn't on duty himself until nine. He hummed a Strauss waltz as he waited, watching a small, grey bird in the back garden through the window.

The joint service headquarters of the UK Support Command, formerly the British Army of the Rhine, at Mönchengladbach, where Sewell was stationed, was a self-sufficient, protected area which, apart from its military buildings, included schools, sports grounds, cinemas, shops, pubs, clubs and churches, as well as the best married quarters Sewell had ever known in all his twenty-two years in the Royal Engineers. The over-small garden he was now looking at was the only thing about the semi-detached house that didn't completely suit. Still, you couldn't have everything, and if he got his promotion to fully commissioned captain, and he'd been working his guts out for that, they'd be moved into a bigger place with a garden to match. Meantime, this one had everything you could want really – four bedrooms, a shower-room downstairs as well as two bathrooms upstairs, and a basement that incorporated garage, laundry and workshop.

The Germans were especially good about building cellars, he mused. They were good about plenty of other things too. That wasn't why he had married Heidi, but it was part of the reason, and why he had learned her language. He'd twice succeeded in having his posting here extended, because of his German wife. He hoped to finish his army career in Mönchengladbach, and even if he didn't, when he left the service he aimed to find an engineering job in Germany. He was sure there were better prospects for his kind here than in the UK, and for the children as well. He and Heidi were making sure that Shirley and Peter were growing up bilingual.

You only had to spend a week in Britain, as he had just done, to be reminded of what he saw as the lack of opportunity there compared to here. He had nothing but contempt for what he had always regarded as the class-ridden social system that had driven his mother to prostitution and an early death – and his prejudice was ingrained enough for him to believe that things hadn't altered much since then. His Uncle John was another example of the way the British exploited their underclass. More than thirty years down the mines and what had John Sewell got to show for it? Redundancy in his early fifties, and only jobbing work as a handyman since then, while he and his invalid wife lived in what was little better than a hovel by his nephew's standards.

The muscles of Sewell's jaw tightened. At least he'd helped to alter one injustice during his trip. It was why he had gone to spend the last night with his uncle.

'Mr Sewell? Major Denison here, Royal Corps of Military Police. Sorry to keep you waiting.' The voice on the phone was sharp and bluff, and the apology peremptory. 'I'm at the post office. Expecting a package from the UK, were you? Padded envelope, ten by eight? Postmark Pon-tie-gla-ass?' He had anglicized the name in the manner of an upper-crust Englishman who considered the Welsh language an anachronism better ignored than indulged.

'I wasn't expecting a package, no, sir. But Pontyglas is my home town, and I was there last week. There's a package addressed to me, is there?'

'Ye-es.' The long drawn out affirmative was followed by silence.

'Is there a problem with it, sir?' It was obvious there was a bloody problem or this sodding major in the military police wouldn't be ringing him, so why didn't the bugger get to the point?

'Something unusual, yes. It was put through X-ray in the usual way.'

'It's not a letter bomb, sir?' More than the usual number of letter and parcel bombs had been showing up at the establishment recently. Anything capable of carrying an explosive device was X-rayed.

'No. More unusual than that. And not dangerous. Look, Mr Sewell, I think you'd better get down here, pronto. Right?'

'Right, sir.'

'Good man.'

Poncey twit.

'Kind of you to make the time, Mr Trimble. So early too,' said Parry, settling into a chair in front of the solicitor's desk, while Lloyd seated himself to his right.

'I was expecting to hear from the police before this. About Mervyn Davies, is it? Shocking event, and no mistake.' Despite the anticipation he had mentioned, Dewi Trimble was wearing his usual look of unexplained surprise, eyebrows arched, and cheeks sucked in to such a degree that their insides must have been touching each other across his tongue. It was possible, of course, that the expression was this time meant to stand as an admonition because he hadn't been approached sooner.

'Yes, well, we were intending to get to you yesterday, sir, but we were concentrating then on –'

'Trying to find the rest of the body?' There was certainly reproach in the interruption, as if the failure to produce a complete corpse showed a woeful lack of professionalism on the part of the police force.

'That, and interviewing the people who'd been with Mr Davies late on Saturday night, sir. At the end of the church supper, and after that.'

'I was with him at the supper. He was my guest, except we were sitting at different tables. My wife and I had to be on the top table, you see? The top table. To look after the archdeacon. He was the chief guest and speaker. Fine man and leader. He'll go far.' The compliments, about a spent and boring cleric, were delivered without true conviction, and had only been voiced at all because Trimble was still irritated at the bishop with whom he and Mrs Trimble should have been hobnobbing.

'We gathered Mr Davies had been with you at the supper, sir,' put in Lloyd. 'But that you and your wife didn't stay on at all, not after the function finished officially?'

'No, we didn't. My wife had had the responsibility of arranging the whole thing, and she was tired out. Tired out.'

'Quite so, sir. We also thought if you had anything really urgent to tell the police, you'd have been in touch with the station. You being a lawyer, like.'

'Is that so?' said Trimble heavily, as if he didn't consider it had to be so at all.

'Did you happen to go out again after you came home from the supper, sir?' asked the sergeant.

'Yes. I took my bull terrier for an airing. Across the park.'

'That'd be the open park at the back of your road? You didn't go down to the town centre?'

'No, I didn't. Why d'you want to know that?'

'Because the last time anyone saw Mr Davies, he was leaving Mr Geoff Godwin's house, which we understand isn't far from yours, and heading back to Condleston Road through the town. If you'd been going that way you might have seen him.'

'Well, I didn't. What time was that?'

'Around eleven-thirty, sir.'

'Ah, well, I set off soon after ten-fifteen, and I was out less than an hour. So it's not likely I'd have seen him in any case.'

'And you didn't meet him walking across the park with Mr Godwin earlier, when they were going to Mr Godwin's house? That was the way they took.'

Trimble shrugged. 'No again, I'm afraid. And there are any number of routes people can take across the park. You'd know that if you were local. Where's Godwin's house?'

'In er . . .' Lloyd checked his notes. 'In Park Rise, sir.'

'Well, that's some way from mine. Much further down the hill, of course.' His stern look implied that the downhill distance between his part of Park Hill and Park Rise was even more significant socially than it was geographically. 'I understand you've found nothing but Davies's head? In the boot of Franklin's car?'

'For the record, could I ask who told you that, sir, and when?' Parry asked.

Trimble's eyebrows arched again. 'It was the rector, Mr Gravler, at the end of the parish communion service at St Luke's yesterday.' And you couldn't have a more innocent informant than that, he thought to himself, as he completed: 'Have you now found the whole body?'

'Not all of it, sir,' said Parry. 'Not by any means, I'm afraid. Since the head, only one of the hands has come to light.'

'Good God!' The lawyer took out a clean white handkerchief, unfolded it, removed his half glasses, and blew his nose loudly. 'Which hand?'

'The left, sir. It was in the pannier bag of a motorbike. I wonder, could you tell us, did Mr Davies have any enemies in the town that you know of?' Parry continued, before Trimble had the chance to ask whose motorbike.

'Not that I know of. He'd been away from here a very long time. You know, of course, he was the main intended beneficiary through the will of my late client Edwin Edworth?'

'We did know that, yes, sir.'

'Everybody did, I suppose. It was in the paper.'

'Not the actual amount of the inheritance, sir. It may be germane to our inquiries to know the size of the legacy, sir. In round figures?'

The lawyer seemed to consider deeply before replying. 'In round figures, about two and a quarter million pounds, including the house. That's after taxes, which will be substantial.'

'Even so, that's less than was reported in the paper, sir.'

'It usually is in these cases, Mr Parry.'

'But very substantial all the same. Would you know why Mr Edworth made Mr Davies his principal beneficiary, sir?'

'Because they were close boyhood friends.'

Parry used his elbows to lever himself slightly forward in

his chair. 'Even though they hadn't been in touch during the whole of Mr Davies's absence from this country?' he said, the tone surprised as well as questioning.

'That's not quite correct. They spoke once on the telephone, some weeks before Mr Edworth died.'

'Even so, isn't it all very unusual, sir? With all the friends Mr Edworth must have made since boyhood, and with his having living relatives, that he left all his money in that way?'

Trimble shrugged. 'It's a free country, Mr Parry. Mr Edworth was slightly eccentric as well as very obdurate.'

'And so far as you know, he was a free agent in what he did, sir?'

'How d'you mean?'

'Mr Davies didn't have some kind of hold over him? A hold that forced Mr Edworth to leave him his money? Something someone else might have known about and resented, to the point where the person might have taken vengeance on Mr Davies by killing him?'

'Oh, that's very fanciful, Mr Parry. Too fanciful by far for my taste. And quite foreign to the relationship of the two men as I knew it. Quite foreign.'

'I see, sir. And to your knowledge, there were no other exchanges between the two of them, except the telephone call you mentioned?'

'None.' Trimble took a breath and made as if to say something more, then didn't.

'You're sure of that, sir?'

The lawyer hesitated. 'I was only going to say, there was a sealed letter Mr Edworth left with me, to be conveyed to Mr Davies after his death. I suppose it was an exchange in the strict sense, but hardly the kind you mean.'

'Had you sent the letter to Mr Davies in Australia, sir?'

'No. I held it here when we knew he was coming. I handed it to him in this office, when he came here early on Friday morning.'

'Do you know what was in the letter, sir?'

'I have no idea, Mr Parry. He didn't open it here. He seemed diffident about breaking a wax seal. People often are.'

'We've taken charge of all his effects, sir, but there was no letter. Can you think of a reason why he might have destroyed it?'

'Not without knowing what was in it. But on the face of it, it'd seem unlikely he'd have destroyed it,' Trimble offered slowly.

'I agree.' Parry glanced at Lloyd who made a note in his book as the senior policeman continued. 'Going back to the newspaper reports of the will, sir – they suggested that members of the Edworth family were left absolutely nothing.'

'That's pretty accurate, yes.'

'And so far as you know, had that produced a feeling of hostility to Mr Davies from members of the family?'

'It could hardly have produced a warm feeling of gratitude, could it, Mr Parry? But it was no more than members of the family had come to expect. Edwin never married, so there were no direct family heirs. And there was a rift many years ago. Between Edwin and his brother Gwilym. It never healed.'

'I see.' Parry nodded. 'You mentioned Mr Davies came to see you here on Friday morning?'

'Yes. He'd only been in the town a few hours. We discussed the will.'

'Anything else, sir?'

Trimble studied the ceiling as though carefully recounting to himself what else had taken place. 'There was nothing of real substance, no,' he responded, ultimately.

'He didn't give you any instructions about his new wealth. How he intended to use it? Whether he'd be giving any of it away immediately, and to whom?'

The lawyer seemed to be taken momentarily off guard. He cleared his throat. 'The answer to that is no. And I hardly see what it'd have to do with his being murdered next day, Mr Parry.'

'It might have a lot to do with the attitude of disgruntled people who expected to benefit, and didn't, sir.'

'Hm, I see. Well, the point still seems hypothetical to me. Very hypothetical.' Trimble looked from Parry to Lloyd, then back again to Parry, sucking in his cheeks the while. 'In any case, instructions Mr Davies may have given me would have remained confidential between the two of us.'

'The two of you, and some of your colleagues perhaps, sir?' Lloyd interjected. 'Was anyone else here involved in the meeting?'

'My legal secretary, Miss Lewin. She was here some of the time.'

'Then we'd like to speak to her before we leave, if you could arrange that, sir,' Parry put in promptly. 'Wasn't it she who sat next to Mr Davies at the church supper?'

'Yes. Miss Lewin was also there as our guest. She er . . . she entertained Mr Davies on my behalf during the meal, my wife and I being committed at the top table. To the arch-deacon.'

'And was Miss Lewin, or anyone else here, involved before that in any legal instructions Mr Davies may have given you?' Parry returned to the earlier point.

Again Trimble frowned, steepled his hands under his chin, and looked upwards, eyes half-closed. He maintained this pose for several seconds. It seemed either that he was debating whether he should reply to the question at all, or that he was praying for divine guidance in composing an answer. 'Miss Lewin took down the draft of a . . . of a will for Mr Davies. It was only a draft. He was due to come here to go over it again today.'

The two policemen exchanged glances. 'That was a new will he was making, sir?' asked Lloyd.

'No. He'd never made one before,' Trimble supplied forcefully. 'At least, that's what he told me.'

'And was it a long will, sir? Complicated?'

'No, it was neither. Why do you ask, Sergeant?'

'I was just wondering why it couldn't have been approved and signed on Friday, sir. Was it Mr Davies's idea to leave it in draft form till after the weekend?'

Trimble gave a myopic sort of blink. 'In my experience, in matters as weighty as the making of a will, speed is rarely of such moment as thoroughness,' he offered in a magisterial voice.

133

'And you advised Mr Davies to think about what was in the draft over the weekend, sir,' Lloyd pressed.

'Almost certainly, yes, though I really can't remember doing so specifically. It would have been standard practice to have done so. There again, it could have been his own idea.'

'And you could neither of you have foreseen Mr Davies's imminent death, of course,' put in Parry with some gravity.

'Obviously,' the lawyer replied.

'Can you tell us what was in the will, sir? The draft will?' Lloyd asked.

Trimble's eyebrows began to rise, this time slightly in advance of his cheeks hollowing, both actions being slow and methodical, like the movements in some mechanical toy. 'You should be aware, Sergeant, that in normal circumstances the answer to that question would have to be no. But er . . . but as things are . . .' He paused for due honour to be ascribed to his decision to waive convention and the Law Society's ruling in the aftermath of a bloody murder. 'Mr Davies intended to leave everything to his two sons and their heirs in Australia,' he completed shortly, and with what turned out to be a bit of an anti-climax.

'And nothing to any member of the Edworth family, sir?'

'Nothing.'

'Nor to Mr Owen Franklin?'

Trimble stared hard at Lloyd. 'Why should he have left anything to Owen Franklin?' He uttered the name with a pained expression, as though it might be a euphemism for putrid fish.

'Because Mr Franklin is reputed to be Mr Davies's natural son by the late Alice Morgan. She was the sister of his adopted mother, Mrs Jacky Franklin.'

'That's an old wives' tale.'

'Mr Ken Franklin believes it, sir.'

'Does Jacky Franklin believe it?'

'Possibly not, sir,' said Parry, 'but her adopted son Owen does. Mr Davies didn't mention Owen Franklin to you, by any chance?'

'Certainly not.'

'As you may know, sir, the story goes that Mr Davies left this country all those years ago after admitting he was the father of Alice Morgan's unborn child.'

'The story has no formal corroboration that I know of.'

'If Owen Franklin were Mr Davies's natural son, would he be entitled to some part of his estate, sir?'

Trimble adjusted his glasses on his nose, and looked grave and judicial. 'It's more than possible, I suppose. Under the present legislation.'

'Would it be a large part of the estate, sir?'

'That would depend probably on the result of litigation.'

'You mean Mr Franklin would need to challenge the matter in the courts? To challenge Mr Davies's will?'

'If he'd made a will, yes, but I'm afraid the whole matter —'

'But since he hadn't made a will, sir, and he died intestate, I assume the same thing would apply, only the process would take even longer?'

'Ah, well, there you'd assume wrong, Mr Parry,' said the lawyer with a high degree of satisfaction in his voice. 'Whether Mr Davies died intestate or not is no longer relevant. I was just going to say that he'd inherit nothing from Mr Edworth, so there'd be nothing to pass on to his heirs either.'

'I don't understand, sir?'

'I mentioned just now that Edwin Edworth was inclined to be obdurate and eccentric. After his retirement, he also became increasingly opposed to paying professional fees.'

'Legal fees, sir?'

'Yes. The morning after I'd persuaded him on the telephone to make a will, he came in here with the draft of one he'd written himself. He'd copied the wording from some household compendium or other.' The speaker moved a hand contemptuously in the air as if to spread scorn on all such outrageous attempts to do an honest lawyer out of a hard-earned crust. 'He insisted we use his draft and make no charge for it. A false economy, of course, and one that is now to have serious consequences.'

'You mean the will wasn't legal, sir?'

'Oh, it was legal, all right. But the standard wording he'd

copied from his household compendium was, in one particular at least, intended for a married person. It included the clause that to inherit, a sole beneficiary must survive the deceased person by twenty-eight days. This is a perfectly sensible and usual proviso when it's to do with a wife surviving a husband, or vice versa. It avoids double duty on the two estates if a couple die together, or nearly together, where the life of one is protracted by only a short period.'

'As might happen if they were both in a car accident, for instance?' Parry put in.

'Exactly, but it was hardly appropriate to Edwin Edworth and Mervyn Davies. Quite the opposite.' The lawyer sighed heavily. 'I started to explain this to Edwin at the time, but he wouldn't listen. Claimed I was just trying to justify a fee. In the end, I let the point go. The proviso seemed harmless enough at the time. Harmless if irrelevant.'

'Except now Mr Davies has died –'

'It completely nullifies the will, I'm afraid,' the lawyer interrupted.

'But won't Mr Davies's sons inherit?'

'No. He was named as the sole beneficiary. There was no mention of his heirs or successors. That was another consequence of Mr Edworth's own drafting. When I mentioned the omission, he misunderstood the point again. Simply insisted it should be up to Mervyn Davies to decide who inherited the estate after him.'

Parry frowned. 'But you said Mr Davies's death nullifies the will, sir. Surely it names a . . . what do you call it . . . a fall-back beneficiary? In case Mr Davies didn't survive?'

'That is precisely what it doesn't do. Mr Edworth was quite adamant on that point. And if it ever came to court, in my view there's no doubt the judge would consider it decisive. Nobody else was named. That was completely against my advice. I tell you again, Edwin Edworth had become quite eccentric, and stubborn with it.'

'So his will counts for nothing?'

'That's right. Effectively, he died intestate. As if he'd never made a will at all.'

'So who'll inherit his money, sir?'

Trimble took off the half glasses, then studied them closely, as if he was valuing them for insurance purposes. 'The law in that regard is quite clear, Mr Parry. Since he was unmarried, and had no children of his own, with no living brothers or sisters of the whole blood, his estate will be divided equally between his nephew and niece. Charles and er . . . and Gail Edworth.'

14

'You reckon Annie Lewin was telling the truth, boss?' asked Lloyd, getting into the Porsche beside Parry. They had parked the car in one of the two spaces reserved for clients in the yard behind Trimble's office.

'About not letting on to Charles Edworth about that clause in his uncle's will? The survival clause. Yes, I think so. But I'm not sure I really know why. Not yet.'

'Was it because she came clean about them having an affair?'

'Eventually came clean, Gomer. After you'd implied we knew about it anyway, which we didn't.'

'Not for sure we didn't, but it was worth a try, boss. After that hint from Jacky Franklin. Anyway, in the end it was almost like Miss Lewin was glad to get it off her conscience, wasn't it?'

'Her conscience? No, I don't think so. She's reached the stage when she needs to do more than just will events along. She's a mistress tired of waiting for lover boy to leave his wife, as he's been promising.' Parry started the car engine as he went on. 'According to Dewi Trimble, Charles Edworth is about to become seriously rich. If, as she says, he's been delaying his marriage break-up for money reasons, he doesn't have to any more. Only our Annie doesn't want the responsibility of being the one who discloses all to his wife. That kind of action tends to ricochet.'

'Because the mistress can be the one who ends up being deserted? After the man finds he can't leave his kids, and blames the mistress for making his wife suicidal. Or homicidal,' said Lloyd, in a deep and morally deprecating tone, as befitted a thinking, if largely lapsed, Methodist.

'Whereas, this way, if it comes out, you'll get the blame, Gomer,' Parry chuckled, backing the car out into the alley and then on to Pentre Street.

Lloyd shifted uncomfortably in his seat. 'If Mrs Franklin knew, I'll bet others do. Anyway, Miss Lewin only admitted it in detail after I said we'd try to keep it confidential.'

'I'm glad you said we'd try. There won't be much trying if it turns out Charles Edworth was Davies's murderer.'

'Ah, well, then all bets would be off, wouldn't they?' The sergeant paused. 'But if she hadn't told him about the twenty-eight-day provision, he really had no motive, did he?'

'Which gets us back to whether she did or not. If she did, it gave him one hell of a motive. And, again, if she did, and he passed on the good news to his sister, that gave her one hell of a motive as well. What's this chap up to?' They had just passed the Coach and Horses on the left, and were now held up by a pantechnicon turning into Somerset Street across the traffic.

'This street ought to be one way,' complained Lloyd, as they moved on some seconds later. 'Anyway, boss, the sister's out of the frame. Name's Gail. Unmarried. Dental nurse. She was in Cardiff Saturday night, with a girlfriend. Didn't get home till late. To the old family house we're going to now. It's been divided into two flats. The mother's on the ground floor.'

'Sister Gail is only out of the frame if she didn't know she'd come into money if Davies died,' said Parry firmly.

'But it wasn't a woman's crime, boss. The beheading, or the rest. Not really.'

'What if she had a big strong boyfriend? Anything known about her love life?'

'No, boss. And she hasn't been formally interviewed. We only know about her movements Saturday night because she happened to be there when Detective Constable Avis Quigley called yesterday to see her mother. The mother was out at the time. We wanted her interviewed because she'd been to the church supper, of course. And she'd talked to Mr Davies at the end.'

'OK. Gail Edworth's a long shot,' said Parry, but not dismissively because he was trying to think laterally. 'But remember the game's just changed. When did Annie Lewin say Charles Edworth left her that night?'

'She said he was with her from just after ten-forty till five past eleven. I noticed she came out pretty pat with that.'

'Yes, I remember now as well. It was the only time when she sounded as if she might be lying.'

'Perhaps she was just uncomfortable knowing she was telling us something he hadn't admitted already.'

'He's lied to us, has he?' Parry questioned quickly.

'Not directly. Detective Constable Innes interviewed him yesterday afternoon. That was also because he'd been at the church supper and talked to Mr Davies. He said he couldn't remember exactly what time he'd left his mother's, but he thought he got home about eleven-thirty. His wife was present at the interview, and she confirmed the time. I read the report last night.'

'So he'd left out he'd been to Annie Lewin's between his mother's and getting home?'

'Yes, boss. For the obvious reason, especially as his wife was present. He also told Detective Constable Innes he was driving to Wolverhampton last night.'

'Not that he was spending the night with the lovely Annie, and driving on there early this morning.'

'Yes, for the same reason as the other. But it was what you might call an incidental omission, wasn't it?'

'No, it's what *you* might call it, Gomer,' Parry responded glibly. 'Anyway, he's got a few things to straighten out with us when he gets back from Wolverhampton. When's that going to be?'

'His office says he'll be back there at four this afternoon. He's bound to admit everything Miss Lewin's told us, because it gives him an alibi.'

'Assuming she's not been lying to us as well. Of all of them, his wife is probably the one most likely to be telling the truth about Saturday night. It's her corroboration that

140

just about puts him in the clear, too. We're not that much interested in what he was doing up to eleven-thirty, the time Godwin said Davies left his house.'

Lloyd scratched the wisp of hair at his temple. 'Like some of the others, he just wouldn't have had time to do the murder, and get rid of the body. And the head and the hand, come to that.'

They had cleared the shopping area, and the traffic lights at the junction with Tawrbach Road, and were heading along St Bride's Road which was lined on both sides by ponderous, genteel sets of Victorian semi-detached villas built of grey, rusticated stone, with minimal front yards, double bay windows, and steps up to the front doors. 'Raglan Avenue is the next turning right, is it, Gomer?' Parry asked.

'That's it, boss.' The sergeant waited for Parry to turn across the oncoming traffic. 'The house should be the last at the bottom, on the left. It's called The Chestnuts. It's on the corner of Raglan Avenue and Condleston Road.'

'So how far is that from Condleston Lodge?'

Lloyd fingered his moustache. 'About four hundred yards, boss.'

'So we're pretty close here to the assumed scene of the crime,' said Parry a few moments later, as he stopped the car outside the house. 'And Charles Edworth lives where?'

'In Tegsarn village.'

'That's two miles north of the town?'

'Yes. Close to where he works on the industrial estate.'

Parry considered the gloomy, redbrick, 1920s house. Although it was the oldest and most substantial building on the street, it had seen better days, particularly since two generations back, when its then owner, Dan Edworth, Charles's grandfather, had been a local builder of substance, as well as a lay reader at St Luke's. The ground floor was screened from the road by a waist-high wall with some of its tile cappings missing, and a tall privet hedge that hadn't been clipped for several seasons. 'And Annie Lewin lives in Woodford Road, which is also north of here.'

'That's right, boss. On the other side of the station. It's not far, though. Late night, about three or four minutes by car.'

'So if we've been told the truth, Edworth left here at around ten-thirty, and went to Miss Lewin's. He was in the area again from ten past to twenty-five past eleven. After that, he wasn't on this side of town at all. Hm. Even so, this is another garden we need to check for ground disturbance. Right, Gomer, let's hear what his mother has to say. I'd like to meet the sister too, if she's in.' He glanced at the upstairs windows as he got out of the car.

The patch of garden in front of the house was as unkempt as the hedge. It was partially overhung by a mature chestnut tree, already in young leaf, to the right of the building and the driveway. The tree's roots were breaking up the concrete of the driveway, and its branches were also overhanging the street corner and the top end of the main garden. There was no street gate, only brick posts where a double gate had once hung. The wooden garage at the end of the drive was old and lopsided. Some crazy paving led off to the left of the drive and up to the front door, which was sheltered under an elaborate wooden porch, with fretworked side panels and peeling green paintwork, like the garage. There was a newish notice where the paths divided which read 'Flat Two at side', but it seemed that the recent conversion of the premises had not included any refurbishment of the exterior.

When Lloyd pressed the bell push he was surprised that it worked at all, let alone that it generated a musical peal loud enough to be heard outside.

'Well, there's quick you were, Mr . . . Mr Felsted, isn't it?' said Winifred Edworth, wiping her hands on a tea cloth as she opened the door. She had a pinafore on over a blue woollen dress. 'It's through there to the right,' she went on, turning about immediately, and leading the way through the hall. She hadn't looked at the identification both men had been proffering. 'Well, you know, don't you? From the other times. Give that door a bang as you come through, will you? Who's this with you? Learner, is he?'

It was Lloyd that Mrs Edworth had addressed from the start, and who she had continued to address as she shuffled along in her carpet slippers, leaving the tea towel bunched on the hatstand. She eyed Parry for the first time after the two men had followed her through into an over-furnished sitting room with French windows on the wall opposite the door. 'It's the middle C sharp and B flat are the worst. Gone off something terrible, they have. Must be the weather we've been having. Pianos don't like rain, do they? Well, people don't either, come to that. I'll get it ready for you.' She went over to the Broadwood upright piano in the far corner and removed some sheet music from the stand on its front.

Lloyd gave her the winning smile he usually reserved for female helpers in police canteens when he hadn't been given enough mashed potatoes. 'Mrs Edworth, I'm afraid there's been a mistake. My name's not Felsted. I'm Detective Sergeant Lloyd from Cardiff CID, and this is Detective Chief Inspector Parry.'

'Well, you're in the wrong house then, aren't you? Funny, you look just like Mr Felsted.' She turned about, holding a small plaster bust of Johann Sebastian Bach which she had cleared from the piano top. 'That's why I thought you'd come to do the tuning. I should have known, because I only rang the shop half an hour ago.' She paused. 'Or was that yesterday? I know the lady said it'd be a few days before Mr Felsted could get here. I hate an out of tune piano, don't you? Grates on the ears, I always think.'

'Oh, yes, specially if you're musical, ma'am.'

'Well, you'll want to get on with the tuning, won't you?' She raised a hand to her forehead. 'No, that's not right, is it? You just said you're from the Council, wasn't it?'

'From the police, actually, ma'am.'

'But you're in the wrong house.' This was a statement, not a question, and Mrs Edworth seemed pleased to have sorted things out as she began moving back to the door, clearly intent on showing her visitors out.

'No, no. We're in the right house. It's you Mr Parry and I have come to see, all right.'

'Why d'you want to see me, then?' Her mouth stiffened. 'I've paid the licence on the telly. Well, my son has. He does it for me. I've got it here somewhere.' She went over to a small desk in a corner beyond the fireplace and began pulling out drawers.

'We're not here about that, Mrs Edworth,' put in Parry. 'It's to do with your son Charles.'

'But I've told you, he's paid it.' She now looked worried as well as confused, and she accelerated her searching of the drawers.

'Why don't we all sit down, and then we can explain, ma'am,' said Lloyd. 'There's really nothing to be concerned about.'

Mrs Edworth seemed unconvinced, but she came over from the desk. 'You're not John Parry's son from up the road?' she asked, peering hard at the chief inspector as she sat down on the edge of an armchair with tasselled covers – part of a matching three-piece suite.

'Afraid not, Mrs Edworth. I come from Port Talbot originally.'

'Ah. I had a cousin there. Peter. He worked in the steel mills. That's years ago, though. He's dead now.' She fell silent, thinking perhaps of her departed relative.

The two policemen settled themselves on the sofa.

'We were wondering if you still remember your son bringing you back here after the church supper on Saturday night, ma'am?' said Lloyd.

'Remember? Of course I remember. Did Charles tell you I didn't?' she demanded hotly, deep suspicion now in her voice and eyes. 'You aren't here about the retirement home in Newton, are you? The one Gail's been on about? Because I'm not going to any retirement home just to suit Gail, and I'm not leaving here to go and live with Charles either, with him and . . . and . . . what's her name . . . his wife.' She scowled because she'd forgotten her daughter-in-law's name again.

'No, no, we're nothing to do with any of that, Mrs Edworth. Like I said, we're policemen.'

'Not from Dr Peebles? He's another one,' she demanded, but with less blatant distrust.

'Certainly not. We just want to know if you can remember what time your son left here on Saturday night. After he brought you home.'

Mrs Edworth looked from Lloyd to Parry, then at the

ticking, silver carriage clock in the centre of the dark oak mantelpiece: the clock was flanked by a pair of porcelain shepherdesses. 'It was late,' she said eventually. 'After nine.'

'You can't remember more precisely than that, Mrs Edworth?'

'I'll try.' She paused. 'Which Saturday was it again, Mr . . . Mr Felsted?'

'Last Saturday, Mrs Edworth,' said Parry with a sinking heart. 'The day before yesterday. Actually, you and your son left the church hall at about quarter to ten,' he offered gently.

'Mervyn Davies was there.' She shook her head, then added: 'You know he's dead? I knew him when we were all young. Well, he was younger than me. Didn't make any difference though. Not to what happened. He was more Alice Morgan's age. He went to . . .' She paused, evidently confused.

'To Australia, ma'am?'

'No, no. That was later. It was when he went to live with his gran. We were all in the choir. Very forward he was, Mervyn. For his age. Big with it, too.'

'He was a friend of Edwin, your brother-in-law,' said Lloyd.

Mrs Edworth's face stiffened. 'I used to say there'd be trouble in the end.'

'Trouble for whom, ma'am?'

'For all of us. For them, I mean,' she corrected quickly. 'Alice Morgan, and Jacky, and . . . and Esme Sewell. And there were others. All too young, they were. But it wasn't their fault. Not any of them. It's God's punishment. What's happened to Mervyn. He shouldn't have said what he did. And *he* shouldn't have done what he did. That was the worst part.'

'You mean what Mervyn Davies did, Mrs Edworth?' asked Parry, even more gently than before.

'No.' She had been studying the bust of J. S. Bach that was still clasped tightly in her hand. Now, in a less reflex response to the question, she looked up with a knowing glint in her eyes. 'Edwin was his father's favourite, and no

145

mistake. My Gwilym never got a look in.' She put the bust on a side table.

'Your husband got the business, though, didn't he, ma'am?' Lloyd put in. 'The building business?'

'Fat lot of good that was. This house was all we got in the end. She wants it, of course. To sell.'

'Who wants it, ma'am?'

'My daughter Gail. Upstairs.' She jerked her head towards the ceiling. 'Wants it now, too. Can't wait till I'm dead and gone. Plotting to get it, she is.' She leaned forward, lowering her voice. 'With Dewi . . . Dewi Trimble, the lawyer. Lawyer!' she expostulated in contrast to before, grasping the sides of her skirt and pushing them closer towards her ankles. 'Shrimp of a choir boy, Dewi was in those days. And only in the choir at all when he was home for the school holidays. All Eton collar and private school uniform. Different now. Plotting, yes. He's always up there.'

'Upstairs, ma'am? With your daughter?'

'Comes after dark. When he thinks I can't see. Or else he's delivering the parish magazines for his wife. "Is Gail upstairs, Winifred?"' she continued, in a nasally imitation of Trimble's superior accent. ' "No trouble. I'll pop up and put it through her door." I know what's going on. Plotting.'

'He was up there recently, was he, ma'am?'

'Who?' She looked at Lloyd blankly for a moment, then her gaze softened. 'I was lucky to get you at short notice, wasn't I, Mr Felsted? Can I get you a cup of tea before you start? It's the middle C sharp and –' She gave a violent start, put her hand on her heart, and stopped speaking as the mobile phone Lloyd was carrying began ringing.

'It's for you, boss. A Major Denison, RCMP in Germany.' He handed the receiver to Parry.

15

'Rum do altogether, what? But a lot clearer now, Parry. That's since you've come on the scene.' Major Denison annunciated the compliment sharply, his consonants as clipped as the bristles in his moustache. 'We've had some bloody crude things in the mail in my time, but this one's the crudest.' The major squared his shoulders, and wrinkled his nose as if preparing to meet an evil-smelling crudity head on.

'The copper who found the other hand took a similar view,' Parry replied with a grin. 'Of course, we're still assuming the two hands came from the same body.'

'No doubt in your mind, is there?' The major's left cheek twitched so hard it momentarily closed his left eye.

'Not really.'

'Good egg, Parry.' There was genuine relief in the tone.

The chief inspector sat back in the front passenger seat as Denison urged the army Range Rover down the autobahn they had joined outside Düsseldorf Airport. He was warming to the major, a stylish driver, who handled the vehicle with gloved hands, rigid arms, and the decision and concentration of a racing professional.

On first encounter, bearing down on Parry at the airport with a parade-ground salute, a thunderous greeting, and a bone-crushing handshake, Denison had better fitted the visitor's image of a Brigade of Guards officer than that of a military policeman. Not that, in a strictly professional sense, this initial impression had been entirely reassuring. Fortyish, six feet four, lean and mettlesome, the major, with his penetrating public school accent and his dated idioms, had the thrusting persona of an old-style military leader – of the kind ready to mount a cavalry charge at no notice, and to impale himself on the colours if the assault failed. He had addressed Parry from the start by surname only, and in a way that indicated this was a mark of equality not superiority, even though the policeman was aware that an army major was roughly one pip ahead of a chief inspector.

Parry had motored the hundred and thirty miles from the centre of Cardiff to Heathrow in less than two hours, and caught the 13.05 British Airways flight to Düsseldorf. He had come largely on impulse – though he had cleared the decision with his divisional superintendent: any overseas trip involved too much time and money to be undertaken without solid reason by members of a police force woefully, many thought dangerously, short on both commodities.

The policeman had also remembered to call Perdita Jones at the hospital, to put off the arrangement they had made to see a movie in Cardiff that evening. He thought he sensed that Perdita had been relieved about the postponement, even though she had been doing her best not to show it in her voice. He accepted that this could have been his own invention, and that, anyway, she was naturally preoccupied with the preparations for her move to London. Simply he had been miffed that she had not shown more disappointment – a reaction on his part which he knew was unjustified since it was he who had been doing the cancelling. Probably it was her final jocular sally that had needled him – something to the effect that, if he couldn't be good, he should be careful, if he spent a night on the loose in Düsseldorf.

It had been Major Denison's initiative that had first extended the murder investigation to Germany. After being called to the GHQ post office to view the X-rayed skeleton of a human hand inside a padded envelope, he had carefully opened the package in the presence of the addressee, Warrant Officer Derek Sewell. This had revealed that the human relic, inside a transparent kitchen bag, was still covered in well-preserved human flesh, as well as a fair amount of congealed blood. After further questioning of the mystified Sewell, the major had telephoned the South Wales

148

Constabulary at their own headquarters in Bridgend. From there he had been switched to the force's Major Crime Support Unit in Rumney, Cardiff, where, following a brief conversation with the duty superintendent, he had been transferred to Parry in Mrs Winifred Edworth's sitting room.

The two men had spoken again on the telephone at some length while Parry had been driving to Heathrow.

'You're letting this Owen Franklin go?' Denison questioned now.

'No alternative, I'm afraid. He was alibied up to the gills over the murder, and the DPP's office weren't prepared to proceed on the other charges.'

'Wouldn't have helped you if they had been, would it?'

'Not immediately, no. He'd have got bail.' Parry had earlier given the major a rapid and professional situation report of the Davies case.

'Of course he'd have got bail,' Denison responded contemptuously. 'Don't know how you chaps cope. Different in the Service. We confine the ones we want, till ready. That's till we're ready, what?' He gave a deep chuckle that came out closer to a gargle.

'I'm afraid Franklin's dropped further out of the frame since we last talked. His blood test showed he couldn't have been Davies's son.' Sergeant Lloyd had called Parry with this news at Heathrow. He had reported at the same time that the earth in Geoff Godwin's flower bed had been dug only to a depth of one spit, and that no other part of Godwin's garden had been recently disturbed. It had also been established during the morning that Mair Jarvis's aged Auntie Olwyn had proved to be a punctilious recorder of the time things happened to her. According to her careful testimony, she had been taken by Gareth Jarvis from Porthcawl at ten past eleven on Saturday night and delivered to her sheltered accommodation in Kenfig Hill at twenty-five past. There had then been some minor trouble with her front-door lock which Auntie Olwyn had insisted on recounting to the police interviewer at length, and in great detail. It transpired that Jarvis had put the lock right, but in consequence, he hadn't left her again until twenty to twelve. His wife's sister and brother-in-law had both confirmed that he had even so rejoined their silver wedding party in time for the midnight toast. Thus, by no stretch of the imagination could he have been to Pontyglas and back as well in the time, let alone murdered Davies and disposed of the body.

Altogether, the list of putative suspects was reducing hourly, with no compensating hardening of evidence against any of those who remained on it. Not that Parry had harboured too much expectation about the possible culpability of Geoff Godwin. And while he still had his own reservations about Gareth Jarvis, despite this most recent report, it was the technical exoneration of Owen Franklin that had set him back the most – something that was now heavily underlining the importance of the German trip in pursuit of the only fresh lead involving hard evidence.

'Except you said Franklin himself thought he was Davies's son?' the major next put in loudly, as he accelerated past an articulated lorry of a length that was still illegal in Britain.

'He did at the start, but he's back pedalled hard on that one since the murder.'

'Naturally. So with your prime suspect kiboshed, you're looking for another?' There was a serious questioning in the other's tone.

'Yes. We've got a few possibles. No actual probables. Not yet,' Parry responded with more optimism in his voice than he was feeling.

'I see.' A certain relief was perceptible again. 'And if Franklin's prints are anywhere on our precious exhibit, you'd get him back in custody toot sweet?'

'Yes.' Parry looked across at the other man. 'You haven't dusted any of it for prints?'

'No. We've done nothing to inhibit our gallant German allies from being free to cooperate. Which wouldn't apply so easily if we had to admit we were starting an investigation here. The hand, with packaging, is in an evidence bag in a top security place. To wit, my drinks fridge. More secure than a regimental safe. Only one key, d'you see? In my pocket now. So it's all ready for you to take away. I brought in the chief of the police criminal branch in Mönchengladbach. Nice enough chap. He keeps Labradors, as a matter of fact.' The major paused to give this last, to him, evidently significant commendation proper time for digestion and appreciation, before he went on. 'He's given his permission for you to take the er . . . the specimen back with you. He cleared it for us with the airport police too. Did I say you're booked on the eighteen-fifty flight this evening?' He leaned forward to read the time on the dashboard clock: it was already four-twenty-five p.m.

'That'll give me enough time here?' Parry asked, uncertain about whether it would, but subconsciously pleased that Perdita's undeserved caution had just become irrelevant.

'Loads of time, yes. You don't want to hang about, what?'

'Not longer than I have to.' Parry accepted that Denison was indubitably a fast mover who encouraged the trait in others. Even so, he felt there might be an undisclosed reason for quite such tight timing.

'I confirmed your return arrangements verbally while I was waiting for your flight,' the major continued. 'They've cut down your check-in time, incidentally. You're getting the full VIP treatment. So, it'll be as if our little bundle had never left Pontyglas.' As usual, he made the last syllable rhyme with farce.

'No paperwork?'

'Good God, no. Because your Mr Davies's hand has never officially been on German soil, d'you see? If you can avoid letting the Germans produce forms in triplicate, they're the fastest little movers on earth.' Denison gave a benign glance at the stout, elderly man and woman they were passing in a minute car which was progressing at the minimum legal speed on the inside lane. 'And there's no sign of the rest of the body?' he inquired.

'No. With your severed hand, the score of bits remains at three.'

'Hm. You said there's some kind of connection between the Franklin chap and our Warrant Officer Sewell?'

'Yes. But it's all historical and a bit tenuous.' Parry had watched as the major negotiated the exit from the autobahn and picked up speed on the still quite wide, but rural road they had now joined. There were freshly ploughed, un-hedged areas of flat farmland on both sides. It was noticeable that a good deal of the road traffic here belonged to the British army. 'The two men are almost exactly the same age,' he went on. 'Their mothers were both from Pontyglas, and they were both in the choir photo I told you about.'

'Which had Davies in it too? And his crony Edworth, who left him all his money?'

'That's right. Both the mothers were unmarried when the boys were born.'

'Sewell doesn't know who his father was. He told me so this morning. Seemed bitter about that. Well, one would, I suppose.' The major blinked twice, very hard, while trying to contemplate what such an eventuality would have meant for him personally – an academic enough exercise since his plain and pious mother, a bishop's daughter, had been unswervingly faithful to her husband.

'Franklin doesn't know who his father was either, of course. Not since the result of the blood test.'

'Perhaps he picked the wrong candidate from the two on offer? Davies and Edworth?'

'We've thought of that one. Franklin could have been Edworth's son. The blood groups fit. Same applies to Sewell, assuming the blood group you gave me on the phone is right. You were going to check it, incidentally.'

'It is right. Lucky for Sewell it's Davies not Edworth who matters in this context, what? Keeps him out of the picture. Well out of it,' Denison commented pointedly as he swung the vehicle off the main road. He lifted his chin and straight-ened his back. 'That's not to prejudge anything, of course, Parry. You must form your own opinion of Sewell. Whether he might be involved in this business. I mean more than passively involved.'

They were now on the short approach road to the British services joint headquarters in Germany with its high peri-meter fence extending, it seemed, indefinitely from both sides of the entrance ahead, and protecting what, beyond, seemed more like a modern town than a military installation. There was a two-storey guard room in front of them on the right, with regimental sentries doing guard duty, and red-capped military police inside and outside the ground-floor, glass-fronted command post. The twin red and white striped pole barriers were raised, and a Union Flag fluttered from the masthead erected some distance after the entrance on a central island.

The Range Rover was promptly waved through with extra alacrity. The major had simply slowed the vehicle while he managed, without excessive arm movement, punctiliously to return the quivering salute of the military police sergeant who had earlier leaned down to check the driver and passenger. From then onwards, the scene about them became so indubitably British, that Parry found it almost incongruous that traffic hadn't promptly reverted to driving on the left.

Some seconds later, Denison turned off the busy central thoroughfare on to a slip road to the right, then parked in front of a square, grey-rendered, three-storey building, identified by a large, free-standing board set in a presently empty flower bed, and painted with the emblem and name of the Royal Corps of Military Police.

'You haven't talked to Sewell since our last phone call,' the chief inspector asked as Denison turned off the ignition.

'No. Thought it best to wait for you.' The major was blinking hard again. 'Warrant officers are the salt of the earth, you know? Particularly sappers. Quite indispensable. Show would grind to a halt without them, if you think about it.' He glanced at Parry to see if he was thinking about it. 'And Sewell's special. He's put in for a full commission. Probably won't get it, what with all the cutbacks, but his CO's backing him. It's why he was sent on that course last week.'

'So you obviously don't believe he's involved in the Davies murder? Except, as you suggest, passively?'

Denison cleared his throat, and tapped the steering wheel of the stationary vehicle with the fingers of one still-leather-gloved hand. 'Since you ask, no, I don't. Chap in his position. Mystery to me why someone's sent him the hand. I'd warrant it's as much of a mystery to him too, incidentally. You get a feel for that kind of thing in this job. Well, you'd understand that, Parry, of course you would. I'm damned sure

Sewell had nothing to do with that package or what's in it. You mustn't think I'm prejudiced in his favour, though,' he added, flinging open the door. 'So off we go, then,' he completed, stepping out on to the concrete, drawing himself up to his full, domineering height, and slapping his trousers with the bamboo carry stick he was now holding, while waiting for his passenger to alight.

The major was clearly satisfied, Parry judged, that he had just made the right utterances to protect the honour, reputation and inviolability of his fellow soldier, Warrant Officer Sewell – not to mention that of his Queen, his Country, and the whole bloody British Army.

16

'Hello, what's your name then, sonny?' asked Gomer Lloyd. The heavyweight sergeant directed his most avuncular smile at the frowning seven-year-old with the red and sore-looking nose. The child had just opened the front door of 16, Somerset Street, though he hadn't opened it wide enough to allow for easy entry through the gap, nor entry of any kind by someone of Lloyd's substantial girth.

'Stuart James. What d'you want, thed?' The fiery nose was blocked, and was also now beginning to run.

'I've come to see your . . . your granddad, Stuart. Is he here?'

'Dow.' The frown had deepened, and had acquired a quizzical aspect.

'Your gran, then?'

The boy gave a very long and, to Lloyd, a very unappetizing sniff. 'My gran and grandda don't lid here. They lid id Pontypool. Mrs Sewell lids here. And Mr Sewell, but he's dot ind. She's ind.' He gave another unendearing sniff.

'Ah.' Just shows you shouldn't assume things, Lloyd ruminated, even in the interests of jollying along new relationships. 'Then I'd like to see Mrs Sewell,' he said, advancing, but not very far because the boy had reacted sharply by nearly closing the door altogether on his toes. 'Will you tell her I'm here then, Stuart? I'm from the police.' He retreated slightly, and produced his warrant card, something he would have done before, except he hadn't wanted to alert anyone, especially prying neighbours who were always up with the action in streets like these – even ahead of it sometimes. And children were exposed to so much police procedure on the telly these days, the sergeant wouldn't have been surprised if Stuart James had demanded to see a search warrant on top of the normal police identity. This last was all very commendable, he supposed, but it had started to rain quite heavily, and he was getting wet standing on this doorstep.

The child had disappeared abruptly, slamming the door shut, and leaving Lloyd to contemplate the recently painted woodwork which the rain was washing – which is what it was also doing to his bare head. It was a narrow, stuccoed dwelling, with only one window on the ground floor, in a long terrace of identical narrow, stuccoed dwellings, though few of the others were as relatively spruce as this one, with its painted window boxes on both floors, polished brass knocker, and pumiced, stone doorstep. Somerset Street was a cul-de-sac, with terraced houses on both sides, the rear side of an old commercial building blocking its far end. Halfway along on this side, a short alley separating two of the houses ran to a lane at the back. The house doors opened on to the street: a minute later the door to number 16 opened again.

'Auntie says you can come id,' the boy offered, opening the door wider this time, then wider still for Lloyd's benefit.

The sergeant knew his way around pre-war houses in the meaner streets of South Wales. He headed purposefully for the kitchen at the rear, along a tight, dark corridor, passing the steep staircase on the left, and, on the other side, the doors to the front room, and the middle room – both parts of the house that would rarely be used, except occasionally in high summer when there would be no need to heat them.

The kitchen door, with a pair of vertical, frosted-glass panels in its upper half, opened on to the bright, over-warm room, where the fire was burning fiercely. The upholstered easy chairs on either side of it, that John Sewell and his nephew had occupied on Saturday night, were now empty, showing their permanently creased extra cushions pressed into the backs. The plump, elderly looking woman who now greeted Lloyd was in a wheelchair which she was propelling in from the back scullery. There was a toy train set laid out in the centre of the unpolished, wooden table in the window opposite the fireplace. Stuart James sidled past Lloyd, mounted a chair, and began winding up the model 0-4-0 tank engine, decorated in the old Great Western Railway green livery. He continued to make sidelong glances at the policeman.

'Afternoon, Mrs Sewell. Detective Sergeant Lloyd. Sorry to disturb you.' He showed his warrant card as he spoke.

She tried squinting at the card, then gently waved it away unread. 'My hubbie John, he's out, I'm afraid. Back soon though. He's got no work today. Just doing a few errands for friends, like.' Mrs Iris Sewell wiped her hands on the pinafore she was wearing. 'I'm making cake,' she added, half apologetically. On a second look she was not as old as Lloyd had first assumed – just worn, and tired, and pained probably, he thought, with a lined, compassionate face, and straight grey hair pulled back to a bun, wisps of it escaping and hanging over her face. 'From the police, you said? Fancy.'

'Is he frob Scotland Yard, Auntie?' asked Stuart.

'No, just Cardiff, sonny,' Lloyd answered. 'Stuart's your nephew, is he, Mrs Sewell? Well-built lad.' He nodded approvingly at Stuart who looked away, scowling at the engine.

'No, no. I'm not his real auntie. He only calls me that, don't you, love?' Stuart didn't respond as she went on. 'He lives next door. Only he couldn't go to school today because of a nasty old cold. That's right, isn't it, Stuart?'

The boy gave another long sniff in adequate confirmation.

'Blow your nose then, love. And wipe it properly on your hanky. And you'd better start putting the train away.' Mrs Sewell had looked at the time on the omega-shaped, mahogany-cased clock on the mantelshelf. 'His mam'll be back from work now just. Cup of tea then, Mr Lloyd?'

'No, thank you very much, Mrs Sewell. Very good of you, but I mustn't stay long. I'll sit down though, if you don't mind. Been on my feet a lot today.' He settled himself in the nearest of the armchairs. 'I'm making inquiries into the death of Mr Mervyn Davies.'

The woman's hands lifted, then dropped again in her lap,

while her head shook slowly from side to side. 'Terrible, that was. To happen here, in Pontyglas, as well.' Her face clouded. 'But someone from the police came to see John yesterday evening. After we'd had our tea. I was having a sleep, but he told me about it later.'

'Yes, I know about that call, Mrs Sewell. Your husband was very helpful.'

'It was a lady who came, John said. A policewoman, in plain clothes. Well, the women do everything these days, don't they? She was interested in the back garden. What there is of it. Pocket handkerchief gardens was all they allowed for when these houses were built. Still, I suppose we have to be grateful we don't live in one of those high-rise flats.'

'That's right.' The woman DC's report had said that the garden was undisturbed. 'It's just that there are one or two more questions we want to ask Mr Sewell. You too, as a matter of fact. Arising from er . . . from further developments on the case, like.'

'Further developments, is it? Well, I'll do my best, of course. You can't say more than that, can you? But I never knew Mervyn Davies. I'm not from here, you see? Born in Tonypandy, I was. That's where I met John. He lodged with us when he started working down the pits.'

'You both came here later, Mrs Sewell?'

'Yes. That was after John was made redundant. He came from Pontyglas in the first place, though.' She moved in her chair awkwardly, and a spasm of pain showed in her eyes. 'Of course, he knew Mervyn Davies, from the time they were children. They were both at the church supper the very night Mr Davies died. They didn't speak, though. Very crowded, it was, so John told me.'

'Mr Derek Sewell was with him at the supper. Would that be his brother?'

Mrs Sewell shook her head. 'His nephew, Derek is. He's John's sister's son. Her name was Esme. She's been dead this long time, I'm sorry to say. Lot of people think Derek was a brother, but he wasn't. It's a long story, that.' She closed her dry lips tightly to indicate, perhaps, that she wasn't offering the telling unless pressed.

'He's in the army. In Germany,' Lloyd stated carefully.

'An officer, yes. He's done well. Very well.'

'You know his address in Germany, do you, Mrs Sewell?'

'Oh, yes. We write to him sometimes. And always at Christmas. D'you want the address? It's on some stickers here somewhere.' She moved her wheelchair over to a table-height cupboard in the corner, the top of which was covered in a disorderly pile of assorted printed paper, catalogues and the like. The inside of the cupboard, when opened, was crammed with more of the same. 'Dear, dear,' she went on. 'I keep meaning to clear this lot out, but . . . take care now, Stuart.' She looked back over her shoulder. 'You don't want to break that, do you? It'd upset Uncle John something terrible again, if you did,' she warned. She and Lloyd had both started when the boy had knocked one of the toy railway carriages on to the mat under the table. Stuart had been doing as he was told, disconnecting the railway lines and stowing them in a wooden box along with the engine and carriages.

'You won'd tell Uncle Jod I knocked it over, Auntie?'

'No, love, of course not. But take care.' She turned to Lloyd. 'That train set was John's father's. Nearly eighty years old, it is. They don't make them to last, today, of course.'

'That's right, Mrs Sewell.' Lloyd had been waiting to examine the stickers she now passed to him. They were small printed address labels on backing paper. 'Did you have these printed, Mrs Sewell?' he asked.

'No, no. They're Derek's. He's always handing them out like confetti at a wedding. Did the same the last time he was here. Well, it saves people writing things down, I suppose.' Her head came up at the muffled shout of 'Coo-ee!' which had emanated from the other side of the high dividing garden fence, visible through the kitchen window. 'That'll be your mam, Stuart, won't it? Off you go, then. Oh, and take that bag in the scullery with you. It's for her. Watch out for the rain making the step outside slippery too. Give me a kiss before you go.'

The boy wasted no time in leaving, possibly because playing with the train set had been his sole interest in staying. He returned from the scullery holding a large, new-looking green, Woolworth's bag, crammed with winter cabbage. He kissed Mrs Sewell on the cheek, shyly, because Lloyd was watching, gave another lugubrious sniff, then hurried out after a final furtive glance at the policeman.

'So, you were saying, Mr Derek Sewell handed these labels out pretty freely, Mrs Sewell?'

'Yes, he did,' a male voice responded from the doorway behind the sergeant. It was John Sewell, whose entry had almost coincided with the boy's departure. The pale ex-miner was wearing a wet zipper rain jacket over a thick, hand-knitted grey sweater. The wrinkled remains of a burning, home-made cigarette were cupped in his left hand, lighted end inwards, and held between thumb and two fingers.

Lloyd got up and introduced himself. He had to explain again why a second police visit had been necessary. 'Did your nephew give any of the stickers away at the church supper, Mr Sewell?' he asked, returning to the previous subject.

'Yes, plenty.' Sewell had removed his wet jacket and handed it to his wife who had deposited it in the scullery. 'And to neighbours and old friends we bumped into when he was here. Knows a lot of people in the town, Derek does, still.' The speaker took a last drag from the cigarette, squeezing his eyes nearly closed as he did so, then threw the end into the fire. 'They've got his new rank printed on, see? Proud of that, he is, and you can't blame him,' he finished with a wheezy cough.

'Do you think you could give me a list of everybody he gave them to?'

Sewell frowned. 'I could try. The names. I haven't got no addresses.'

'Just the names would be fine, sir.'

'Why d'you want them?' The eyes had narrowed again.

'Just routine really.' Lloyd had used the meaningless answer that usually reassured, or at least prevented the same question being put again. He believed even innocent people didn't ask a second time why the police wanted to know something, for fear of arousing suspicion. 'And perhaps you could include anyone he gave a label to last time he was here. Can you say when that would have been?' he added.

Sewell thought for a moment. 'About a year ago, wasn't it, Iris?' His wife nodded in response as he too went over to the corner cupboard. He bent down, and with some difficulty extracted a pad of lined paper from the pile of things inside, then sat himself at the table. 'Stuart been playing with the train, has he?' he asked his wife.

'Yes, love.'

'Put it back right? No breakages this time?' The voice was stern, and the question evidently a serious one.

Mrs Sewell was looking at Lloyd as she answered. 'No, no. He was good as gold.'

'Have either of you sent anything to your nephew since he was here? A parcel of any sort?' Lloyd asked.

'No.' It was Sewell who answered, looking up over his glasses from the list he had started.

'And while he was here, as far as you remember, did anyone promise to send him anything? Anyone on your list, for instance?'

'Yes.'

'Indeed?' Lloyd's interest sharpened. 'Who was that, then, sir?'

'Mrs Gravler. The rector's wife. He paid for her to send him photos of the supper. She was taking photos all the time, with that flash camera of hers.'

'Your nephew paid for the photos in advance?'

'Yes. For a . . . what's it? . . . a commemorable album of twenty-four pictures –'

'Commemorative it was, love,' Mrs Sewell put in with a smile.

'Was it? Anyway, twelve quid that cost Derek, including post and packaging. I should think so as well. Special thick envelope the packaging was, that's all. The price was overdoing it, I told him, specially with the photos being sight unseen, like. But he said he didn't mind, the profits being for church funds. Generous-hearted, he is, Derek. Isn't he, Iris?'

161

'To a fault, sometimes,' his wife replied. 'He's been so good to us, you wouldn't believe.'

'And the special envelopes, were they being addressed on the spot, Mr Sewell?'

'Yes, yes. Derek gave in one of his labels for that, of course.'

'And who had charge of his envelope after?'

Sewell shrugged. 'Mrs Gravler, I expect. In a pile, they was, by the door, as we left. Lot of people asked for albums, but not all to be posted. There was ordinary envelopes for people picking up photos at the church next Sunday. Cheaper, that was. I said I'd do that for Derek, thinking to save a bit of money, like, but he didn't want it. Not to cause me trouble, I expect.'

'And the photos weren't going to be ready for a week, sir?'

'That's right. So what have they got to do with Mervyn Davies's death, then?'

'We don't know they have yet, sir. You mentioned to my lady colleague yesterday that you and your nephew got back here from the supper at er . . . at twenty past ten.' He had been checking with his notebook as he spoke.

'Near as I remember, yes.'

'And you didn't go out again after that? Either of you? It's just a routine question again, sir,' Lloyd added, forestalling the challenge he thought was formulating in Sewell's eyes.

'I see.' Sewell paused. 'No, we didn't go out after. Had a few beers and a chinwag round the fire here, then we was off to bed at er . . .'

'Quarter past eleven, it was,' his wife interrupted. 'I know because I was still awake when you came in. Our bedroom's next door to this, Mr Lloyd, not upstairs. I can't manage stairs any more, see? There's a bathroom and lav through there.' She nodded towards the scullery, before completing: 'We had them put in last year, with a council grant.'

'Derek was leaving at half past five in the morning,' said Sewell. 'Driving to London airport in his hired car. So he needed his sleep. I saw him off; well, that's natural, isn't it? Made him a bit of breakfast before he went. Couldn't do less than that.'

'And he couldn't have gone out after you went to bed, sir?'

'Why should he?'

'We'd have known if he had,' put in Mrs Sewell quickly. 'Those old stairs of ours creak like a ship at sea.'

'There's your list then, Mr Lloyd,' said her husband.

'Thank you very much, sir. Very helpful of you.' Lloyd scanned the piece of paper Sewell had given him. There were more than twenty names on it, laboriously printed in capital letters. 'Mr Charles Edworth. He's a friend of your nephew's?'

'Yes. They aren't close, though. Never were.' Sewell had started rolling one of his own cigarettes. 'Young Edworth played rugby for the Pontyglas under sixteens,' he went on. 'That was around the time Derek played for the town reserves, at least when he was home on leave. They knew each other through the rugby. Keen player, Derek was in those days. It's the army, see? They like you keeping fit. Derek's not big built. He's more like me. Strong with it, though.'

'Like you again, love,' his wife contributed with a smile.

'That's right. Derek played scrum half. Fast as grease lightning. He'd tackle men big as oxes. Bring 'em down too, every time. He could have played for Wales, easy. They used to say that about me as well. Except we didn't have no advantages at the beginning. Not like some. We both had to leave school too early. To make a living. Derek was as good as any Edworth, any day. Better. He –'

'Sure you won't have some tea, Mr Lloyd?' Mrs Sewell had hurriedly interrupted her husband's increasingly heated soliloquy. He was becoming carried away, almost angry in his vehemence, and dropping tobacco through quivering fingers as he licked the gummed edge of the thin cigarette paper.

17

'So you think you recognized the envelope, Mr Sewell?'
Parry asked the uniformed soldier who was seated across
from him, wearing a dark-blue army beret with a cloth ver-
sion of the Royal Engineers emblem on it. Below this he had
on the straight-necked, regulation, heavy-duty khaki jersey
with leather insets on the shoulders, and the lion and unicorn
insignia of a warrant officer first class sewn to his sleeves,
just above the wrists.

'Well, it's like any other padded envelope, isn't it?' Sewell
replied cautiously. 'But, yes, it looks like the same one. The
one I put the label on Saturday night. For the photo album
to go in.'

Major Denison, on the opposite side of the desk from the
other two, swayed in his chair, making it creak. He had done
this several times since the interview had begun, and always,
Parry had divined, when he was prompted to put a question
himself – except that he had agreed to be present as an
observer only, and not to interrogate Sewell. He was here to
underline that, in the army's view, there were no grounds
for believing that the warrant officer was directly involved
in the murder of Mervyn Davies – that it was not his fault
that some nutter, presumably the murderer, had sent him a
severed human hand.

Sewell had provided a set of his fingerprints for the South
Wales police before Parry's arrival, after Denison had
explained to the donor that these were required for elimin-
ation purposes only. They had already been handed to Parry
with some ceremony, as if they represented some kind of
concession on the part of the army.

The major's entrenched attitude on the whole affair had been clear to Parry before the interview. The sooner the hand was carried back to its place of origin, Denison believed, the better for all directly concerned with it – as well as for those he considered were only incidentally concerned with it, which very much included Derek Sewell. Parry had privately found this last view difficult to accept, but it had cost him nothing to give the impression he was going along with it.

The three men were in Denison's own office, smallish, spartan, and equipped with only the bare essentials – a deal desk, four matching chairs, and two telephones, one black and one red – the red, Parry had facetiously decided, reserved for imminent nuclear alerts. This was before Denison used it to order tea and biscuits. Otherwise, apart from a grey filing cabinet, an open bookshelf neatly filled with army manuals, and an empty, gargantuan-sized metal wastebin, there was only a small, brown refrigerator, and a Bonsai tree of indeterminate age perched on the windowsill. The fridge and the twisted Bonsai were clearly not regulation fitments like the rest of the furnishings. Parry decided the miniature tree was meant to be saying something about Denison as an individual, but he hadn't yet decided what. He was sure, even so, that a Bonsai was a more subtle piece of social intelligence than a framed snap of the wife and children would have been, if not perhaps as clearly informative as a mounted fox's head, or even a photograph of the major in the First XV at Wellington College or somewhere.

'And you stuck the address label on the envelope yourself, Mr Sewell?' the policeman now asked, while still trying to identify who it was the chap beside him looked like – someone he had been with recently.

'That's right, sir . . . Mr Parry.' Sewell, sitting tense and ramrod straight, swallowed with difficulty, his Adam's apple making a tortuously slow up and down movement in his thin sinewy neck. He was nervous, and although he had decided at the start that it wasn't required of him to address a senior civilian copper as 'sir', he hadn't been able to stop himself doing it. His attitude to those wielding army authority over him was always deferential – calculatedly so – and, in the present circumstances, he had equated Parry with that group.

Sewell's dogged aim was to work for further promotion to improve his living standards, as well as his eventual service pension. Anything that threatened his purpose had to be avoided, even if it involved indignity to himself. None of this balanced with his inward disdain for what he regarded as the British 'system' which gave privilege to the few and none to the others. He had beaten that system so far in his career, and was determined to go on doing so, even though it meant sensibly keeping his radical views to himself.

It was the brooding presence of Major Denison that was really throwing Sewell. The major was dressed in similar gear to himself, except he was wearing a peaked cap which was why Sewell had to keep his beret on. It was Denison's cap, and his pointed decision not to take it off, that was giving the whole occasion an overly formal atmosphere. Sewell reasoned that if the bugger was on his side, like he said he'd be this morning, why was he fixing him all the time with that look. Once, when he had been a witness at the courts martial of a staff sergeant, Sewell had watched the President of the Court look that way all through the hearing before eventually voting the prisoner to be guilty as hell.

'So your fingerprints are going to be on the label and the envelope, of course, Mr Sewell.'

Denison gave a sigh of what could have been relief at Parry's last statement, though Sewell immediately translated it as an expression of the worst sort of significance.

'That's right, su . . . Mr Parry. Unless they wear off in transit, like.'

Parry smiled. 'They don't usually. Even sometimes when they've been rained on. Very durable things, fingerprints.' He took a sip of his tea, noting that Sewell hadn't touched his. 'Anyway, if your fingerprints are found on the outside of the envelope, we'll know why.'

'They won't be on the inside. I can tell you that,' Sewell responded roundly. 'Or on the plastic bag the hand was in.' They had all viewed the complete exhibit earlier. It had now been returned to the locked fridge in the corner nearest to the major.

After the last response, Denison's chair creaked again, and not just because he was replacing his empty teacup on its saucer. He didn't believe a possible defendant needed to volunteer anything, particularly not so definite a disclaimer. He had earlier warned Sewell about this.

'You're sure there weren't any transparent bags on the table in the church hall? As well as the padded envelopes? That might have been for putting the albums in later?' Parry offered helpfully, with a glance in Denison's direction.

'Not that I remember, no,' Sewell replied. But then, because the major had made another abrupt movement, he added hastily: 'I mean, there could have been, I suppose, without me seeing them. Or touching them,' which indicated that he thought he had got the message – except it was the wrong message.

'And just in case we find the rector's wife still has the padded envelope you stuck your label on, Mr Sewell, can you remember doing the same with any other similar envelope?'

Sewell frowned. 'Not that I can think of, no. I'm pretty sure the envelope with the hand in must be the one from the church hall.'

'But you did give out address labels to other people at the supper? To some of the people you've listed for me here, for instance?' Parry fingered the list of only eight names, the best Sewell could manage, and which he had compiled at the start of the interview.

'That's right, Mr Parry.'

'So any of them could have stuck one of your labels on one of the rector's wife's envelopes? A different one.' He read through the names again. 'For instance, Mrs Jacky Franklin, or er . . . Mr Geoff Godwin.'

Denison cleared his throat, and made a neck movement so close to a nod of assent that it could hardly have been mistaken for anything else.

'Yes, I hadn't thought of that,' Sewell responded obediently.

167

'But if that happened, your fingerprints wouldn't be on the envelope, because you only handled the one?'

'Right again.'

'You're quite sure of that?'

Sewell glanced at Denison. 'So far as I can remember, sir, yes.' Beads of sweat were now forming at the side of his face. Unconsciously, he had begun rubbing his upper thighs with both hands.

'I tell you what surprises me . . . Mr Sewell,' Parry went on. He would have preferred to call such a nervous witness by his first name, except that such informality would have made the heavily correct Denison more demonstrably uncomfortable, and so offered no easement to Sewell. 'What surprises me is how quickly the package got here. I mean, so far as we can estimate, the earliest Mervyn Davies could have met his death was eleven-thirty Saturday night. The package containing his severed hand was delivered here at the base by seven this morning.'

'There'd be a Sunday collection from the main post office in Pontyglas, I expect,' Sewell volunteered.

'Well, there'd have to be, wouldn't there? No other way the thing could have got here in the time. Is the post always so quick from the UK?'

'It's usually pretty fast, yes. Hardly ever takes more than two days. All airmail, of course.' He paused, then added, 'It's not very often things come in a day, but it happens sometimes. Like it did this morning. And the main services sorting office for Germany is right here.'

'I see.' Parry stroked his cheek with the flat of his hand. 'And you spent Saturday night at your uncle's house in Pontyglas, leaving at five on Sunday morning?'

'Yes. I was coming back on a civilian flight. BA from Heathrow.'

'And you'd just finished a week's course in Hereford. Getting to Heathrow via Pontyglas was quite a detour for one night. Was there a special reason why you wanted to see your uncle?'

'Sort of, yes. Except I always try to see him if I'm in the UK. He's the only family I've got left there, really.'

'But there was a special reason this time?' Parry pressed.

The soldier hesitated. 'He and my Aunt Iris haven't had a proper holiday for two years. Couldn't afford it. Heidi and I – Heidi's my wife – we thought that was wrong . . . and unfair as well. People of that age, and she being in a wheelchair and everything.'

'Arthritis, is it?' Parry asked, finishing his tea.

'That's right. Well, last summer I wrote offering to pay for them to go to Tenby for a fortnight, all found. They wouldn't accept. Wouldn't hear of it, even after I rang them about it twice. I thought if I came in person I could talk them into it for this year. I did too. Took some doing, I can tell you. They're proud. A lot of Welsh are, aren't they?' He looked at Denison who blinked what could have been agreement, or incredulity. 'Anyway, my uncle and I fixed it all up Saturday lunchtime. At the travel agent's in Pentre Street.'

'That must have given you a lot of pleasure, Mr Sewell. Very kind thing to have done,' said Parry, then nodded at Sewell's still full cup. 'Your tea's getting cold,' he commented, then went on. 'And you and your uncle returned from the church supper at ten-twenty Saturday night?'

'About then, yes. We had a couple of beers, and a chat in the kitchen, then we went to bed.'

'And you neither of you left the house between then and five next morning?'

'I didn't myself. I can't speak for my uncle, not for certain, but I don't believe he'd have gone out after we went to bed. Oh, unless it was to put a dust sheet over the car I'd hired.'

'Why would he have done that?' Parry asked.

'He was worried about overnight frost on the windscreen, because of the early start. I said not to bother, and I don't think he did. There was no sign the car had had a sheet on it next morning. There'd been one over the front of his old van though, from before we left for the church supper in my car. It's one of his things, see? Frost on windscreens. Oh, and keeping engines warm.' Sewell grinned for the first time since the start of the interview.

'The van's a bit of an old banger, is it?' asked Parry, conversationally, and encouraging Sewell to relax even more.

'That's right. Of course, he has to have transport for his handyman tools. Matter of fact, it was the same thing at the supper. He insisted on taking a sheet from his van with us to put over my car then. The sheet had ruddy great blotches of gold and purple paint on it, I remember. I said I hoped they were dry.' The soldier chuckled. 'We never used it, of course. Anyway, I'd told him I had old bags and newspapers in the boot for covering the windscreen if needed. It was such a mild night, but he was wearing his parka and gloves, all the same.' Shaking his head at the habits of the elderly, he leaned forward and picked up his cup.

'So why did you go to the supper by car? As I understand it, your uncle's house is only a few minutes' walk from the church.'

Sewell drank the whole of his tea before replying, with Parry noting that it must have been unpleasantly cold by this time, and so less likely to promote nervous sweating. 'I'm afraid that was just my uncle wanting to show off. Needing people to see we'd come in my posh car, as he said. It was only a small Ford, but he knew I had a Merc here, and the hire car was a symbol of . . . oh, how well I'd done, I suppose. It's all linked up with me being a warrant officer. He was disappointed I was in civvies too, but I didn't have a dress uniform with me, and I couldn't have gone like this.'

'Even though you look smart enough. Those badges of rank are pretty impressive,' Parry commented amiably.

'No, no. It would have been against general orders to go to something like that in working kit.' He looked at Denison. 'Anyway, that's why I sort of indulged my uncle over the car, if you follow? Probably it all sounds daft to you.' The speaker glanced again at the major, then leaned forward and back again heavily, evidently embarrassed.

'Not at all, Mr Sewell,' said Parry quietly. 'Anyway, it's a very complete answer to my question. And later on, was the hired Ford parked outside your uncle's all night, with his van?'

'Yes, in the alley at the back. It's not really suitable for parking, too narrow, but my uncle thinks it's safer than the street. It's another of his fixed ideas.'

'And when you came out in the morning, the Ford was in the same spot where you'd left it? In the alley?'

'It had been. But my uncle had brought it round to the front for me by the time I was up, to save trouble. That's on top of having my breakfast ready. A boiled egg and everything. He wasn't even supposed to be up before I left. He's a good sort. The best.'

'I'm sure, Mr Sewell. And I imagine he thinks the same of you.' Parry made a tick against something in his notebook, then looked straight at Sewell, very hard, and holding the other's gaze. 'And can you think of any reason why anyone, anyone at all, might have sent you the severed hand?'

'The murderer, you mean?'

'For the moment we're assuming it must have been the murderer, yes.'

Sewell shook his head slowly. 'Nobody I can think of would have killed Mr Davies.'

'And sent the head and the two hands to different people, before disposing of the rest of the body,' Parry continued in an almost ruminative voice. 'You can't think of anyone?'

'No, I can't.'

'Didn't think you would.' He balanced his ballpen between thumb and forefinger, tapping the top end against the notebook. 'But you know Mr Davies left for Australia forty years ago under a cloud? It's said by some that he'd seduced a young girl called Alice Morgan, and made her pregnant.' It was at that moment that Parry realized it was Alice's son Owen Franklin that the man beside him resembled – the more so when he was relaxed. The likeness wasn't all that acute, but it was definitely there, around the eyes and mouth, and the colouring was similar.

'I've heard talk of that, yes.' Sewell crossed and uncrossed his legs, then sat further forward on the chair, back still straight, while he held the edges of the seat with both hands.

'Alice died shortly after childbirth,' Parry continued. 'Her child, Owen Franklin, was brought up in Pontyglas, by her sister Jacky Franklin and her husband. You know Mrs Franklin. Do you know Owen?'

'Yes. We went to the same schools.' He took out a handkerchief, wiped his nose, and then both sides of his face.

'Has he ever said anything to you suggesting he had it in for Mervyn Davies?'

'No. Anyway, I haven't spoken to him for years.'

'I see. You mean you didn't see him on Saturday night?'

'No. My uncle noticed what he thought was his motorbike in the yard of the Coach and Horses. We stopped there for a quick one when they opened. On our way to the church supper. Uncle thought some of his cronies would be there. They weren't, though. Too early.'

'Was the bike still in the yard when you left?'

'I can't remember. There were a lot of other cars there by then.'

'Off the record, would you say it's possible Owen Franklin might have been gunning for Mr Davies? For deserting him and his mother?'

Denison drummed his fingers on the desk. 'Time's getting short, Parry,' he observed. It had been his only spoken comment so far, and it had nothing at all to do with the time.

The policeman had agreed before Sewell's arrival that his questions would deal only with matters of fact, that he wouldn't be seeking to elicit opinion. Although the major's interruption had underlined that he had just broken that agreement, or been close to doing so, Parry continued to stare expectantly at Sewell, waiting for his answer.

'I suppose it's possible,' Sewell responded guardedly.

'And if he did kill Mr Davies, accidentally say, during a fight, can you think of a reason why he might have sent you the hand afterwards?'

'No.'

'Not as a symbol of . . . retribution, perhaps? If he knew, or thought he knew, that Davies had been your father as well?'

Denison was about to say something again, but Sewell was ahead of him. 'Who told you he was my father?' he questioned.

'Could he have been?'

'Not so far as I know.'

'But I gather you don't know who your father was, Mr Sewell?'

Sewell had begun breathing heavily, as if he had been exercising. 'That's right, but –'

'It was generally known Mr Davies had come into a lot of money. On his death, his children, legitimate and otherwise, stood to inherit that money between them. Owen Franklin could have been one of them. You could have been another, couldn't you?'

'I say, isn't that rather –'

'Couldn't you, Mr Sewell,' Parry insisted firmly, cutting off Denison's attempted intervention.

'I didn't know anything about any of that,' Sewell recited, looking from Parry to Denison.

'I see. And you're absolutely sure you didn't see Owen Franklin on Saturday? It'd be better to say so now if you made a mistake over anything you've said earlier. And to correct anything else that wasn't er . . . wasn't strictly accurate.'

'I've told you the truth, sir,' Sewell replied, sweat trickling down from his temple, and a pulse beating furiously at the side of his neck.

Denison had been tapping his fingers on the desk for several seconds, and he had become increasingly red in the face. 'I'm sorry, Parry, but I have to insist –'

'Yes, you're right, Major, I must be off,' the policeman interrupted again, this time with a disarming smile. 'Thank you for being so helpful, Mr Sewell. Sorry to press you, like that. I accept completely what you've told me. I don't think we'll need to trouble you again.'

It was difficult to be sure who it was who looked the most relieved – Denison or Sewell. Parry had been watching the reactions of both and decided, with reluctance, that it was the major.

Exactly four hours later, Parry was hurrying across the non-slip, gleaming floor tiles towards the lifts in the entrance foyer of the Prince of Wales Hospital, Pontyglas. Lloyd was beside him, trying to keep up, but treading more carefully because he wasn't sure if the tiles were non-slip – and wouldn't have trusted them if he had been sure.

The chief inspector had driven almost directly from Heathrow, stopping only to leave the second severed hand at the morgue of Cardiff Royal Infirmary. Lloyd had been waiting for him half an hour later at the reception desk of the Pontyglas hospital.

'And it happened at eight this evening?' Parry questioned, smiling in a reflex way at a group of chattering nurses who were going off duty. Otherwise, there were very few people about. It was now nine-fifteen – except for the policeman it felt a lot later. It had been a long working day, even before he had regained the hour on the flight from Düsseldorf, changing back to British time.

'Yes, it was just before eight. And like I said on the phone, boss, it was Mrs Jarvis who sent for the ambulance.'

'Is she in better shape than he is?'

'She's recovering quicker. Seems like she'd taken a pasting before she had a chance to defend herself. She's badly bruised, with an open wound to the head, and a cut lip. She seems stable enough mentally, but the doc said there's a chance she could develop concussion. That's why they're keeping her in.'

'It's all right for us to see her now?'

'Sure. I've cleared it with the doc. Mr Jarvis has had some stitches to his stomach, and he's heavily sedated. Behaving like a banshee at the start, he was. There won't be any more talking to him till morning, I'm afraid.'

'We're sure he started things by assaulting her?'

'Oh, yes. He admitted it. He was proud of it, even. Pissed, of course. But sobered up a lot by the time I got to see him.'

'Where was that?'

'Here in casualty. The two of them came in the same ambulance.'

'And you got preliminary statements from both of them?'

'Yes. Enough to establish roughly what happened. They're in separate wards on the second floor.' Lloyd was pressing the lift button as he spoke.

The Dwynwyn Ward, when they reached it, contained four

174

beds, but only one was occupied – by Mrs Mair Jarvis. A uniformed WPC had been seated outside in the corridor. The patient was propped up, and sipping tea, but awkwardly, through a glass tube. Her face was drawn, greyish, and devoid of any of her usual make-up. There was a large, upstanding, stiff white plaster dressing across her left temple that immediately reminded Parry of the price ticket in the Mad Hatter's topper. The eye below the bandage was badly bruised, and her lower lip was split at the side. Both uncovered wounds glistened with medicament.

'Oh, my Lord, do you have to see me looking like this?' Mrs Jarvis complained, speaking through a nearly closed mouth, and with no strength in her voice. Instinctively her hand went to finger her yellow, tightly waved hair which had largely withstood the onslaught she had suffered, as well as the following ministrations at the hospital.

'We won't stay long, Mrs Jarvis,' said Parry. 'Just a few questions to ask you. We've got the basic facts of what happened already.'

'My drunken husband tried to half murder me, that's what happened.'

'And you warded him off with a potato knife?'

'Yes. Self-defence, it was. It was all I had handy. I was doing the washing up.' She paused. 'If he goes to jail, will we lose the money Mr Edworth left us?'

'I shouldn't think so, Mrs Jarvis. But perhaps you should ask a lawyer about that. You're going to press charges against your husband, are you?'

She sighed, and her hand returned to her hair. 'Do I have to?'

'No one can force you.'

She sighed again. 'Gareth didn't mean it, I suppose. Like I said, he was drunk. He came home late for his tea. Quarter to eight. I ask you? Playing billiards all afternoon, he was. The drinking was after. I'd cleared by the time he walked in. Put his plate in the oven. There was something on the telly at eight.'

'The argument was about Mr Edworth? Your husband accused you of having er . . .'

175

'Relations with him. Yes,' she interrupted. 'And with Mervyn Davies. Well, how could I have had relations with Mr Davies? He was only here two days, God rest him.'

'In the case of Mr Edworth, did your husband have grounds for his accusation?' Parry was knowingly taking advantage of her plain-speaking mood, not her frail state, nor the tranquillizers she'd been given – though he would have admitted that the first condition could well have been produced by the other two.

Mrs Jarvis shrugged her shoulders under the hospital issue, slightly starched and faded, but, appropriately for her, pink nightgown, then winced because the movement had hurt. 'I never had relations with Mr Edworth. Not the way Gareth meant.'

'So he had no grounds for accusing you, in any case?' put in the sergeant, with a note of pious expectation in his voice.

'That's not what he'll tell you. But he knew well enough I never went to bed with Mr Edworth. I just did . . .' she hesitated, looking down at the bed tray. 'I just did the exhibitions, that's all. God, I'd give anything for a ciggy.' She looked about her desperately through the undamaged eye.

'Exhibitions?' Lloyd's hopefulness had withered.

'Yes. That's what Mr Edworth called it. Every Saturday teatime. When Gareth was out bowling in summer, and watching his old rugby in winter.'

'That's when you did these . . . these exhibitions?'

'Yes. I used to sit in front of Mr Edworth and er . . . show a leg. Nothing more. Well, not much more. I've got nice legs, if I say so myself.' She moved her knees under the covers, then touched the side of her eye very gently, testing for pain. 'But it was all harmless, and it pleased him. Nothing like what you see on telly these days, I can tell you. Yes, harmless,' she repeated, more to herself than to anyone else. She looked straight at Parry, then at Lloyd. 'And he never touched me. Not in any . . . any intimate place, like. Not in all those years.'

'How many years would that have been exactly, Mrs Jarvis?' Lloyd questioned, in a tone implying the answer was of only passing interest.

176

'Since the exhibitions started? Oh, getting on for nine, I suppose.'

Looking for mitigation, Lloyd thought that wasn't as long as the Ideal Homes or the Motor Show, after all. 'Would you care for a peppermint, Mrs Jarvis?' he asked, proffering a tube. 'I used to find they helped with the not smoking.'

'No thanks, all the same. I'd rather suffer,' she said in a martyred voice, but jokingly.

'And your husband found out about what was going on, did he?' the sergeant resumed.

'He guessed, or something, yes. Long time ago. Perhaps he saw us. I don't know. I wouldn't put it past him to have looked through the keyhole. Only he never complained at the time.'

'Not in nine years?'

'That's God's truth. He knew well enough how we kept the job. It wasn't because of his gardening, I can tell you, or his driving. It was my cooking, and the way I kept the house, and . . . and what I just said.' She nodded. 'The same reason Mr Edworth left us all that money. He told me that himself. Well, good as.'

'Could your husband have thought Mr Davies might be expecting . . . exhibitions as well, Mrs Jarvis?' Lloyd inquired earnestly, as if they were discussing innocuous events like floral arranging or hot-air ballooning.

Mrs Jarvis looked down again at the crockery on the bed tray. 'He was bothered because Mr Davies paid me compliments, like any gentleman would. Any gentleman who admired a lady.'

'I see. He hadn't had words with Mr Davies, by any chance?'

'Who, Gareth?' So far as Mrs Jarvis was physically able to give a sarcastic smile, she did so. 'No chance,' she said. 'He knew which side his bread was buttered, all right. Never said anything to upset Mr Davies, nor Mr Edworth for that matter. It was me he took things out on.'

'Has he ever struck you before, Mrs Jarvis?' asked Parry.

'Yes. Not as bad as today, though. And only when he's been one over the eight.' She picked up a handbag mirror from the bedside table and gazed at her face in it. 'Oh, my Lord,' she sighed, hardly moving her lips.

'And you've struck him back? Defending yourself?'

She considered for a moment. 'Not properly. Not till today.'

'And you've never reported him for assaulting you?'

'He's usually sorry after,' she replied grudgingly.

'And although he may have known something about the harmless exhibitions, he could never have seen you, say, in bed with Mr Edworth? Having sexual relations with him?'

Mrs Jarvis's expression went blank. 'Mr Edworth never had sexual relations with anyone. He was, what d'you call it? . . . er, he was impotent. I mean, he couldn't manage it, if you follow?' Parry looked as if he followed. Lloyd looked dumbfounded as she went on. 'He said it was through that illness he had. When he was young. Twelve, I think he was. He told me that two years ago. Said he'd never told anybody else. Not ever. It was a compliment, I thought. Well, it was, wasn't it?'

18

'So bang goes the idea that Mervyn Davies took the blame for Edwin Edworth's bastards, boss,' said Lloyd, hanging his jacket on the door hook in the office he and Parry were sharing. 'Edwin Edworth couldn't have children.'

The two men had left the hospital together, but Lloyd had returned to the police station in Greenlow Street ten minutes later than the chief inspector, after making an important call on the way.

Parry, in shirt sleeves, was seated behind his desk. He pushed away the bunch of accumulated reports he had been scanning. It was late, but he was anxious to compare notes with Lloyd on the day's developments. 'So Dr Amor definitely confirms what Mrs Jarvis told us,' he said. They had Amor listed as Edwin Edworth's GP. It was he Lloyd had just come from seeing.

'Well, as good as, boss. Mr Edworth was sterile. Result of glandular fever before puberty. Dr Amor had looked after him for thirty years. Knew all about it. Very helpful, he was. Didn't mind the late call, either. He said Mr Edworth didn't know about his condition till he had some tests done in his late twenties. Then knowing he was sterile made him impotent as well, which was what Mrs Jarvis said he was. That was a psychological effect from the other, according to the doctor. Anyway, he said he thinks it was the reason Mr Edworth never married. Bad luck, of course. Could have been what made him bitter, I suppose.'

'Bitter and jealous, perhaps?' said Parry in a seriously speculative tone. 'Making a reason why he didn't leave his money to his brother's children? That kind of thing affects

179

people in different ways.' He got up and paced across to the open door connecting with the main incident room. There were two men and a woman still on duty there, the men hunched over word processors, the woman speaking on the telephone. 'Anyway, as you sáy, it wipes out one reason why he left everything to Davies. There's still no sign of that sealed letter he left?'

'None. We've been through everything again, looking for it. His room, belongings, and luggage. He only brought a grip with him, of course. We've taken that apart in case he'd shoved the letter in the bottom lining. Chances must be he still had it on him when he died.'

'Meaning his killer's probably got it now. Unless the Jarvises nicked it, as you suggested this morning.'

'Mr Jarvis, most likely.' Lloyd still had sympathetic feelings about Mrs Jarvis. 'We're double-checking on that now, boss. Their being in hospital gave us a chance to go through their rooms again. We did it with Mrs Jarvis present Sunday morning, but we didn't know about the letter then. We've had no luck tonight though, not so far.' He paused to put a peppermint in his mouth. 'About the other possibility,' he went on, sucking noisily, 'that he sent the letter to Australia. We've been trying to check that out as well. We faxed the Perth police this morning asking them to contact his sons to tell them he'd died in suspicious circumstances. We got their names from Mr Trimble, but he didn't have addresses. Perth police faxed back they're on to his ex-wife through an address they found at his flat. They're contacting the sons through her, asking them to hand over any letters they get from their father. Especially anything he sent enclosing one to him from Mr Edworth.'

'And they'll be told it could give us a clue about who killed him?' Parry put in.

'We stressed that to the Perth police, boss. They're also arranging to check the mail at Mr Davies's flat for anything from the UK. It could be he sent the letter to himself, for safekeeping, like. People do that sometimes. They'll also check with his bank. The bank may know if he had a solicitor. Mr Trimble doesn't think he did. Oh, and we've checked with all the Pontyglas banks in case he deposited the letter with one of them. He didn't.'

Parry frowned. 'And we have to accept Dewi Trimble's word for it that Davies didn't read the letter in his office, then give it back to him to keep.' There was a brief silence as both police officers considered the consequences of the opposite scenario, before Parry went on, 'And you've asked him about his relationship with Gail Edworth?'

'Yes, boss. He says he knows her because she works for his dentist, but otherwise he only sees her when he delivers the parish magazine to her flat. His wife is supposed to do that, but he does it instead when he's in the area walking his dog.'

'So Mrs Edworth may be putting two and two together to make five?'

'That's about what he said. And that she's getting senile. Imagines things. He also said the daughter will confirm what he told me.'

'And does she?'

'We haven't asked her. Not yet. I wondered if there was any point.'

'Probably not.' The chief inspector stopped pacing and stared through the glass into the outer office. 'I've just read the report that Charles Edworth now admits he was at Condleston Lodge Saturday night.'

'Yes, boss. Straight after he left Miss Lewin's. The trip to Wolverhampton seems to have cleared his mind no end. He's scared out of his wits we'll tell his wife he's got a mistress. And he doesn't want us going back to his mother either, to tell us the time he left her Saturday night.'

Parry turned about, folded his arms and stood with his back against the partition wall. 'That chap's definitely not got the stamina to lead a double life, has he?'

'That's right, boss. Anyway, he now swears he left Miss Lewin at five past eleven and drove straight to Condleston Lodge. There was no answer when he rang the bell, but he says he waited till eleven-twenty, parked in the drive.'

'At least fifteen minutes before Davies could have been there?'

'More than that, boss, if Mr Godwin's telling the truth, and we now believe he is, because we've got four probable sightings of Mr Davies walking back through the town between eleven-forty and midnight.'

'I saw the report, yes.'

'Anyway, Mr Edworth says he was hoping to talk Mr Davies into putting money in a company he's setting up. As a business investment.'

'Not just to hand him part of the inheritance?'

'He says not.' Lloyd's eyes betrayed serious doubt, as he added: 'Except, as well as the other, he was hoping Mr Davies might help his mother financially.'

'Not his sister?'

'He didn't mention his sister. But it's all the same really, isn't it? If Mr Davies had given money to the mother, her two kids would have got it when she died.'

'Assuming she hadn't spent it already.' Parry shook his head. 'The second part of his story depends on the word of his wife, who confirms he was home at eleven-thirty –'

'Eleven-thirty-five actually, boss,' the sergeant corrected. 'And she swears he never went out again.'

'In which case, he can't have done the murder. And the two women providing his alibi are not likely to be in cahoots.' Parry moved back to a spot behind his chair, and for a moment seemed to be considering the veracity or logic, or both, of what he had just said. 'And someone's going over Jarvis's movements again for Saturday night?'

'Yes. Now we know he had a motive for killing Mr Davies. Or thought he had. But we'll need to establish he left his sister-in-law's place in Porthcawl in the middle of the night. Someone may have seen him. Or heard him. We said already there wasn't time for him to have done a murder and got rid of the body before he got back to the party earlier on. And there's a dozen witnesses to that.'

'What about his doing the murder, and disposing of the body later?'

'Possible, boss. But if he did, the body wasn't moved in his car. That's been taken apart by forensic. Nothing. No trace of Mr Davies's blood or anything.'

182

'OK, so let's go back to the fact that he's the one person who could have killed Davies at say, three a.m., and rigged things to make it look as if it happened before midnight.'

Lloyd smoothed both sides of his moustache with thumb and forefinger. 'Like he could have got Mr Davies outside, done him in, reset the house alarm, because he's the only one who knew the code –'

'Except for his wife,' Parry broke in. 'Remade Davies's bed, so it looked as if it hadn't been slept in.'

'Dressed him in his day clothes again. Ah –' Lloyd paused, frowning.

'Yes, there's the problem,' said Parry. 'We can't know he was in his day clothes. Not till we've found his body.'

Lloyd pulled out his own chair and sat in it. 'It's just that we haven't found the clothes he had on at the church supper,' he said.

'So we've assumed he was still wearing them. But if he wasn't, if he was in pyjamas when he was killed, or naked even, it might have been easier for the killer to take the dead body away than to try dressing it. Especially if the killing was by decapitation, and it's pretty certain it was.'

'Messy, you mean, boss? Bloody? For dressing the body after?'

'Yes. But the killer might still have taken the clothes with him. And, once again, Jarvis had access to them.' He shrugged. 'At least we've found a credible suspect with a motive. And one who had the means to make the job seem to have been done earlier than it was.'

'Except it doesn't fit Dr Ironmonger's time of death, boss.'

'He wasn't positive about that.'

'And pathologists are sometimes wrong,' Lloyd added.

But the expression on Parry's face was a long way from indicating conviction. 'I just wish we were sure Jarvis fitted as a killer, not just a wife-basher when stoned.' He moved the telephone by his right hand a little further away. 'And I wish I knew why he'd have wanted to distribute bits of Davies like he did. The head and the hands.'

'To put suspicion on Ken Franklin, and Mr Davies's illegitimate sons, boss? After all, Mr Jarvis didn't know young

Franklin and Derek Sewell couldn't have been Mr Davies's sons, did he? And it seems to have been well known Ken Franklin believed Mr Davies was Owen's father.'

'And incidentally, Owen Franklin and Derek Sewell couldn't have known Davies wasn't their father either,' Parry responded, changing the subject slightly. 'Not at the time of the murder.'

'So what about Warrant Officer Sewell then, boss?'

The chief inspector leaned back and crossed his arms tightly across his chest. 'I can't make up my mind about him. I don't believe he's nervous by nature, but he was nervous as hell when I interviewed him. And warrant officers are usually sure of themselves. Entitled to be, too, because they know their business. Promoted on knowledge and experience. And merit.'

'Like coppers, boss?'

'Exactly.' He gave a good-humoured snort. 'With no old school network privileges. Major Denison says that applies especially to the Royal Engineers. He believes their warrant officers are the salt of the earth. And this one's even up for promotion to captain.'

'Hm. Very nervous-making thing, doing a murder, boss,' said Lloyd slowly.

This time Parry made a pained face. 'Sure. But having met him, I've got a gut feeling that if Warrant Officer Sewell had topped somebody, it wouldn't have been on the spur of the moment. He'd have planned it. And that includes what was done with the head and hands, and with the disposing of the rest of the body where we can't find it.' His eyes narrowed. 'It wasn't a rushed job. Too many phases involved, despite the lack of time, or the apparent lack of time.' He paused. 'It was a cool operation done by someone working from his home base. Anyway, not someone on a fleeting visit from overseas, pushed for time.'

'So you wouldn't expect this killer to be jumpy as soon as he's confronted, boss? But, for the sake of argument, if it was Derek Sewell, he could have been nervous if someone else was involved with him. Like his uncle, say? Someone who was around to do the finishing touches, like?'

Parry considered for a moment. 'Could have been. But I still can't accept Derek Sewell is a killer. I notice your report says the uncle has a council allotment?'

'Yes. I found that out later than I should have done, too. It never came out the first time we saw him. Detective Constable Susan Flowers did that interview, while a forensic team checked his van. She never asked him about an allotment, and he never volunteered. She checked the back garden at the house, of course. Wasn't enough bare earth to bury a body, not even one put in vertical. The rest was concreted over years ago. I didn't ask about an allotment either, not when I was there today. Then, after I'd left, I remembered Mrs Sewell giving a neighbour's lad some shopping her husband had done for his mother. Well, that's what I thought at the time. Winter cabbage, it was, in a Woolworth's bag.'

'And Woolworth's don't sell veg?' Parry grinned.

'That's right, boss. I don't know what I was thinking about. Anyway, I figured after that Mr Sewell had probably grown the cabbage himself. We checked with the council. He's got a double-sized allotment on a site just up the road here, beyond where Greenlow Street goes under the railway.'

'And?'

'We went over it late this afternoon with the GPR machine, with Mr Sewell present.' Lloyd sniffed. 'Nothing,' he ended.

'He didn't object?'

'He wasn't pleased, but he didn't object. Understood why it was necessary, like. He was up there anyway, not specially for us. According to the council superintendent of allotments, he's their keenest tenant. Up there all the time. Probably means his handyman business isn't busy.'

'You said we found nothing suspicious on Godwin's allotment either.'

'That's right. But he stopped renting it a year ago. It's on the same council site, of course. Next plot to Mr Sewell's, as a matter of fact. We'd checked it yesterday. And his tool hut. We didn't use the GPR machine. Didn't need it. The plot's too overgrown. Earth not dug since he gave it up, by the look of it. Funny, keen gardeners used to snap up council allotments in the old days. People without the growing space

185

in their own gardens, I mean. Doesn't happen now. They say it's mostly because of vandals. Allotments are hard to protect, of course. On the other hand, I think people have mostly given them up because it's too easy to buy cheap vegetables in the supermarket. Never as fresh as home grown, of course,' the sergeant deplored, while easing his trousers at the waist. Parry was expecting him to add his standard homily about the merits of organically grown radishes – a Lloyd family garden speciality – but the sergeant was already too preoccupied, searching amongst the reports in front of him as he went on: 'So if Warrant Officer Sewell isn't the killer, and he wasn't nervous on his own account, was there some other reason he was jumpy, you think?'

'I'm not sure. It could be just that Major Denison unnerved him. He did me, at times. Or it's still possible, of course, that Sewell's somehow got tied in as an accomplice with Owen Franklin who he doesn't trust.'

The sergeant looked up sharply. 'Well, you couldn't blame him for that, could you? I wouldn't trust that slippery bugger with the date of my birthday. They know each other, then?'

'Knew each other, Sewell says, at school, and later probably. Except he soft pedalled on the second bit. But if they both believed they were Davies's sons, it gave them a reason to renew the acquaintance. I mean after Davies came back, and everybody knew he'd come into Edworth's money.'

'And pretty livid Derek Sewell and Owen Franklin would have been if they knew Mr Davies wasn't cutting them in.'

'But *did* they know, Gomer?'

As Parry asked the question, one of the detective constables still working in the incident room tapped at the open door of the inner office. 'What is it, Phil?' Lloyd asked.

'Fax for the guv. Marked urgent.' The constable handed over the sheet.

'They found Derek Sewell's thumbprint on that padded envelope,' Parry announced, scanning the print-out. 'I wonder why only one thumbprint?'

'It's enough, though,' said Lloyd.

'Yes, but don't get excited, Gomer. His prints almost had to be on it somewhere. That's if it was the envelope he stuck

186

the address label on himself, at the church supper, and it looks pretty certain now it was. Better check with the rector's wife in the morning that she doesn't have it any more. She might have ideas about who could have nicked it, too.'

'Right, boss.' Lloyd made a note as he continued: 'Doesn't stop it from being Derek Sewell himself who nicked it, does it? To put the hand in later?'

'And posted it to himself. Why?' Without waiting for an answer, Parry went on. 'His prints weren't on the clear film bag inside the envelope. He told me they couldn't be.'

'Because he wore gloves for that bit, boss? And he could have sent the hand to himself to draw off suspicion. The same kind of thing could have happened with the hand put in Owen Franklin's bike pannier. I mean, to draw suspicion off Franklin. That's if those two were in it together. Or even if they weren't.' Lloyd never missed an opportunity to keep suspicion on Owen Franklin.

'Your report said Derek Sewell couldn't have left the house Saturday night without the older couple hearing him. Something about creaking stairs.'

'That's only what Mrs Sewell said, boss.'

Parry frowned, then looked at the time. 'Gomer, it's late. Let's pack it in for tonight, shall we?' He pushed his chair away from the desk and reached for his coat which was hanging over the back of it. 'How did the news conference go?' He had missed the first scheduled news conference on the case at five that afternoon.

'It was OK. Lot of newspaper reporters came, and people from the radio. BBC Wales, and the local commercial stations. Oh, and ITN came with a camera.'

'Not BBC TV news?'

'No. I did the talking, and Superintendent Jenkins took the chair. Like we agreed, I asked for anyone to come forward who saw Mr Davies walking home Saturday night. We could still do with more definite sightings for the earlier part of his walk.'

'Many questions?'

'Not really. Usual ones about did we have a prime suspect, and whether an arrest was imminent.' The sergeant made a tutting noise. 'Too simple for them, isn't it? Of course, they'd had a hand-out already about the second severed hand. We're monitoring all the news bulletins, radio and telly. There's been something on every radio bulletin since five o'clock. Nothing on the box so far.'

Superintendent Ted Jenkins, an old friend of Parry's, was uniform branch, and currently attached to the Pontyglas Division. He had been the ranking officer at the station during the afternoon relief.

'So no Oscar again for you this week, Gomer,' Parry joked, then leaned forward to examine the titles of the files on the desk. 'Look, I want to take home all the reports covering those old relationships Davies had. People who were in that choir photo who are still alive, and anyone else he knew from those days who's still living in the town. Or who came here for that supper. There were a few of those, weren't there?'

'You've got most of what you want there, boss. All updated late this afternoon,' Lloyd replied. 'But I'll get you copies of anything printed out tonight.'

As the sergeant walked through to the incident room, Parry dialled Perdita's number. The call was answered by her machine. He was leaving a message to say he had rung when Lloyd returned. The chief inspector checked the time again, then replaced the phone.

19

It was nearly an hour later – close on 11.15 – when Parry let himself into the flat in Westgate Street. The drive had taken only thirty minutes, but he had looked in on Ted Jenkins, who was just coming off duty at the time, to thank him for chairing the news conference, and to give him an update on the case.

Parry went to the sitting room and switched on the television set, hoping to catch a news bulletin. Pleasant as the flat was, he still found it a good deal less welcoming than his own home used to be, especially when he had gone back to it late at night, and even in the months he had soldiered on there as a widower.

He had ultimately given up the first and only marital home he and Rosemary had made together, in Tawrbach, ten miles away, because he felt it had too often stirred up memories of her. Now, surrounded by other people's furniture and pictures – an ambience far grander than anything he and Rosemary had ever enjoyed – he found himself wishing, perversely, that there were more things in the rented flat that did evoke memories. His cello, in the corner, was the only big personal possession in view, but he hadn't played it for months. He and Perdita were always planning to spend an evening playing duets, but somehow it never happened. It was music that had brought them together, the three of them, he ruminated poignantly. Rosemary had played the violin, though not as well as Perdita played the piano. Still contemplating his cello, he gave an involuntary shrug: now was certainly not the time to break his performing fast with a solo.

There were no news bulletins on either of the Independent TV channels, and he looked about for a paper that would tell him when the next one was scheduled. He was still half hoping that Lloyd, who hated addressing news conferences, might be featured doing just that, pressing recalcitrant witnesses to hurry forward in the public service. As he was turning the pages of a surviving Sunday newspaper supplement, the phone rang. It was Perdita, returning his call.

'I did try to reach you earlier, from the car,' he said, as soon as they had exchanged greetings.

'Sorry. Been out to dinner. With Jeremy.'

'Jeremy who?'

'Oh, come on, darling, there's only one Jeremy in my life. Dr Jeremy Bates. My old anatomy tutor. The sub dean at St Mark's Hospital Medical School. Where I'm going at the end of the month. You haven't forgotten that too?'

He supposed it was the wine she had drunk at dinner that was making her arrogant. 'Of course not,' he said. 'Dr Bates is in Cardiff?'

'Unexpectedly for the night, yes. He rang at the last minute and offered me dinner. Pity you were in Germany, you could have joined us. How was good old Germany?'

'So, so. And *he* could have joined *us*,' Parry corrected lightly, but with just a hint of peevishness. 'We had a date, remember? I had to break it. Call of duty.' He vaguely recalled now that it was Bates who had fixed the last-minute place for Perdita at St Mark's. 'Anyway, I'm sure the venerable doctor wanted to talk shop.'

'Don't you believe it. We had a Chinese, a heated argument about Benjamin Britten, and then we went dancing, to that club you like. He's not venerable either. He's only just had his forty-eighth birthday. But don't worry, he's very much married.'

Irritatingly, he found he was worrying – and had been, mountingly so, since near the beginning of the conversation. 'You're still here till the end of the month?'

'Yes,' she answered, then added, after a brief pause: 'Well, for the next two weeks, at least. Actually' – there was another pause, this time more blatantly awkward – 'actually, there may be a problem about June. Our holiday? It . . . it looks as though I'll have to use all the time between April and September for revision after all. No rest for the wicked.'

'Dr Bates's orders?'

'Well, I do owe it to him. For getting me the place. I don't want to let him down.'

'And he'll be around to help with your studies?'

'Well, yes. A lot of the time. He and others. Everybody's ready to help plucky young Perdita with her cramming, apparently, and . . . well, it seems ungrateful not to be there to take advantage. You do understand, Merlin?'

'Of course I do.' Except he couldn't help wondering who would be taking advantage of whom.

'I just have to be up to fourth-year standard by October.'

'That's right,' he agreed stoically.

'I mean, I couldn't bear to be put back a year. Or dropped altogether. That'd be awful, at this stage. You see, it's all so competitive. You do see that?' she pressed, almost belligerently.

'Sure.' Pedantically, he was trying to work out how you could be at a stage with something before you started it. 'So, can I come over?' he asked.

'What, now?'

'No time like the present,' he offered, knowing already from her tone that she was going to say no.

'Oh, darling, do you mind? I'm so tired, and I have to be up at the crack. I'm doing an extra hospital session first thing.'

'OK. I'm pretty whacked too, I suppose.'

'The German trip was tiring, I expect. Try to get a good night's sleep, darling. You need it when you're stretched. The case not working out?'

'Difficult to say.' It was the kind of blocking answer he gave to interested strangers. 'How about tomorrow night, then?' he asked.

'Fine. Well . . . provisionally, anyway,' she went on, more carefully. 'Could you call me at lunchtime? I'll be here. I'm seeing private patients up to one-thirty.'

'You bet.' It might have been his imagination, but he

thought the line had picked up the background sound of ice being dropped into glasses.

'You sure I'm not disturbing you, ma'am?' Parry asked, as Winifred Edworth invited him into the end house in Raglan Avenue. 'It's very early, I'm afraid,' he added, wiping his shoes. 'You said you were an early riser, though, and I wanted to catch you before you went shopping or anything.'

He had already spurned a gnawing, unworthy impulse to drop by at Perdita's place in Tawrbach and innocently invite himself for breakfast. He had been too well aware that the reason behind the prompting had been anything but innocent, and that, thus, it would have been more shaming for him to have discovered that Dr Bates had not stayed the night, than it would have been hurtful to discover that he had.

It was now just on eight-fifteen – at the beginning of the last day when the detective chief inspector could count on keeping anything like all the personnel assigned to his present team. But at least all the initial, labour-intensive work had been covered on the case. The police man and woman hours involved since Sunday morning had been prodigious, but the information was now logged on computer and available for any number of instant, permutable cross-checks. It was his reading and rereading of the accumulated data in the small hours of the morning that had brought him to Winifred Edworth's door so early, convinced that she should have more to tell than she had provided so far.

Mrs Edworth straightened the collar of her red jumper and fingered the topaz jewel hanging from the thin gold chain. 'Not early for me, this isn't, Mr Parry. At my best early mornings. Always was,' she responded in a confidential voice, as though she had just shared a secret of some significance. After she closed the front door, her head inclined, her eyes narrowed and her mouth opened a fraction as she next gazed quizzically at the silver-coloured, cylindrical container she was holding in her hand. 'Now, what in the world . . . ?' she began, then the expression cleared as she flipped open the hinged lid. Inside was an opened packet of Typhoo Tips. 'I

192

was just going to make a pot of tea when you rang the bell,' she went on. 'I never bother with proper breakfast these days. You'd like a cup yourself, I'm sure, wouldn't you, Mr . . . Mr Parry?' She was leading the way now, but had hesitated in front of the closed sitting room door.

'That'd be very nice, thank you.'

'Right you are. Come into the kitchen, then,' she said with sudden decision, and moved off again in that direction.

'You remember I was here the other day, Mrs Edworth?'

'Yes, yes. With the other plainclothes policeman, wasn't it?'

'That was Detective Sergeant Lloyd, yes. He reminded you of your piano tuner.'

'Mr Felsted? Never. I remember Mr Lloyd. He's a big man. Mr Felsted's only little. Perhaps it was the voice? Or the eyes? You can never tell, really, why people remind you of other people, can you?'

'Quite true.' There were more important things on his mind than the relative sizes of Gomer Lloyd and Mrs Edworth's piano tuner.

'Sit down at the table, then, Mr Parry, while I make the tea. More questions, is it?'

'In a way, yes. But it's more your girlhood reminiscences I want to hear about, really.'

'Oh, I'm not sure they'll be fit to tell,' she responded skittishly, before she became embarrassed and confused by her own boldness, reddening a little, and putting an extra spoonful of tea in the pot by mistake.

'Now I'll bet that's not true, Mrs Edworth. I'm sure you've led a blameless life.'

'I'd like to think that, Mr Parry.' She paused, then added: 'And by today's standards, it's true enough, I'll grant you that.'

'You told me before that you knew Mervyn Davies when you were both teenagers.'

The sunken eyes narrowed again, but out of interest, not mistrust. 'Yes, I knew him then, but not all that well. And he was quite a few years younger than me. Three, I think. But he didn't always behave as if he was. Very forward, he was, in more ways than one.' Mrs Edworth's mouth tightened as she moved over to join Parry. She was carrying the teapot on a tray, with an extra cup, saucer and tea plate to match the single setting already laid on the table beside a milk jug, a slop basin and a sugar bowl. There was another, larger plate too, holding a selection of biscuits. Mrs Edworth observed formal table standards even when taking tea alone in her kitchen. 'Very forward, Mervyn was,' she repeated, as she sat down.

'Yes, I've been learning about other people's memories of him. They say the same.'

'Mark you, he had to stand up for himself. Wouldn't have had much chance otherwise, with no mother and father. And his old gran being a tippler, I'm sorry to say. He lived with her, of course, till she died. Explained a lot, that did.' She looked up from pouring the tea. 'Who else has been saying he was forward?'

'Mr Geoff Godwin, for one.'

'Ah, now he used to be jealous of Mervyn who was better-looking than he was. Mervyn had all the girls after him. Geoff didn't. Bit of a mother's boy. Help yourself to sugar, Mr . . . Mr Parry.'

'Thank you. But Geoff was a friend of Mervyn's, wasn't he?'

Mrs Edworth thought for a moment. 'I suppose so, yes. Not so close as Edwin, though.'

'Edwin Edworth, your brother-in-law?'

'Brother-in-law that was to be, yes. He and Mervyn were always together. Thick as thieves, too. Now there was a good-looking boy. Edwin, I mean. Like his brother Gwilym, my late husband. I've got a photo of them together here somewhere.' She pushed her chair back, got up and went to a deep drawer under a working-top near the door. 'In this album, I think it is,' she said, returning to the table with an old-fashioned photograph album, its blue silk cover worn at the corners. 'Yes, this is the one they're both on. In their late teens they would have been when this was taken.' She held the album open near the centre page and handed it to Parry. 'My late husband's the one on the left. The older one.'

194

The photograph was the only one on the page. It wasn't a casual snap, but a half-plate, posed studio portrait of two young men. 'Very like each other, weren't they?' Parry commented, while thinking to himself that Gwilym Edworth was almost the double of Derek Sewell. 'You're right, Mrs Edworth. They were both fine-looking young men.'

'Ran in the family, you see. There were strong family resemblances too,' the widow responded, and there seemed to be more thought behind the last remark than a passing comment would have rated.

'John Sewell. Was he a close friend of Mervyn's too?'

'No, no. Far from it. There was jealousy there, as well. Over Alice. John was crazy about her, but it wasn't mutual. Have a biscuit, Mr . . . er . . . They're fresh.'

'That would be Alice Morgan?'

'That's right. They were all after Alice. Geoff Godwin as well. Of course, he fancied Esme Sewell too, but it didn't get him anywhere. He fancied me, come to that, and that didn't get him anywhere either. What a sauce.' Mrs Edworth's tiny eyes seemed to cloud at the recollection, and her voice had softened. There was no self-conscious blush over what she had said this time either. It was almost as though she had been talking to herself.

For a woman of mature years who, at their earlier meeting, had shown distinct problems over recalling contemporary issues – as she was now with keeping Parry's own name in her mind – Mrs Edworth seemed able to recollect the events of forty years before with unusual facility.

Parry bit into the biscuit he had taken and found it anything but fresh. He thought that it had probably been stored with cakes – as his hostess's son would have confirmed. 'You mentioned to me before,' he said, 'when we were talking about Mervyn Davies, that he shouldn't have said the things he did. Can you tell me what you meant by that, exactly?'

Mrs Edworth gave a little grunt. 'He shouldn't have told my mother-in-law he was the father of Alice Morgan's unborn child.' She looked up, straight at Parry. 'He wasn't, d'you see?'

'And you know who the real father was?'

The widow's face was suddenly suffused with sadness. 'Oh, yes. I know all right.'

'And how did you know he said that to your mother-in-law?'

'Because she told me so, years later. And about Mervyn putting it in writing for Dan, her husband, for him to keep. He wanted that.' She looked hard at Parry. 'He paid Mervyn money for it.'

'A lot of money?'

'I don't know. But to Mervyn, anything would have been a lot. It got him to Australia, and that's what he'd wanted.' She took a biscuit from the plate. 'I don't believe he could have made a fortune from what my father-in-law gave him. Not from the way he was looking the other night. Perhaps he was extravagant at the start. Prodigal with his money, like the younger son in the Bible parable. St Luke's gospel, isn't it?'

'I think so, yes.' Parry smiled. 'Or could it have been that Mervyn was only paid just enough for his passage?' he commented. Trimble had suggested to him that Davies had arrived in the far country as a penniless immigrant.

'That's right, perhaps. Dan Edworth wasn't generous by nature,' Mrs Edworth vouchsafed in one of her musing asides, while absently dunking the biscuit in her tea.

'I believe Mr Edworth senior was a very respected member of the community?'

'Oh, he was respected all right. Town councillor for a long time. Pillar of the church, of course. Lay reader at St Luke's. And well off, with it. His building firm was the biggest in the town in those days.' She consumed some of the biscuit, then delicately touched the sides of her mouth with a newly laundered blue-bordered, white handkerchief.

Parry frowned. 'Would you say he bribed Mervyn Davies into confessing something he hadn't done?'

'Good as, yes,' she replied with no hesitation.

'But what did Alice, the girl, say?'

'She was too ashamed and frightened to say anything, I should think, except what her father told her to say. He was standing by her, d'you see? That was more than she expected. Times were different then from now, Mr . . . er . . .'

'But did Mervyn Davies need his passage paid for?' Parry asked. 'Wouldn't he have got a free ticket to Australia in those days? Under the immigration scheme?'

'Yes, but it would have meant waiting a bit. A year, my mother-in-law said. And they wanted to get him out of the country. Out of the way. Quick like.'

'Who were "they", Mrs Edworth, besides Dan Edworth?'

Mrs Edworth had her teacup halfway to her mouth. She held it there, in midair, until she had said: 'Edwin Edworth, and . . . Mr Sewell, Esme's father. Ianto his name was, come to think.'

'Edwin because he and Alice were friendly, and people had thought it was he who'd seduced her?'

'That's right. And fair dues, he'd been ready to say so, as well. That's before Mervyn confessed, like,' she put in promptly. 'It was to protect someone else, of course. My mother-in-law told me that as well. It wouldn't have been the truth, though, and it would have ruined Edwin. His father wanting him to be a clergyman and everything.'

'Edwin could have married Alice, couldn't he?'

She hesitated. 'No,' she answered slowly, 'he couldn't have done that. They were both too young for marriage, and it would have been . . . well . . . awkward, all said and done.'

Parry was ready enough to accept as much, now that the truth of the matter was becoming crystal clear. Even so, he wasn't ready yet to stem Mrs Edworth's account. 'And why was Ianto Sewell also involved in Mervyn being hurried out of the country?' he asked.

Mrs Edworth took two quick breaths. 'For the same reason Dan Edworth paid for the Morgan family to move to Llandovery. And bought them a cottage there. Of course, that made up for what had happened to Jacky as well.'

'Jacky? You mean Jacky Franklin, Alice's older sister?'

'That's right. Jacky Morgan as she was then. She'd been led away from the straight and narrow as well. Earlier that was, though, and her father had found out about it.'

'But she didn't have a baby too?'

'No, no. She was lucky. It's wrong to say luckier than she deserved, because it wasn't her fault in the first place, I suppose.' But Mrs Edworth didn't sound wholly convinced about her last comment.

'But it was the same man?'

'Oh yes, it was the same man all right.'

'I asked you about Ianto Sewell because wasn't it around this time that Dan Edworth gave him a job in the firm?' asked Parry.

'Yes.' She looked inquiringly at the policeman. 'But how did you come to know that, after all this long time?'

'Just routine police work, Mrs Edworth.'

'It was a well-paid job Ianto got too, even though he didn't have a proper trade, like bricklaying or carpentry.'

'The job was given him to compensate for something, was it? You said in the same way as the Morgans were paid to move to Llandovery?'

She breathed in and out, ponderously. 'That's right enough, but Ianto never knew it. Only Esme knew. It meant Ianto closed his mind to believing anything bad about Dan, of course.'

'But did Mervyn Davies ever admit to anyone that he was the father of Esme Sewell's child, as well as Alice's?'

'He didn't have to. Not after the rumour was spread saying he was the father. And people believed it. Before then, they'd thought it was Edwin was responsible, and for a bit he did nothing to stop them. Ianto Sewell believed it for one. Edwin did have a reputation with the girls, you see? But fair's fair, he never did anything to hurt any of them. Not that I know of.'

'So the rumour about Mervyn Davies was spread on purpose?'

'Oh, yes. I'm afraid so.'

'And once he'd left the country, it would have been hard to prove he wasn't the father of either child?' Parry didn't wait for an answer before adding: 'So Mervyn Davies took the blame for another man's indiscretions. But the other man wasn't his friend Edwin, was it, Mrs Edworth?'

'No, but they may have let Mervyn think it was. I'm not

sure on that.' She looked solemnly into the cup she had just emptied, as though she was reading her fortune in the tea leaves. 'It could have been Edwin. Like I said, for a bit, he was ready to take the blame in any case. My husband never gave him enough credit for that.' She lifted her gaze to stare at Parry. 'Mark you, Gwilym might have done the same himself, only he was never asked. Not that anyone would have believed he'd been seducing young girls. Especially not two at the same time. He wasn't like that. And anyway, we were engaged already.'

There was a simplicity and innocence in some of Mrs Edworth's reasonings that Parry found refreshingly disarming. 'And Mervyn didn't marry Esme Sewell,' he said, 'because apart from their also being too young, that might have been awkward as well. I mean in the circumstances, as you said just now?'

Mrs Edworth hesitated for a moment. 'Yes, if it meant Mervyn staying. Not going abroad. Nobody would have wanted that. In any case, Esme wouldn't have had Mervyn for a husband. She was more independent than Alice. Proper little madam. She might have given the game away early on, except she was given some money.'

'Like Mervyn Davies?'

'More, and spent it quicker, no doubt. She was good to her parents, though. Getting her father that job. They were very strict Baptists, I remember. Her mother pretended the baby was hers, of course, to save the disgrace.' She shook her head. 'You know both those girls died quite soon after all this? Alice committed suicide days after the baby was born, and Esme died of pneumonia in London, the winter after she delivered Derek.'

'So I understand. Tell me, Mrs Edworth, did the father of both children mend his ways after all this?'

'Oh, yes. It all scared him rigid. He knew he could have been prosecuted, even. But he was very contrite after. Stopped all his old lusting after young girls.'

'And Jacky Morgan was one of his earlier . . . conquests?'

'One of the first I knew of, yes. The girls respected him, d'you see, which meant they trusted him as well.'

'And it was he you meant when you told me Mervyn Davies's death was God's punishment?'

'Did I say that? Yes, well I didn't mean it quite like that. But Mervyn shouldn't have admitted what he did. It was a lie, d'you see? But God's punishment should have been on the real sinner.'

'You mean your father-in-law? It's Dan Edworth we've been talking about, isn't it?'

'My father-in-law, yes.' She had opened the photograph album at the same page as before, as though she was studying the image of the two brothers again, except, quite soon, her eyes made it plain her thoughts were on other things. 'I promised his wife I'd never tell anyone. But there it is. I prayed about it a lot yesterday. With Mervyn dying like that. I think it's only right you should know the truth about him. I'm glad you came back.' Her bosom heaved, and she let out a long sigh, as if a great weight had been lifted from her. Then she looked up, blinked several times, smiled at Parry, and drew her chair a little closer to the table. 'More tea, Mr . . . Mr . . .'

20

'We've got a SOCO team on the way, have we?' asked the waiting Parry, as Lloyd hurried to get into the Porsche beside him.

'Yes, boss. DS Wilcox has been organizing a new group for that. They'll probably be there before us. The GPR machine is on its way too. Sorry to keep you waiting.' The detective sergeant did up his seat belt more quickly than usual: it was a gesture indicating he was responding to Parry's mood. His apparent tardiness was because he'd been left a lot to do before he could leave the police station as briskly as his boss had done.

The chief inspector had been issuing orders rapidly, but without going into their purpose, since his arrival at the incident room ten minutes before this. Because Parry was normally a good communicator, Lloyd figured that he was too preoccupied with proving a hypothesis to want to start explaining it. That Parry was fired by something important was evident from his whole demeanour.

'And Mrs Edworth told you all that business was to protect Dan Edworth?' said Lloyd, as Parry steered the car to the right, out of the police station car park, away from the town, and up into the newly redeveloped end of Greenlow Street. The sergeant was referring to the only bit of fresh information Parry had vouchsafed to him so far, because, by the sound of it, it had offended his moral susceptibilities.

Parry didn't respond for some moments. 'Sorry, Gomer? Oh, yes. He was a sanctimonious lecher, that one. And greedy with it,' he replied eventually, his words even more clipped than usual. 'He'd put two young girls in the club at the same time. *Two*. He was a lay reader. Probably seduced the girls in the church vestry. Some bastards are hard to credit.'

'Ah, the pious ones are always the worst.' Lloyd smacked his lips loudly, adopted a holier than thou expression, then indulged his own prevailing weakness by running his tongue familiarly around a fresh peppermint.

'I wonder how many other families he had to square in his time?' Parry speculated. 'Incredible he's never been given away till now.'

'Yes, but that sort aren't. Or weren't in those days, boss. Girls who had sex with respectable, older married men couldn't very well tell anybody. In case no one believed them. And if they got pregnant, the men made sure they still didn't tell, one way or another. Illegal abortions, for instance. They were commoner than people remember, and twice as dangerous. Took a lot of money, too.'

'Yes, but our godly Dan Edworth didn't hold with abortions. For religious reasons, probably,' Parry commented drily. 'He bought his way free, all the same.'

Lloyd was bending his substantial trunk forwards as he tried to knot a broken shoelace while strapped into a moving car, and without being able to see his foot. 'He must have had a strong hold over Edwin, though,' he grunted, getting short of breath from the effort, and with his chin now resting on the dashboard shelf. 'That's if the boy really was ready to take on a paternity rap for his father.'

'Edwin was genuinely devoted to his father, weaknesses and all,' said Parry with conviction. 'Anyway, he never had to take any rap. Mervyn Davies took it on for him. In return for not much more than his passage money to Australia.'

'With no inconvenience to Edwin, and Dan Edworth left with his reputation still intact,' Lloyd observed. 'I suppose all he had to do on top of that, in the case of Alice Morgan, was buy her family a house miles away from here. Expensive, again, but worth it for him.'

'Different with Esme Sewell, though,' Parry put in. 'She had a mind of her own. Dan Edworth must have paid her never to say who fathered her child. He also gave a job to

202

her unskilled, unemployed father, with Esme, not her father, knowing why.'

'There's a touch of old-fashioned melodrama in that one, isn't there?' said Lloyd, a romantic at heart.

'Case of a wronged daughter suffering her father's wrath, you mean?'

'And dying without him ever knowing her silence was for his benefit? *Duw, Duw,*' the sergeant lamented, in his dungeon bass. Two of his five children were girls. 'And do you think Mr Davies knew it was Dan Edworth he was really protecting, boss, not his mate Edwin?'

The car had been stopped by the traffic lights at the top of the road. 'Yes, Davies knew all right,' Parry answered, still clipping his phrases. 'The two boys were such close friends. They'd have confided everything to each other. Especially anything involving sex.'

'So if young Edwin had been sleeping with those girls —'

'Which he very probably had been, but without knowing at the time there was no chance of his making them pregnant.'

'Yes, yes. But if he had been sleeping with them, you're saying Mervyn Davies would have known about it, for sure?'

'I'm certain he would.' Parry squinted through the rain-spattered windscreen. 'It's straight across here, is it?'

'That's right. Then under the railway bridge. Nasty, this rain.'

The sky had been blue and cloudless an hour before when the chief inspector had called on Mrs Edworth. Now it was a cheerless grey, with the falling rain becoming heavier by the minute.

The upper end of Greenlow Street was a dismal, lifeless area at the best of times. Once a property developer's paradise, the four-storey office blocks built two years before, on both sides of the road, had remained obdurately unlet. Sombre, neglected concrete elevations were now showing ugly weather streaks of black. The unfinished, starkly pillared ground floors, intended for shops, were rubbish strewn and more forlorn even than the empty areas deteriorating above them.

'I can remember when this was all allotments too,' remarked Lloyd lightly, because he could see Parry was getting irritated with the wait. 'Not that long ago, either. When they built the new police station,' he added, wiggling his foot to make sure the knot in his shoelace was holding, and glancing from side to side of the still stationary car.

'Allotments probably made more money for the landlords than empty buildings, as well,' Parry observed cynically.

'For British Rail it would have been, boss. They owned the land this side of the bridge. The site we're going to on the other side belongs to Pontyglas District Council. The gate's just after the bridge on the left.'

'If we turned right here now, is the alley that runs down the side of the Coach and Horses the first or the second turning to the right?' Parry snapped suddenly.

'The third, boss.' Lloyd knew the area a lot better than his chief. Still studying the empty buildings, he added: 'My grandfather worked on the railways. He had an allotment. Didn't have to pay rent for it, either.'

'Because the wily old railway barons and mine owners were glad to give strips of useless land to their workers. To grow food. To satisfy a primeval need. Good for industrial relations, that was. Only because the workers didn't know any better. These lights are bloody slow.' The lights changed as Parry spoke, and just after a police Ford Transit twelve-seater, coming from the right, had turned across the traffic at the crossroads in front of them. Parry moved the car off and followed the Transit under the railway bridge.

Beyond the bridge, the area was rural. To the right, there were cows at pasture. On the left, a six-acre field had been divided into allotments, each measuring a hundred feet by twenty-five feet, each having its own tool shed, and narrow boundary paths, and with communal water taps and butts at reasonable distances. The tool sheds, provided by the tenants, were anything but uniform in appearance, and most of them looked fairly ramshackle.

'It's local councils that mostly let land for allotments now, of course,' Lloyd commented.

'Yes. As a senior council employee, I suppose Geoff Godwin

had the pick of the ones here,' said Parry as, still following the Transit, they drove into the field through the open, tubular metal gateway. The hard-core path they now joined, just wide enough for a car, ran alongside the fence, which followed the foot of the railway embankment.

'That's more than likely, boss,' Lloyd agreed. 'The patch he used to rent is the last one along this side. It's away from the road, and the vandals, but it's handy for this car track round the field. If your allotment's in the centre, you have to hump everything to and from, like.'

Parry was moving the Porsche in low gear to the far corner of the uneven way where the Transit had already stopped. 'But this is a wilderness,' he said, as they drew up beside what had been identified as Godwin's patch.

'That's right, boss. Mostly rhubarb, cabbage and potatoes, all gone to seed,' commented Lloyd the gardener, with perfect accuracy. 'When it was checked Sunday, they reckoned nothing had been touched on it since last year.'

'Looks like it. And no new tenant, yet,' said Parry absently, because he was thinking about something else, as they both got out of the car.

'Like I said, people can't be bothered to grow their own stuff these days.' Lloyd narrowed his eyes against the driving rain and pulled up the collar of his rain jacket. He nodded across the overgrown patch in front of them. 'That's one of Mr Sewell's allotments next along. He rents two. The other's next door to that again. Neat, they are, both of them.'

'That's allowed, is it? To rent more than one?'

'If there's not much demand, it is. We checked the freshly dug bits of Mr Sewell's plots yesterday. Where he'd been picking winter veg, and preparing for his spring seeding. Nothing suspicious seen or found.'

'And you saw inside his tool sheds?'

'Tool shed. He's only got the one. The other fell down, he said. The one that's left has seen better days, too. But it's weather proof all the same. He's been a handyman by trade since he gave up being a miner.'

'And this one is the shed Godwin still owns?' said Parry, moving forward, his step as purposeful as his words.

'Morning, everybody. Sorry about the weather. Hope I haven't got you here on a wild goose chase.' He pulled the tweed cap he had put on further down his forehead, after acknowledging the six men in white SOCO gear who were getting out of the Transit. The two vehicles had been parked on the outside verge of the track where it cornered to the right.

'This shed's miles better for the job than the rest here, sir. More practical, as well. Kept an allotment myself once,' volunteered Alf Vaughan, the first of the detective constables to join Parry and Lloyd. He was fortyish, with a tanned, open-air sort of countenance, and he seemed to be enjoying the rain.

Parry continued to examine the oblong, cedar structure set at the corner of the allotment. Two sides of it backed nearly up to the track. It was ten feet long by six wide, with a high-pitched roof, and padlocked double doors in the narrow side facing on to the track. It stood on a base of two-foot square, concrete paving stones, some of them lifting slightly at the joins where weeds had begun to thrust through.

'Hm, the shed itself looks like something out of *House. and Garden*,' the chief inspector commented. 'Why has Godwin never taken it away?'

'A leaving tenant usually looks to sell on his shed to who-ever comes after, sir,' offered DC Vaughan. 'This one's pretty secure, as well as right for the job. The window's even got bars on. We noticed that Sunday. As near vandal proof as you'll get.'

Parry moved round to look at the single window in the other short side of the structure. 'There's a closed curtain as well,' he remarked. 'Did you notice that on Sunday?'

'Yes, sir. Anti-vandal, that is, again. We opened it, but I remember Mr Godwin closed it again before he locked up.'

'The report says he was here with you when you inspected the shed. The whole time, was it?'

'That's right, sir. He brought the key up. As soon as we'd checked inside, he locked up and we all left. We'd gone over his old allotment before he arrived.'

'You haven't got a key to the shed now?'

There was a brief silence as Vaughan looked to Lloyd.

'No, boss. I told SOCO not to trouble Mr Godwin again, just for the moment,' said the sergeant pointedly.

Parry nodded. 'And when you were here yesterday, nobody looked inside this shed again?'

'No, sir. Yesterday we were concentrating on Mr Sewell's two allotments next door,' said DS Wilcox who had just come from the Transit. He was dressed, like the others, in fresh white coveralls, gloves and overshoes and, like the others, he was pulling on the hood.

'Sewell was present all the time you were here yesterday?' Parry asked, while his eyes were searching the area from the shed doors across to the far side of the car track.

'That's right, sir.'

'And he was here on Sunday too?'

'Mr Sewell was working on his allotments both days, sir,' Vaughan volunteered unexpectedly. 'Sunday's the most popular day for allotment holders, of course.'

'Except we didn't know till later on Sunday that Mr Sewell was anyone connected with the case, sir,' Wilcox explained, as puzzled as the others to know why the chief inspector was so concerned literally with going over old and, from the police viewpoint, infertile ground.

Parry's eyebrows had risen a touch at the last statement. 'And nobody spoke to Sewell here on Sunday, of course? I see,' he went on without waiting for an answer. 'So have we got something that'll deal with this padlock?'

'In the van, sir,' said Vaughan, who disappeared for a moment, then returned, carrying a pair of heavy metal cutters.

'OK. I think we can run to a replacement padlock if we have to. Get this one off, and put it in an evidence bag.'

The cutters went through the thick steel arm of the padlock at the first attempt. When the doors of the shed were swung open, the air that wafted out carried a pungent, clinging smell of turned earth and human sweat.

Nine square paving stones, similar to those around the outside of the structure, were stacked upright against one another at the far end. It was fairly evident that they had earlier formed part of the inside floor. They were now standing on a line of three undisturbed, matching stones which spanned the width of the rear wall, and looking as though they had been doing so for years. Leaning against the stacked stones was a pick, a heavy shovel, a long narrow steel surface grader with a spirit level set into the centre, and two big electric torches. Next to these was a ball of twine with toggles stuck into it, a trowel, a board that had been used for mixing mortar, a dented metal bucket, and two open bags of sand and cement. Three more paving stones, making a total of fifteen, had been recently repositioned, their edges newly cemented against the three that had remained in situ, with more fresh cement under the exposed corners of the relaid stones. The rest of the earthen floor had been compounded, levelled, and sanded, ready to take the remaining stones.

'And it wasn't like this on Sunday?' Parry asked, knowing what the answer would be.

'Nothing like it, sir,' the astonished DC Vaughan replied. 'It was just an empty shed, with the floor paving intact.'

'So this is it. Must be,' said Parry quietly.

'Nice going, boss,' said Lloyd, wiping water off his forehead. 'Neat job of work, isn't it? Nothing slipshod, or done in haste. Wish my garden patio was as well laid.' He was pulling his radio from his pocket. 'D'you want the full team up now?'

'Yes.' Parry turned to Wilcox. 'Tape off the area and tent over the shed before anyone goes in. You got a photographer in this group?'

'Yes, sir. And the fingerprinter can be here in five minutes.'

'Right. Don't think we'll bother with the ground radar machine.' For some moments after Wilcox had left him, and while Lloyd was finishing giving orders over his radio, the chief inspector went on studying the shed interior. The rain, still falling without let up, was doing nothing to dampen his elation. Eventually, he turned to Lloyd. 'He must have done all the heavy work since Sunday evening after dark. Probably stayed here most of the night. Same last night, I expect. Must have been a tight operation inside here, with a body and the doors shut. There's not a sign of what's gone on from the outside.'

'Another hour or two, and his secret could have been safe for years,' Lloyd responded. 'For ever, perhaps. So what about him? D'you want him brought in now, boss?'

Parry shook his head. 'Not yet. We know where he is. He'll keep there for a bit. I'd like to be sure of what we've got.'

Except he was fairly sure already.

'Four foot under. That's a tidy depth for an amateur grave-digger,' short, thickset, weather-beaten Dr Maltravers remarked cheerfully. The sixty-year-old police surgeon had arrived in his mud-caked Range Rover only minutes after Mervyn Davies's fully clothed remains had been exhumed from his unorthodox resting place.

'Deeper than we expected, Doctor,' said Lloyd. 'We think his killer may have been worried about the floor subsiding after the body decayed.'

'Hm. Knows about such things, does he? A thinking man's assassin?'

'An experienced digger, at least, sir.'

'Ah.' The horny-handed Maltravers was delicately brushing earth off his dilapidated Barbour jacket, as though the tattered garment was new and previously unblemished. 'Well, there's not much decay, yet. Torso's beginning to niff a bit, of course, and you don't need me to tell you it's been dead about three days. And that it's headless and handless. Clean bit of dissection, in the circumstances. Done with a machete, not an axe, you think?' He paused. 'Well, the neck was severed from the rear probably, with a back-handed swipe from a left hander.' He pursed his lips. 'Or it just could have been at an angle from the front, by a right hander. Difficult to tell without a longer examination. Did the forensic pathologist tell you anything helpful about the head?'

'It was Dr Ironmonger, sir. He told us more or less what you've just said.'

'Ah.' The doctor plunged a hand into a side pocket of his waxed jacket, from which a broken zip was hanging loose, and pulled out a stubby pipe with some difficulty. 'It's this

Davies bloke who was in the paper yesterday, of course,' he added. 'Did Ironmonger hazard a time of death from just the head and the hand?'

'Roughly between eleven-thirty Saturday night and two o'clock Sunday morning, sir,' Lloyd provided.

'Well, he'd know better than me. All I can tell you is he wasn't killed here, but I expect you knew that already.' Maltravers blew violently into the pipe, scattering bits of old tobacco in all directions. 'Sorry about that.'

'That's all right, Doctor, we're out of the protected zone here,' Parry countered with a smile. They were inside the recently arrived long, black police incident van that was drawn up across the waterlogged car track some yards back from the tool shed. Half a dozen more vehicles were now parked along the increasingly muddy outside verge, humped there at various angles. The shed itself, and its immediate surroundings, were completely shrouded under orange-coloured, plastic tenting. The full investigating team had been busy inside for nearly an hour.

'If Ironmonger isn't planning to come out here, and I wouldn't blame him if he isn't,' said Maltravers, looking at the rain outside, 'so far as I'm concerned, you can ship off the corpse to him when you like. That goes for the coroner's officer as well, I gathered from him just now. Afraid I can't complete the paperwork till the head's been officially matched to the rest of the body.'

'Thanks, Doctor. We've got what we most needed from his pockets.'

'Oh, what was that?'

'These.' Parry picked up two transparent evidence bags from the collapsible shelf behind him. One contained a white envelope with a broken wax seal, the other an opened-out, single-page letter, roughly typed on a piece of white, A4 stationery with the Condleston Lodge address printed on it in blue.

'Does that give you the name of your murderer?'

'Not exactly, Doctor. But if the killer had read this first, which I don't believe he could have done, he might have spared the victim, and himself a long term in jug.'

'Is that so? May I see?'
Parry handed the letter to Maltravers. It read:

Dear Mervyn,
By now you will know I have left you as good as all my
fortune. I believe this is no more than your just reward
for falsely confessing, in that letter to my father, that it
was you who was responsible for the pregnancies of the
two choir girls, Alice Morgan and Esme Sewell. Oddly
enough, I don't believe the letter was shown to anyone
afterwards. The fact that it existed, and that my father
made it known it existed, was enough to kill the rumours
about me that were rife just before you left the country.
You and I know that it was my father who had
seduced the girls. If that had come out, he would almost
certainly have gone to prison, since I am pretty sure they
were both under age at the time of their conceptions. In
any case, his reputation would have been ruined, along
with the fortunes of every member of the family. As it
was, we all survived, thanks to you. Although he had
not been willing to let me take the blame for what he
had done, he had no misgivings about allowing you to.
For my part in letting that happen, I am deeply
ashamed and anxious to make amends to you.
Although my father felt that paying you the pittance
of your fare to Australia was enough compensation for
what you did, I never took that view. I am sorry that
in the nine years since his death I have made no real
effort to trace you till now, despite a long-held intention.
I did have an idea of coming out to Australia and
surprising you, but that won't happen now. I have been
finally driven to take action because my own death is not
far off. I hope very much that you will have enough
years left to enjoy the money you will inherit.
My father gave me your original letter just before he
died. I burned it the next day. So if you come to Pontyglas,
there is no longer any proof that you said you were the
father of those children, both boys, and both of whom
have survived. Their names are Derek Sewell and Owen

211

Franklin. If it came to it, I imagine a blood test would prove you were not the father of either of them. If it didn't, this letter will. Even so, I suppose I would be happier if you never had to tell anyone who the real father was. I would like to think he kept his promise to my mother, and never interfered with another young girl after the fright and threatened ruination of all of us those two pregnancies represented.

I am sorry we were not able to meet again, but glad that we talked on the phone.

Your grateful friend,
Edwin Edworth

21

'You see, contrary to what you told us before, we believe you drove from your house to Condleston Lodge last Saturday night, about eleven-thirty,' said Parry, slowly for him, to emphasize the importance of the statement. 'You were driving a Ford Escort, the one your nephew, Derek, hired a week before from Hertz. We know he left the car keys with you when he went to bed. Otherwise you couldn't have brought the car round from the lane before he was up again next day. I believe you told him you might have to move it, if it was found to be blocking other vehicles in the lane.'

There was no verbal response from John Sewell, only a deepening of the sullen, diffident expression he had adopted from the start. The weedy man's hollow eyes were focused on his heavily veined hands which he was clasping tightly. He was seated opposite Parry and Lloyd, across a black-topped table in a windowless interview room in the basement of Pontyglas Police Station. Behind the two detectives, a uniformed constable was standing at the closed door of the room. A tape machine, recording the proceedings, was on the side table beside Lloyd.

Sewell had earlier been brought to the station for questioning from his home, after he had returned there in his van for lunch. He was still in faded blue overalls. He had spent the morning doing a carpentry job at a shoe store in the town. Advised of his legal rights, he had so far declined the services of a solicitor, saying, sourly, that he didn't trust lawyers. This had been the only statement he had made extending to more than a curt 'yes' or 'no'. More often he was making no response at all to anything said to him.

'We believe you waited in the drive of Condleston Lodge for Mervyn Davies to get home,' the chief inspector went on. 'And when he arrived in the drive, you attacked him with a machete from behind, severing his head from his body.'

When Sewell failed again to show any reaction, it was Lloyd who put in. 'Do you want to tell us why you took the machete with you in the first place, Mr Sewell? Was it to threaten Mr Davies with?' There was no response to this either, so the sergeant put another question. 'Did Mr Davies provoke you in some way. Did the two of you have an argument, like?'

Sewell raised his eyes to look at the speaker. While he still didn't utter a word, his expression had changed momentarily, showing now more despair than hostility. It seemed, at least, that Lloyd might have come close to a truth.

'Do you want to tell us about the argument?' the sergeant pressed.

There was another long silence, then Parry said: 'All right. Afterwards, still in the drive of Condleston Lodge, we believe you cut both the hands off Mr Davies's dead body. You put the head in one shopping bag, and the left hand and the machete in another. The right hand you put in a smaller, polythene bag which you posted next day in a padded envelope to your nephew. You acquired that envelope at the church supper, didn't you?' He waited for an answer, and when, as expected, one wasn't forthcoming, he added: 'It wasn't the one Derek addressed for the rector's wife, because that's still at the rectory. It was an extra one that you addressed later to Derek, using one of the labels he'd given you. That's why we found only his thumbprint on the label, but none of his fingerprints on the rest of the envelope. Was that why you took the extra one? One that Derek couldn't have touched. One you picked up when you were wearing your gloves?'

Lloyd leaned forward. 'Why did you take the envelope, Mr Sewell? It's important you tell us. You see, as things stand, it looks as though you knew you'd need an envelope for posting the hand before you left the supper. It makes

214

what you did later look premeditated. Intentional. I mean, your attacking Mr Davies. Do you understand?'

This time there was only the merest acknowledging look from Sewell to Lloyd, though this again was more than Sewell had so far offered to Parry.

'Next you wrapped the torso in a dust sheet,' Parry went on, believing, as he had from near the beginning of the interview, that the way to break Sewell was to let him understand the extent and detail of the police case against him. 'You'd left a dust sheet in the car earlier in the day. Derek mentioned to me it had some gold and purple paint on it. The one Mr Davies was wrapped in is the same. Funny combination, gold and purple.'

'It is, isn't it, Mr Sewell?' Lloyd took up the point. 'Not colours you'd expect to use much when you're decorating houses. You might if you were doing up a church, of course. Like the Lady Chapel of St Aloysius in Gwyn Street. We checked with all the churches this morning. Seems you did some painting there after Christmas. Father O'Conner said you did a very thorough job, too, and reasonably priced.' The sergeant put a peppermint into his mouth, then, as an afterthought, offered the tube to Sewell who ignored the gesture as firmly as he had the last comments.

At this point there was a knock on the door. A pert young WPC then appeared with a fax in her hand which she delivered to Parry. He read it and passed it to Lloyd, after giving the girl a cheerful nod which she returned twofold, before leaving.

'When you were finished at Condleston Lodge, you drove to the allotments,' said the chief inspector, 'and left the torso in your tool shed for the time being. But that wasn't where you intended burying it, was it? By that time you probably had Geoff Godwin's shed in mind for that. Only you didn't take the body there right away. Perhaps there wouldn't have been time to start an operation of that size on Saturday night. Not with Derek leaving at five in the morning. Or did you delay the job because you'd seen Davies and Godwin leave the church supper together, and figured Godwin was bound to be investigated? That's if he was the last person to be with

Davies before he died? You'd have been right about that too. But you were certain Godwin's shed was safe enough after you watched the police go over it on Sunday. Reckoned we'd never go back there, I expect. Lucky for you we didn't ask to see the inside of your shed till yesterday, wasn't it? But you had to take a calculated risk with that. It came off too.'

Sewell's jaw muscles hardened, inflating the skin around his mouth.

'We had to cut open the padlock on the door of Mr Godwin's shed to get in, same as you did on Sunday night, I expect,' said Lloyd, putting the fax on the table in front of him. 'The key we borrowed again today from Mr Godwin, before lunch, didn't fit. The one we found just now under a flower pot in your own shed did, though. Pity we'd already bust the new padlock you'd put on by then.'

Sewell reached into a top pocket of his overalls and took out his black plastic tobacco pouch and a packet of cigarette papers. Slowly, he began rolling a cigarette, holding the paper in his right hand, and spreading the tobacco expertly with his left. He still said nothing, but was intently regarding his own actions as Parry went on.

'When you left the allotments Saturday night, or rather early Sunday morning, you stopped near the top of the lane behind the Coach and Horses, and walked down to the pub yard, so as not to wake the Franklins. Mrs Franklin didn't hear you in the yard, but she did hear the car when you came down the lane in it later without stopping. That was after you'd put the hand and the machete in the pannier of Owen Franklin's motorbike. Did you originally intend to leave the head at the back door of the pub?' The chief inspector paused long enough for Sewell to reply. When he didn't, but only placed the newly rolled cigarette on the table in front of him, the speaker continued. 'Since Ken Franklin's car was left open, it was more appropriate to leave the head there, of course, especially since the Tesco bag in the car already was identical to the one you had the head in. We wondered what you did with that ham.'

'That's till we found it this morning,' said Lloyd, 'buried with Mr Davies's body. It was a tidy size, that ham. Pity to waste it. Worth a bit, too. Were you going to keep it, Mr Sewell? Then thought better of it?'

Parry leaned back in his chair. Both policemen were beginning to despair of ever getting a verbal response. 'We were also puzzled to know why you did what you did with Davies's hands,' he said. 'We understood why you left the head at the Coach and Horses – to get us thinking Ken Franklin had done the killing. But the hands?' He shrugged his shoulders. 'Then we figured you saw them as proof of vengeance to the two sons you believed Davies had deserted. Your sister, Esme's child, and the child of your girlfriend, Alice Morgan, the one you've believed, for all those years, had preferred Davies to you as a serious boyfriend. Serious enough to have gone to bed with.'

For the last minute, Sewell had been fixing Parry with a look of mounting hatred. His breathing was becoming increasingly noisy, as well as painfully wheezy. Now, without warning, he leaped to his feet, knocking the chair over behind him. 'I won't listen to no more bloody lies!' he shouted, his arms rigid at his sides, fists clenching and unclenching. 'It's all lies. Lies.'

'You'll listen for as long as we want you to listen, Mr Sewell,' Parry answered back instantly, in an uncharacteristic, stentorian tone, as the constable on the door moved forward ready to restrain Sewell. 'So sit down again, please,' Parry continued firmly, but less loudly. 'Constable, pick up Mr Sewell's chair for him, will you?' He held his detainee's gaze until the red-faced figure dropped his eyes and, with every appearance of unwillingness, lowered himself into the chair.

'The other thing we found in that grave, Mr Sewell, was a pair of canvas gloves,' said Lloyd, as though nothing untoward had happened. 'Caked with blood, they were. Suppose you thought it was better to get rid of them that way. I'm afraid the gloves will be enough to convict you, all by themselves, that's once we've got the DNA test results back. The shirt and the trousers you were wearing Saturday night had blood on them too, didn't they? But it was too expensive to get rid of them in the same way as the gloves. So you' –

he paused – 'well, you or somebody, washed the shirt and sponged the trousers. We took both of them from your house before you got home today. Your wife picked them out for us, and two other people who were at the supper have identified the trousers as belonging to the suit you were wearing.' He tapped the note on the table in front of him. 'Our forensic people are working on the shirt still, and the gloves, of course. But we've just heard the trousers have heavy traces of Mr Davies's blood on them. So if you didn't kill him, how does it happen you've got so much of his blood on your clothing?'

With his bent elbows resting on his knees, Sewell covered his sweating face with his hands, but he made no response.

Parry leaned forward over the table. 'Since you must have been out of the house for several hours on Saturday, when you were supposed to be in bed,' he said, 'we have to assume your wife knew you were out. Did she know what you were doing? Did she see you when you came back, with blood on your clothes? Was it she who washed and sponged them? You know that could make her an accomplice to murder?'

His head still down, Sewell's hands moved to knead the back of his neck, but he still remained silent.

'Of course, it's possible you told your wife you were just going to put the sheet over the Escort, and that er . . . well, she fell asleep waiting for you to come back,' Lloyd offered. 'That way you could have done the washing and sponging yourself, and she wouldn't have known the time when you got back. Is that what happened?'

Sewell lifted his head slowly and looked at the sergeant. It was the same nearly supplicant expression he had focused on him earlier. His lips seemed to move for a moment, then stopped without his uttering audible words.

'Of course, we think it more likely that your nephew Derek was your real accomplice,' said Parry, and noting the look of heightened concern that immediately suffused Sewell's face. 'He must have hated Davies as much as you did. More, perhaps, for deserting him and your sister. Did you and he decide to kill him out of revenge? It was a fairly big job for one man, after all, even a tough ex-miner like you. Easier if it had been the pair of you, perhaps.'

'Or did Derek do the job on his own?' Lloyd put in. 'It was his car that was involved, we know that. By the way, we've recovered the car from Hertz. It hadn't been hired out again since Derek brought it back Sunday morning. It hadn't been cleaned either. Lucky for us, it had gone straight to the workshop for brake work. Unlucky for you though, and Derek, perhaps. We haven't got the full report on it yet, but a first examination showed bloodstains on the carpet in the boot. It's a black carpet. Did you hope they'd never be noticed?'

Parry cleared his throat. 'Or is it Derek who's been doing the hoping?' he asked. 'We'll know soon if the blood is Mr Davies's. I expect it will be, don't you?'

Sewell was sitting up again, his dark eyes darting from side to side. For the first time, his expression seemed to be mirroring the alarm in his mind.

'Derek's fingerprints are all over the car, Mr Sewell,' said Lloyd in a concerned voice. 'Of course, they would be, in the circumstances, like. He'd been using it all week, hadn't he? Except, that's something a jury might not make enough allowance for, on top of his thumbprint being on that old envelope.' He shook his head. 'We all know there's an innocent explanation for that, of course. On the other hand, you've got to worry about what a prosecuting counsel will make of it. In the end it might be very awkward for Derek.'

'Was it the envelope Derek rang you about last night, Mr Sewell? From Germany?' Parry asked quickly, as soon as Lloyd stopped speaking. 'Oh, we know about the call. We've got the numbers of all calls made to and from your home since yesterday. Was Derek warning you? Or trying to find out where we've got in the investigation? He's very vulnerable, of course. Even being on the fringe of a murder case would be bad for his military career. His next vital promotion. And if it turns out he was in any way involved with you in committing this crime, well, that'd be the end of him in the army, wouldn't it?'

Sewell moved back in his chair after reaching out first for the cigarette that was still lying on the table. Then for some moments he studied the cigarette, smoothing the paper around it. No one else spoke until eventually he looked up and said: 'It had nothing to do with Derek.' The words came slowly and woodenly, but, this time, with no high emotion in his voice. 'I wouldn't have let Derek near a punch-up even with Mervyn Davies, let alone anything serious. And Iris wasn't part of it, neither,' he went on. 'She was asleep before I went out, like you said. Derek was as well. He never heard me go or come back. Neither of them did. Derek rang yesterday to tell me about getting the hand in the post. He didn't understand nothing about it. Only he was worried for me.' His fingers were still caressing the wrinkled cigarette. 'I did it all. Putting down Mervyn Davies. Taking his life because he took the lives of others. Alice Morgan and our Esme. And I'd kill him again, too. I hated him. Hated him for forty years. Longer. And him getting all that money, too. Blood money, it was. I always said I'd do for him given the chance.' He paused, and then gave a slow sigh. 'Perhaps I didn't always mean it. And I never planned on killing him Saturday. Not the way you said. About taking the envelope for the hand, and that. It was on the floor when we were leaving the supper. I picked it up. Put it in my pocket. Finders keepers, like. Come in useful after, that's all. It was only later when Derek told me our Esme ended up on the streets.' He swallowed awkwardly. 'I never knew that before, see? If I had I'd have gone to bloody Australia to kill him. All I wanted when I went there Saturday was to do for the bastard. And I made sure after the two he'd harmed the most knew about it. The most besides me and the two girls, that is. And there wasn't no argument with him neither. I never spoke to him. Just cut the bugger's head off. I made up my mind on that in the car going.' His defiant gaze, matching his words, came up and held Parry's for several seconds, then his head dropped, not in shame, but because he was vainly searching in his pockets for matches.

'Got a light, Constable?' Parry asked the uniformed policeman behind him, but without taking his eyes off Sewell. Then, when the cigarette had been lit, he added, 'Right, Mr Sewell, before you say anything else, I'm insisting, in your own interests, that a solicitor should be present. While that's being organized, we'll have what you've just said typed out ready for you to go over.'

Gomer Lloyd settled himself more comfortably in the front of the Porsche. 'Soon as it was clear we were going to involve the nephew,' he said, 'you could see Sewell was going to cave in, boss.'

It was just after nine that evening. John Sewell had been formally arrested, had signed a statement in the presence of the solicitor now acting for him, and was due to appear before the local magistrates next morning. All the required support-ing evidence and paperwork on the case had either been produced or was in train. A brief news conference had been held, and the chief inspector and the sergeant had just left a modest celebration party in the already half-dismantled incident room at Pontyglas Police Station.

Parry gave a half smile as he started the engine. 'Sewell didn't exactly rush to clear his wife of blame the first chance he had, not like he did when exonerating his nephew,' he commented drily.

'But you reckon she really was asleep, boss?'

'Since her doctor makes her take two sleeping pills before she goes to bed, every night, as well as the analgesics for the pain she gets, I reckon that's a reasonable supposition, yes. In fairness, I think probably he'd have cleared her when we finally cornered him. That's even if we hadn't tried to involve Derek Sewell, who he obviously idolizes.'

Lloyd nodded with enthusiasm. It had already been agreed with the DPP's office that no charges were to be laid against the wheelchaired Iris Sewell, nor against Warrant Officer Sewell.

Parry moved the car off down Greenlow Street, and left into Pentre Street. He was heading for his Cardiff flat, drop-ping Lloyd on the way, at his home in Penymaes village.

'No question he'd have done anything to save his nephew, or even just to stop his name being tarnished,' said the ser-geant. 'Not that it needed to be. Not after Sewell said what he did. Terrible thing, an obsession of that weight. Could drive you mad. Like it did him, really.'

'And in this instance without any valid foundation,' Parry observed.

'But Sewell wasn't to know that, was he, boss?'

'Hm, he might have figured Davies wasn't the father of his nephew, or of Owen Franklin, just by looking at them both. There's no resemblance there at all to Davies. Others might have come to the same conclusion in the same way.'

'You mean Ken Franklin, boss? But he blinded himself with what he thought were the facts. That Mr Davies had admitted he was the father before he left for Australia.'

'I suppose so. Those two look a bit like each other, and Owen Franklin in particular looks very like the young Gwilym Edworth. The resemblance was really very marked. Winifred Edworth showed me a photo of him this morning. Taken with Edwin when they were both in their teens.'

'Well, we know now all four men had the same father, of course,' Lloyd put in. 'But then John Sewell also believed Mr Davies's phony confession to Dan Edworth. He wouldn't have been looking for likenesses.' He offered Parry a peppermint, which was refused, before he put one in his own mouth. 'Funny, with so much of Edwin's money at stake, in the end the motive for Mr Davies's murder was just revenge,' he said. 'Even if John Sewell had got away with it, he didn't stand to gain a thing except satisfaction.' He turned to look at Parry. 'Anyway, it was a nice bit of deduction, you knowing it had to be him.'

The chief inspector shook his head. 'It's Winifred we have to thank. For deciding to unburden when she did. It was pretty clear from what she told me that Sewell had a unique reason for hating Davies. But even Winifred never knew Esme Sewell had ended up as a prostitute. That's what made him homicidal, of course. Derek telling him.'

'Pity he didn't even know Derek stands a chance of inheriting part of Edwin's estate, boss.'

Parry frowned. 'Because he and Owen Franklin are both natural half brothers to Edwin? But they're not half brothers of the whole blood, as Trimble would say,' he corrected. 'The

222

other doesn't confer legal rights. Well, not automatically, anyway.'

Lloyd moved the seat belt again over his large middle, made larger through the recent ingestion of three Marks & Spencer Scotch eggs, two sausage rolls, a chicken pasty, and four miniature pork pies. 'But you reckon Derek Sewell and Owen Franklin will apply to the court for a share of Edwin's money?' he asked.

'Possibly. In the case of the hard-up Owen Franklin, pretty certainly. That's if he can raise the money for the legal fees. On the other hand, it's a big enough inheritance for Charles and Gail Edworth to agree some sort of settlement out of court if they choose.'

'Otherwise, they'll get the lot between them, boss?'

'Under the intestacy rules, yes. Unless Davies's sons in Australia try to prove that survival clause in Edwin's will really is invalid. If they do, a settlement could be held up for years while the lawyers do battle.'

'And get fat on the proceeds. Glad I'm not a contender for great riches,' said Gomer Lloyd, sucking on his peppermint. 'Too much time and trouble involved,' he added, belching quietly.

Parry let himself into the flat at nine-thirty. He had refused an enthusiastic offer of supper from Lloyd's ebullient wife – the jolly paragon who endlessly knitted her husband warm sweaters, cooked him gourmet meals, who had been a dutiful wife and mother for all of thirty years, and while weighing in at only a few pounds less than he did, still whisked around the ballroom floor with him, featherlight and inexhaustible.

For no reason that he wanted to define, the chief inspector had found the prospect of such congenial, maritally blissful company less attractive than being on his own for what was left of the evening. To be precise, he had decided that since Perdita had cancelled their provisional date again when he had called at lunchtime, he preferred to wallow in loneliness, and to oppress himself with speculation. Perdita had explained that her private patient session had been extended, and that when it was over she would still have to go back to the hospital again, with no idea when she would be finally free. He had chosen to believe that her indefinite plans might have had more to do with the continued presence in Cardiff of Dr Jeremy Bates — though he had no foundation for assuming that presence had continued.

The light on his answering machine was flashing as he went into the darkened sitting room. He rolled back the tape, then listened to the message.

'Hello, darling,' came Perdita's voice. 'I'm on my way home at last. Had enough of patients and hospitals for tonight. And doctors. Come and join me, *please*, even if it's late. If you haven't eaten, I'll do you an omelette. And another one for breakfast, but only if you're good. Very good. Love you.'

He switched off the tape, nodded at his cello in the corner, and briskly moved back towards the front door of the flat.